MILWAUKEE BLUES

MILWAUKEE BLUES

BY **LOUIS-PHILIPPE DALEMBERT**

A NOVEL

TRANSLATED BY
MARJOLIJN DE JAGER

SCHAFFNER PRESS
TUCSON, ARIZONA

Copyright © 2021 by Louis-Philippe Dalembert
Translation copyright © 2022 by Marjolijn de Jager
MILWAUKEE BLUES was first published
by Sabine Wespieser Editeur
13 Rue de L'Abbe Gregoire, Paris VI
© 2021
Manufactured in the United States
First Paperback Edition by Schaffner Press,
Tucson, Arizona
All rights reserved.

Cover design and illustration by Evan Johnston.
Book typesetting by Evan Johnston.

*This work received support for excellence in publication and
translation from Albertine Translation, a program created by
illa Albertine and funded by FACE Foundation.*

*Although inspired by two real dramas, this novel is nevertheless
a work of fiction. Any resemblance to individuals, living or not,
is purely coincidental*

ISBN: 978-1-63964-009-6
Ebook: 978-1-63964-034-8

For Sarah, Larry, Anita, Mary, Anne,
who taught me to love their city of Milwaukee.
For Big Sam Dalembert who welcomed me there.
For Melissa, who helped me understand the
athletic scholarship system and the American
college championships

CONTENTS

"Hickock tells us you're a natural-born killer. Says it doesn't bother you a bit. Says one time out there in Las Vegas you went after a colored man with a bicycle chain. Whipped him to death. For fun."

—Truman Capote, *In Cold Blood*

I left Atlanta one morning 'fore day
The brakeman said, "You'll have to pay"
Got no money but I'll pawn my shoes
I want to go west, I got the Milwaukee blues
Got the Milwaukee blues, got the Milwaukee blues
I want to go west, I got the Milwaukee blues

—Charlie Poole, "Milwaukee Blues"

9-1-1

I SHOULD HAVE NEVER dialed that bloody number. If I could, I'd delete the 9 and the 1 from the face of my smartphone forever. The way a cyclone or a flood wipes an entire village off the face of the earth from one day to the next. I would have a special application with a keypad not including those numbers. I'd give my right arm for it if need be. Having said that, if it were possible it would be so anywhere else in the world except here, because for this country's inhabitants *nine-one-one* is an inescapable necessity. A bit like the image of our minimarket for the residents of this part of Franklin Heights. The fingers' natural extension when the slightest thing goes wrong: a squabble between spouses, a kid who's fed up with his parents, an unfamiliar passerby walking with his head down or hugging the walls, a tramp who mistakes a fire hydrant for a urinal, the bodybuilder type who forgot to pick up his dog's mess; not to mention far more serious problems, like the drunk or the crackhead who beats up his lady—sometime it's the reverse, but that's less frequent—before she starts to shriek out her pain for all the neighbors to hear; or the perverse predator who stalks a child in broad daylight; all those things they talk about all day long on television or the internet; that force you to spy on your kids, search their phone contacts, be on their back 24/7 for fear that they'll get raped then murdered, or the other way around. In short, get on their nerves and turn them into tomorrow's neurotics, a large part of their salaries landing as cash in the pocket of a shrink, no invoice to show for it.

God only knows, though, if there are any problems in this city. It may well be the biggest one in the state, but that doesn't mean it's any less of a jerkwater town. Even if there are those with a few bucks to spend on their private clubs, their opera, with their blasted Wisconsin accent, which they do their utmost to hide from the ears of the rest of the country. They only have to be a little tired or have downed a small glass of champagne, and they lose their ar's, swallow a vowel in the word 'M'waukee', stress another one too much, '*baygul*' instead of '*bagel*'.

I would've been better off getting out of here a long time ago. After high school, when my buddies wanted to go to Chicago, the closest metropolis, to continue their studies. The universities there are much better than the ones we have here, besides they have a higher rating in the labor market. For most of my friends it was just a pretext anyway because ultimately they never even set foot on a university campus.

Maybe for lack of money. In this bloody country of America, even when it's a public institution it's never 'public' except in name only. When you get out, you may find yourself in debt for one, or even two, generations. As if you'd bought a fucking house.

Last I heard, all, or almost all, these pals are scraping by making a living job to job. What's the point of leaving if it's only to do the same shitty work elsewhere? Like one of my cousins who ended up opening a minimarket in Evanston, a suburb north of Chicago where almost one out of every three inhabitants is Haitian, when he could have simply taken over the one his parents have here. Basically, these guys just wanted a change of scenery, breathe different air in a place where everything seemed possible. Where the craziest dreams are permitted, even encouraged. That's the great strength of this country. Not like in Pakistan where I spent two summers with my parents as a child and then as an adolescent. Here, there's always some place to set up shop and try to turn your dream into a reality. Even if, when you get there, you wind up being cheated by someone more cunning than you and croaking mouth wide-open without ever making it. At least you die with hope as your flag. There's nothing worse than dying without hope.

Of course, I should have taken off with my friends. Gone as far as New York even, like the most intrepid of the group. A matter of really creating distance, leaving all of this behind. That can be healthy sometimes, crossing out the past. In a manner of speaking that is, because crosses for Muslims like us, you know. In the end, I stayed, buried in this hole. Without a diploma in my pocket, I got stranded in my uncle's minimarket, taking the place of the cousin who'd left for Chicago. What else could I've done? Besides starving or scrounging off my parents with this girl who got knocked up right away and found nothing better to do than stick me with two brats one right after the other. She refuses to take the pill, like all those women who can't say two words without bringing religion into it. So, it's all well and good to have a hard-on in bed at night, but you're afraid to get near her. When you finally get your courage up, you do it with fear in your heart. Afraid she'll get pregnant again. Another mouth to feed, and all the expenses that come with it all the way to the end of high school, if the kid doesn't get lost along the way. Uncle Sam gives nothing for free. Me, I don't want a slew of kids like you see among the Blacks and Latinos. It only increases the problems for people like us who don't have unlimited credit at the bank.

I should have listened to my cousin, gone to Chicago with him and our pack of pals. I wouldn't have had to dial that damned '*nine-one-one*'. I wouldn't have spent all those sleepless nights. After the first night I thought I wouldn't have given it any further thought. At least, it would've faded, even if it were to come back from time to time; and I would have slept eight hours straight, unless my own snoring woke me up as it sometimes would before. But no. It actually tends to be the opposite. And gets worse every night. I've gotten to the point where I can't close my eyes anymore. I can bust my butt all day long, yet at night I no longer drop into bed. The rare times that I manage to, I fall into a bottomless hole without anything in the wall to grab onto. It really lasts just a few minutes but in my sleep it seems like an eternity. And all the way down a pack of black faces accompanies my fall, shouting: 'I can't breathe! I can't breathe!' I wake up with a start, in a sweat. I can't catch my breath. I'm suffocating, too. I rush over to the window, whack it open, but I still can't breathe. It takes several minutes for my heart to get back to a normal rhythm that's more or less tolerable for a person like myself.

The imam with whom I talked about it, looking for some reassurance, told me I'd made the right choice. 'The right thing. It's the law.' You're obliged to call the police when you suspect a customer of passing a counterfeit bill on you. Otherwise it's you who pay the price. It can land you in jail. He said it in different words, precious and controlled, the words of men of faith, but it comes down to the same thing. Nevertheless, I'm the one who dialed that damn number. As a reflex. The extension of our fingers, I tell you. A bit out of cowardice also. These days, it's not good for a Muslim to have to deal with cops. Even for something like counterfeit banknotes. They'll quickly accuse you of laundering money to finance terrorist activities, Daesh and other organizations that are anything but holy, whose names you didn't even know until they yelled at you, or worse, had you in custody and scared the living hell out of you. So, I dialed 'nine-one-one'. Anyway, I still don't know if that bill was really counterfeit or not. The cops took it and the guy away with them. As a piece of evidence, they said. And nobody paid for the pack of cigarettes he'd bought.

When I dialed that bloody number, I didn't tell them right away that the guy was black. I just said that he was big and brawny. Starting to go bald on the top of his skull.

I noticed it when he bent down to pick up the bill that had fallen on the ground. Had he been white, or like us, he might have been able to hide it with a lock of hair. It's the kind of baldness that's easy to cover up unless it's frizzy hair like his. I also told them the color of his clothes. A loose-fitting black T-shirt and a faded pair of jeans. Not the fashionable ones with holes everywhere, that they sell for a pile of money. You could see that these had faded over time. They must have been through the mill or else their owner was very attached to them. Or he couldn't afford to get a new pair. Who knows. He also wore heavy beige ankle boots, like the ones that construction workers wear, with a reinforced tip to protect the toes from heavy falling objects. He must have been about forty or fifty years old. It's hard for me to be more specific. I never know how to tell the age of Blacks and Asians. With Whites it's easy: once they're barely past thirty they look fifty. Had the guy been Pakistani it would have been easier. You see, I grew up with them.

The lady's voice at the other end of the line was more demanding than reassuring. She insisted. What kind of man was he? I understood very well what she was after, but I pretended not to get it. I instinctively put on my Pakistani accent. At that game I'm unbeatable. My friends and I would often provoke parents who came from there, like mine, to take revenge for being punished. So I put on the Pakistani accent, even though I was born here. Just so I wouldn't get into trouble if you get my drift. Not with the cops, not with the neighborhood guys who would have considered me a snitch and given me the treatment that comes with it afterwards. It was a way out. You can never be careful enough. I could always say that I hadn't understood her very well.

However, I got it, I sure did. But I pretended I hadn't. I gave her other details. His size, his beefiness. The type and color of his clothes, things like that. I believe I even gave here the label of his jeans. The construction worker's shoes. But she insisted, getting brusque with me. She didn't care. With my accent, she no longer handled me with kid gloves. She began to threaten me, and more. It was a serious offense, liable to prosecution. At the very least I was risking a heavy fine for inappropriately disturbing the police, there are other constituents in danger who truly need help, stuff like that, you see.

As an Asian, and what's more, a Muslim, I'm not fooled by what goes on between the police and the Blacks. When you see your friend's beard on fire, you'd better take heed and give yours a good soaking. It's a proverb I picked up from the Haitians in Chicago when I was staying in their neighborhood. But as long as it has nothing to do with you, you keep your mouth shut so you don't invite any trouble. See what I mean? I wasn't going to hand the guy over to them with his hands and feet bound. It's the law of our community: never squeal on anyone to the cops. That's not a written one, for once. So when the lady on the other end of the line, almost shrieking at me in that shrill tone they use here, which makes you shout without even being aware of it, I went on yet another tangent. I told her he was a little tipsy but not aggressive. He was actually smiling. He had exchanged a few words with a woman in the minimarket as if they'd known each other for years.

It was the first time I'd ever seen him, although I know most of the customers as they all live in the area and since nobody ventures out here, unless it's a tourist, there are no other people. As a result, I know almost everyone, and their families, too: mother, father when there is one, children.... We often comment on the weather and on sports—the Bucks, the Brewers, even the Green Bay Packers. We sometimes have a good laugh together. The one who makes me laugh hardest is Ma Robinson, a retired former prison warden who became a preacher. She just has one of those looks. But seriously, what I really like is when the former prison warden gets the upper hand over the minister. She then comes out with the kind of spicy talk that doesn't very often show up in the Bible. Or so I assume. Because I haven't read any holy books other than the Koran. And even then only a few passages, when as a teenager I had to please the imam and my parents. In short, she must have learned some good ones in prison. Speaking of prison, I also talked with Stokely a few times, another one of the neighborhood's historic characters together with Ma Robinson and Authie. Ten years in jail behind him. He has since settled down and tries to teach the young how to avoid it. But the two of them, he and Authie, better not run into each other. They always kick each other's ass; apparently that's been going on for ages. When one of them is already in the store, the other stays outside and doesn't come in until the first one has left.

All of which to say that I'd never seen the guy before. I never even had any contact with his mother, whom I must have at least run into once or twice. But he'd never set foot inside the store before. Or I would have remembered. Maybe because of the two years I spent with the Haitians in Chicago. I did end up leaving, in fact. With my wife and the two kids. It was too tempting once the others had given me an earful.

I'd even gone there before for a weekend, just to check out where I was going to land. The others, well, they gave me the grand tour and everything. But I need time. I'm not the kind to set out on a whim. I have to chew it over, ruminate, digest the idea. Then one day I came home and said to my wife: 'Pack the bags, we're going to Chicago.' I waited for the summer and the end of the academic year so as not to disrupt the kids' school. That's how we left.

Two years! I lasted two years. Then I went back to my place, I mean here, in Milwaukee. I should have gotten out a lot sooner, at the end of high school, with the others. After a certain age it gets harder. You're accustomed to where you are, you see? Like with your wife. You may want to broaden your horizons and sometimes you actually do. The grass is always greener somewhere else, right? '*Aina*?' as they say in Wisconsin, instead of '*ain't it*?' But then it's stronger than you and you go back. The warmth of her skin reassures you. That said, time had passed as well. My friends had changed. We weren't the same group of buddies anymore, messing around with this and that. They all had responsibilities that were too heavy to bear. So I went back home.

The guy in question had returned to Franklin Heights in the two years that I was gone, so I gathered. That's why I didn't recognize him when he showed up with his forged banknote. Had I known him before, I would have talked to him frankly. I would've said: 'Where did they stick you with this monopoly money, man?' So as not to accuse him directly and run the risk of losing a customer. It's only after this whole thing happened that I began to learn about him. How he'd been a local celebrity, how he'd played championship football at the university. What did I know? I was just a kid at the time that they're talking about. Not to mention that my uncle's family and my own had never lived here. We always lived in Wilson Park, the neighborhood where I was born and raised. My uncle bought this minimarket in Franklin Heights because he got it into his head that he wanted to make money. He already had two others in our area and another one on the South Side where the Latinos live. It was his dream to have them all over Wisconsin, then the Midwest and, in the end, all across the United States. Creating an empire, like the Asians; not us, the other Asians.

When I started working in Franklin Heights—the family held a meeting to force me to do so, because I couldn't figure out what to do after high school—the guy had already left to try his luck elsewhere. And not to go chasing after small stuff like me when I went to Chicago. He was aiming for bigger game. In the end, it didn't work out. After that he preferred slaving away rather than coming back home to live from hand to mouth. Out of pride or out of shame. An error many people make. Me, I understood that very quickly, which is why I turned back after two years. Tail between my legs, true enough, but I came back in time. If you persist too much, you just move from one failure to the next. That's what the imam says: 'Pride is never a good counselor'. Later you'll find yourself without anything, you're neither the Pope at home nor a mufti in Chicago. But he held out before coming home until he realized he had nowhere else to go. Like a stone sliding down a slope, once it hits bottom it's forced to stop. That's why I'd never met him before and didn't recognize him.

Of course, I didn't unpack all that for the 'nine-one-one' lady, so she wouldn't get any angrier. But my answers became less and less convincing. Sensing my hesitation, she pulled out her story of fines and other hassles, enough for a lifetime. So I finally spat it out and told her the guy was black. Still, I held out for quite a while, only squealed when I felt I was on treacherous ground. The imam assured me that I should be proud of myself. I didn't really grasp why, whether it's because I'd done my duty as a citizen or because I was in no hurry to play along as a collaborator. I didn't dare ask him. The lady added that if I'd said that sooner it would have saved everybody a lot of time. After asking me once more to confirm my name and the store's address, she said she was going to pass on the suspect's description to the police. They'd be there in no time. It makes you wonder if she would have gone out of her way had the guy been Caucasian. I'll never know.

Indeed, the squad didn't waste any time. About ten minutes at most, sirens screaming. There were four of them, in two separate cars. The guy had already emerged from the store. He swaggered when he moved, as Blacks often do. You only have to watch Barack Obama walk, or Denzel Washington when he first appears in his films and you'll know what I mean. The guy was heading for his car, a huge gleaming burgundy vehicle, with the blurred outline of a doll in the front. When I saw the car—I'd gone to the doorstep of the store to watch the operation unfold—I wondered if I hadn't fucked up. Either the guy had spent every last penny on it before going into debt up to his ears to pay for the rest. Or he was a dealer. Generally, cops prefer the second hypothesis. Basically, when you own a car like this, you don't try to palm off such a small bill. Unless it was a test before passing off larger ones.

In the end, I felt reassured because one of the cops was African-American as they say here to avoid mentioning skin color. As a matter of fact, his skin was very light but you could see he wasn't all white, white. There was also a little Chinese stockiness to him, well Asian, though I wouldn't be able to say what country exactly. It's like us when they confuse us with the Indians although we have nothing in common. It so happens that he was born here, just like me. That's why I prefer to be specific. I told myself there wasn't any risk for things to get out of control, their presence would prevent the other two from making a blunder with the guy. Well, I was wrong. I still have trouble admitting it. If only I hadn't dialed that bloody number.

The entire planet knows the rest down to its slightest details. It's all on the internet. How they tackled him from the front, put handcuffs on him while he was on the ground. And as if that weren't enough, the Caucasian with the bald head like Kojak—the actor of a series I used to watch as a child—kept his knee between the shoulder blades, nonchalantly, the way you do with a sheep at Eid so it'll stop wriggling and bleating before its throat is slit, while his colleagues were busy keeping the bystanders at bay. He, too, was watching the little group of people that had gathered around, without paying any attention to the guy beneath his knee. Did he feel the man's last fitful breath? Like when you touch an electrically charged person and he in turn gives you a shock. I'm not even talking about the words, which will undoubtedly be turned into book or movie titles worldwide. People can cheat with words. But breath! You don't pretend with breath unless you're up for an Oscar like Denzel. How can you not feel that? And still let the other one die without turning a hair?

As for me, for the rest of my life I will regret that I dialed that unfortunate number. I was coming back from the bathroom when the cashier gave me the agreed-upon sign. I moved away discreetly to make the call. As the manager it's I who should have been at the register, which my status as the boss's nephew allows me to do in my cousin's absence. I would have done better to follow him or join him much sooner in Chicago. I said that already, I know. The guy would be alive today and his three daughters wouldn't be orphans.

'It's the law,' the imam said. 'What happened afterwards isn't up to you. All you did was respect the law.'

'The law of men,' I replied. "What about Allah's law?'

For once I left the imam speechless. He took even more time to answer before he came out with some hackneyed saying like: 'His ways are impenetrable.' 'It's the law.' That's what I tell myself when remorse takes over too much. In the meantime, I still can't sleep, and the rare times that I manage I can't breathe when I have nightmares. The fact that my uncle, the owner of the minimarket, stated he wants to help defray the funeral costs hasn't changed any of it very much. The shouting black faces persist in disturbing my sleep: 'I can't breathe! I can't breathe! I can't... '

I

FRANKLIN, THE
YEARS OF CHILDHOOD

I, too, sing America.
[...]
I, too, am America.
Langston Hughes
'I Too'

THE TEACHER

'WILL THIS NEVER STOP?' That was the first thought that entered my mind when the news flash began, scrolling nonstop at the bottom of the television screen reporting the death of yet another black man at the hands of the police. It's been feeling like a veritable epidemic ever since the death of that family man who was asphyxiated under the weight of several white police officers in New York City a few years ago, simply for illegally reselling some cigarettes. Not counting all the other victims of the systemic violence that's destroying this country. 'Will this never stop?' Words that were actually revealing an immense weariness. In part because of my age that, I agree, nibbles away at me with little bites of reckless incisors, sure it has the last word. Be that as it may, I'm tired of keeping this unwholesome count. Of repeating the same refrain ad nauseam, like in the song where Gregory Porter gives homage to the Reverend Dr. Martin Luther King, Jr., relentlessly returning to: '1960 *what?* 1960 *who?*' It's never easy to tell yourself you've struggled all these years for a pittance, or even for nothing at all.

'Will this never stop?' But it wasn't the end of my woes yet. When smack in the center of the screen the name and the picture were shown, the face came back to me immediately, clear, precise. Like a vicious stab right in my heart. *Oh my God!* It was thirty-five years ago already. Maybe a bit more. My heart started beating at a pace that's unbearable for a woman of my age. How time flies! Would my lovers of yesterday recognize me in this frail, mostly crumpled little lady whose step keeps slowing down and whose skeleton creaks at the slightest gesture, piercing her flesh with recurrent untold aches and pains? Would they recognize the beautiful, dashing young woman—let's dare be immodest—who made them turn their head, a pure product of the generation that's known today as the boomers? And my little Emmett, whose sweet face has just been flung at the frantic consumers of images from every corner of the world, would he have recognized his former schoolteacher in this useless thing, this worn-out old bag? A very strange era, indeed.

The complete opposite of that faraway period when dreams were blooming and ablaze. We were in the middle of the Cold War. Only a few years after the peoples of Africa and Asia rose up to put an end to centuries of European colonialism. Young Westerners in turn couldn't stop making—mostly dreaming of—a revolution. In Europe it set the streets on fire on either side of the Iron Curtain: Rome, Berlin, Belfast,

Warsaw, Belgrade, with the Prague Spring and May '68 in Paris as the climax. Here in the United States, we created our own revolution, against the Vietnam War, as we sang the "Vietnam Blues" by J.B. Lenoir who was making the government and society confront their contradictions. We wanted to be part of the Woodstock scene, too, that world of wild excess to the acid-drenched music of Jimi Hendrix and so many others.

I dreamed of change among the hundreds of thousands of others who were young like me. And, in my opinion, equal rights had to be the starting point. For men and women, that goes without saying. But, in a country such as ours where human relationships remain tarnished by enslavement, it's even more for Blacks and Whites. That was the level I wanted to change, not the world but the United States. Side by side with tens of thousands of others I'd loudly sing The Stones' "Sweet Black Angel" or John and Yoko's "Angela" at the demonstrations on behalf of our icon Angela Davis. Her stunning beauty touched the heart of more than one man of my generation. In their eyes, her perfect features beneath the Afro were the incarnation of the unadulterated face of the Revolution.

I came from a tidy white neighborhood, the East Side of Milwaukee, one of the most segregated cities in the United States. For those of my social condition, Franklin Heights, a ghetto in the north of the town, was on another planet, much farther in short than Florida, or even Cancún in Mexico, which was our vacation spot. It was in the mid-seventies when, armed with a B.A. in literature from Marquette University, a Jesuit institution—which I'd earned at an age when others of my generation were already parents and well-established in active life, I was recruited as a teacher at a public school in Franklin Heights. It was my way of having a finger in the pie after long years of spending time with my theoretical dreams of changing society, in the hazes of discussion until all hours, smoke of all kinds, alcohol, and mingled bodies.

My close circle carried on about the waste. My friends' parents, who had always seen me as the bad seed influencing their offspring, spoke of mental illness. It hardly surprised them, they concluded, that my use of illegal substances had fried my brain. In the opinion of these self-righteous members of the bourgeoisie, except for my skin color, I was a junkie weirdo, although I'd only smoked a few joints every now and then, like so many of my generation. Certainly, carried away by the atmosphere, I'd ventured one night to try a more detrimental drug but had the self-protective reflex to stop the experiment in its tracks. On their end, if my parents didn't go as far as to disown me altogether, a cold war settled into our relationship. It didn't come to an end until the birth of their first grandson, conceived with a fine white man, good in every respect, though I was well past thirty and had more or less given up on motherhood.

Before him, my previous lover had proven to be incapable of accepting my positions, which were too bold for his taste. He just barely tolerated my relationships, some of which dated from that period of transgression; even though most of them had already fallen in line after their brief escapade on the other side of conformity. Besides, he didn't understand that I'd waste the best years of my life in a fight that was neither mine nor that of my community. All the more so, he figured, because I didn't need to work at all, he was earning enough for two, even for the family we'd soon begin.

The idea of a single and unique human community, outside of ethnicity, class, and gender, was beyond him. Ultimately, he forced me to choose. Between my ideal and him. I didn't hesitate for a second: I chose my ideal.

Such was my situation when I was hired at the Benjamin Franklin Elementary School, a large red brick building, typical of the early twentieth-century architecture, where I would get to know Emmett about ten years later. I'm not ashamed to say that with time he became one of my pet students. In principle, teachers aren't supposed to differentiate between their pupils. A matter of ethics. But we're no less human than anyone else. The main thing is to be fair to everyone, particularly where children are concerned. At that age, they don't have the words to express what they feel in an almost animal way. Any sense of injustice may lead to irreversible damage, especially in children who are already victims in their everyday life because of their social condition. I would be hard put to explain this strong liking for little Emmett. Why him and not another child? It certainly wasn't because of his academic accomplishments. Far from it! In that respect he tended to get on my nerves. At my age, I accept the fact that one can't understand or explain everything. My affection for little Emmett was of that order.

The first thing that drew my attention was his name. Calling your child Emmett—twenty years after the Black teenager whose murder by southern white racists had made the headlines—said a lot about the parents. They must have been activists from the very beginning, in far more dangerous situations than those I'd fought against using our slogans before I started working at Benjamin Franklin. At least, that's what I chose to believe. I was a little girl when that ghastly lynching was committed and had already, thanks to television, shaken the entire world. Nevertheless, the killers were acquitted after a mock trial that contributed in worsening the already deplorable relationships with the police, the legal system and, worse, between our communities. Emmett's classmates, on the other hand, could care less but, because he was overweight, chose to saddle him with the ungraceful nickname Fats Domino. What they didn't know was that, long before Emmett, the name for the slices of greasy pizza their classmates were so fond of belonged to one of the precursors of rhythm and blues. No one could have seen the strapping young man he was ready to become in this somewhat clumsy, chubby child. But he already had character. When the other kids called him Fats Domino he didn't let himself get stepped on. And, he only settled accounts as a last resort. He was happy to have the dirty work done by his two homies who were by his side all day long, so that I ended up calling them 'the three musketeers', despite the lack of a fourth rascal that would have given my comparison more meaning. The others saw the two close friends as watchdogs who blocked any access to Emmett, nicknaming one 'Bodyguard' and the other 'Gorilla'. As if, with his football player's build, Emmett would have been unable to defend himself. But I understood him. It's a good thing to have friends defend you without your having to involve yourself. It's sweet. It's a way of being told 'I love you' without using any words. Most likely why Emmett let Stokely and Autherine put the bullies in their place. Surrounded by Gorilla and Bodyguard, he enjoyed perfect peace in the building's hallways and on the playground.

In class, the three had to be separated to cut short unwelcome whispering and prevent them from copying each other's work. The same nonsense, anyway, since from a strictly academic point of view not one of the three was very smart. When he was successfully removed from his two male sidekicks, Autherine, the girl, was the one who worked the hardest without being particularly brilliant, however. Stokely was the least gifted although the most reckless, a little troublemaker always ready to hatch a dirty trick. I wouldn't be surprised if he ended up badly. If he, too, became the target of a police blunder; or, in a less macabre scenario, if he increased the statistics of Black men behind bars in the United States. Emmett had great potential but school didn't seem to be a priority for him. Which really set my teeth on edge. It almost seemed as if he didn't see the point of it. But God only knows he had the ability to do much better. With a little effort and a minimum of consistency on his part he would have been among the best in the class. It was asking too much of him. He always waited until the last minute to work hard enough to pass with just barely average results. That was the kind of student he was.

I had him in two different classes at the elementary school. The administration had instituted a rotation system whereby we changed class levels every three years. The second time I had him he was in fourth grade. Emmett habitually came to class with a football that literally had to be pulled out of his hands. Otherwise he'd keep it on his desk or between his knees, and fiddle with it all day long. How could he possibly focus with that thing in his hand? It was the year that he began to slim down a little. Not only because he was growing, as I thought at first. Mahalia, a colleague to whom I was close, lived in Franklin Heights. She was the only one, however. The others had moved to Halyard Park where the black middle class had begun to group together. But she refused to leave. This confirmed spinster had turned her profession into a sacred vocation, wanting to serve as an example to the girls of the neighborhood.

Mahalia knew the family well. She was the one who told me that Emmett's father had left home. This information was later confirmed by the mother, an easygoing heavy-set woman with a compelling smile. A lady with great dignity, she didn't go into any details. She was so anxious for her only son to succeed that she'd frequently visit the teachers—all women—to demand they'd be more strict with him. Otherwise he'd become a deadbeat like his father who, she said, would back away from the slightest problem before completely taking off when the situation became intense.

She was alluding to the recession of the early Reagan years, which hit the country hard, especially hounding the Midwest and greater Milwaukee even after the recovery. Like the hurricanes that descend upon Florida and the interior of the United States every year now. In my time we didn't complain about those so much. The A. O. Smith Corporation, which employed most of Benjamin Franklin's parents, almost went bankrupt before other stockholders bought it up. The new management cut back on hundreds of personnel and relocated a good part of the production to countries where labor costs were even lower than here.

Emmett's father was part of the huge wave of layoffs left behind. After a while, undoubtedly weary from his fruitless search for work, unless it was out of the laziness that his wife accused him of, he ultimately got it into his head that there was nothing anymore for people like them here in Milwaukee. It would be better to go back South where he had some family. According to Mahalia, he convinced his wife to let him go on ahead to Alabama and check things out. She and their boy would follow him in three, four months, a year at the very most, once he'd found work and a house where he could receive them decently. Because sooner or later bad luck was bound to grow tired of dragging them down and would drop anchor in deeper waters, as he put it, embellishing his words. Once he'd left Franklin Heights the good woman never heard from him again. Nor did his son.

It was around this time that young Emmett's body began to slim down. Surely because he was growing but also, and most of all, because of the sudden disappearance of his father to whom he was very close, and also because he didn't get enough to eat. Since he wasn't the only one, my colleague and I encouraged the school's administration to establish a system of free breakfasts at the cafeteria and, occasionally, afternoon snacks for those who were very needy. Very quickly the initiative became a victim of its own success. Large numbers were going to the cafeteria during those lean years. Unless my memory fails me, I'd say it was more than half the school, and I don't think I'm wrong. The principal scraped together every last dollar but it wasn't enough. We had to call upon the houses of worship of all denominations in the area and even beyond. The supermarkets cooperated and let us have products close to the expiration date at cost or they donated them. So did the Rotary Club, through my parents who were members and saw no reason why they shouldn't help finance my whims, harmless as they were, now that I was married and a mother.

At first Emmett wouldn't set foot in the cafeteria. He already had that pride that's close to arrogance that generally modest people sometimes demonstrate, surely a sign of the education that the home provides. The father's absence must have brought him closer to his mother. 'You have to go through her,' Mahalia suggested who attended the same parish church as she did. 'Otherwise we're not likely to see him any time soon.' The friendship of this colleague, who was younger but better integrated in the neighborhood, was a true school of life for me. Without her, I would have missed a lot of things. I would have misconstrued so many obvious facts. One morning in the faculty lounge she announced that she'd had a word with Emmett's mother. From then on, he could go to the cafeteria, like Gorilla, Bodyguard and his other little friends. And he wasn't the one with the smallest appetite. Far from it!

In spite of it all, I sometimes caught him away from the others, even from his two sidekicks, a veil of sadness in his look. Oh, hardly noticeable to his friends, for he was a proud little guy and good at masking his feelings. Lazy in class, but proud. He was one of those who would never inform on a classmate, never snitch as they put it. And the day I heard him humming "Alabama Blues" by J. B. Lenoir as he wandered through the hallways of the school, I had to force myself not to run to him and hug him tightly in my arms. In the best case scenario he'd have taken me for a crazy lady and so would've the rest of them. Worse, he might have felt assaulted by this outpouring of unwelcome affection.

The song was too grim for a child. How, at that age, can you be singing a blues where they talk about a white police officer who killed a Black sister and brother in Alabama?

Swearing through the voice of the blues singer never to return because of the unjust release of the killer? The words of the lament, written in the sixties during the brutal period of segregation, that we were to pick up again in the demonstrations after every homicide of a Black man by a white cop, come back to me sometimes. They reverberate inside me so strongly today and make my already weak heart bleed.

> *I never will go back to Alabama,*
> *that is not the place for me*
> *You know they killed*
> *my sister and my brother*
> *And the whole world let them*
> *peoples go down there free*

Having heard Emmett sing this strange song, I told Mahalia of my concern, but she had a ready explanation. According to neighborhood hearsay, it was one of the favorite blues songs of his father, who had left a year earlier for some place in Alabama. The parents originally were from there, from Selma. Emmett's father was the one who had chosen his son's first name against the wishes of his furious wife. She would have preferred Matthew, Paul, Andrew, Zachariah. . . . in short, a more Christian first name. I accepted Mahalia's very plausible clarification but still couldn't stop wondering for days on end why in the world the boy had remembered those lyrics.

The following year in fifth grade Emmett left my class for my colleague's. Knowing I had a weak spot for him, Mahalia made it her business to bring me news about him regularly. Imagine my surprise when, at the end of the academic year when only the principal and two or three teachers were still there to deal with the final administrative reports before leaving on vacation, I saw him arrive at the school accompanied by his mother. They brought me a bouquet of flowers and cornbread wrapped in aluminum foil that his mother had carefully slipped into some Tupperware. It was her way of thanking me for having mentored Emmett a little during his time at elementary school, for having been both indulgent and yet quite strict with him to shake him out of his laziness and help him cross this first hurdle on his life's path.

Mahalia must have told Emmett's mother that I was crazy about cornbread, a mild sin left over from my childhood and from my nanny who came from the southeast. It was my form of Proust's madeleine. I was so deeply touched that I couldn't control my tears. It was a good thing that my colleagues weren't around. The woman didn't hesitate for a second to draw me to her ample bosom and very nearly wept with me. Enveloped by her arms, I could have sworn I found my nanny's scent again. I grabbed the opportunity to invite them to our house the following Sunday. Noticing his mother's hesitancy I took her two hands in mine and told her that it would not only be an honor but it would give me immense pleasure as well. My two boys would be just as happy to meet Emmett, while we adults could talk.

Three days later they showed up at the house in their Sunday best. And when Black people here go to church it's really something. I've never understood why we Whites don't look and learn from them. It's not as if we were going out to the supermarket for God's sake! Or to some damned baseball game. Despite the disagreements with my parents, who'd been living there all the way to the end—may God welcome them in his Kingdom –after my marriage I'd also gone back to live on the East Side, where I'd grown up and knew my way around. I wanted my children to be born there too. It reassured me. A little like a female sea turtle who swims thousands of kilometers to lay her eggs on the same beach where she was born.

It was summertime. People on the street were cooling off on their porches. Neighbors were talking with one another, watching their kids playing in the field adjacent to their homes. Emmett's and his mother's arrival in this exclusively white neighborhood didn't go unnoticed. Adults stopped talking, children stopped playing, to watch them go by. Emmett and his mother weren't dressed like the domestic servants who came into their prosperous homes during the week. The silence that accompanied their steps was as heavy as the air that month of July. Waiting for them on the veranda with my husband I imagined their discomfort. It was then that I considered the incongruity of my invitation, especially on this day and at this time of year; and also the distance that separated us from each other. All I managed to do that afternoon was go out to meet them and walk the final yards to the house together.

Once inside, my husband did everything he could to lighten the mood and put Emmett's mother at ease. He told her he was originally from Chicago where as a child he'd gone to school with a Haitian boy, his best friend, whose mother loved to invite him to their house and serve him dishes whose ingredients reminded him of Southern cooking. These fiery, spicy dishes would make him turn red as a beet.

He'd be perspiring up to his ears but it was so delicious; and, food lover that he was, he never refused. At that memory, the woman had to laugh heartily. With the first shaky moment behind them, the children had taken Emmett to the back-yard. I'd told them that he was a huge football fan. Thank God there was no inappropriate curiosity whatever in their eyes. Not long after we could hear their racket and the noise of the football as it sporadically bounced on the tile strip placed like a bridge down the middle of the lawn to keep us from drag-ging mud into the house.

After that summer Sunday I no longer saw Emmett; he'd gone on to high school. For a while we exchanged two or three letters in which he gave me his news briefly and brought me up to date on his studies. Although he'd made some progress in spelling, his handwriting was still as diffi-cult as ever to decipher. In that area my work hadn't borne much fruit. I encouraged him, in my return letter, and re-minded him that he had to persevere and believe in his lucky stars: 'Work always pays off, my little Emmett.' It felt funny to me to affectionately call him 'little' when he surely must already be almost as tall as the guy whose photograph the journalists were showing on television. Above all, he shouldn't hesitate to call on me if for one reason or another he needed my help. I would be happy to help him out. He never did, nor did his mother. Pride? Or maybe he didn't need it at all. Now it's too late to find out.

In the meantime, under the pressure of the kids and my husband, I'd asked to be transferred to another area. Franklin Heights was becoming a more dangerous place with every passing day, one of the most deadly in Milwaukee. Becoming more insular and open to others only for specific reasons, not necessarily good ones. My continued presence as a 'foreigner' was troublesome in the eyes of the big shots, despite the kindness shown me by former students or their parents. That's why, with a heavy heart, I left the neighborhood and the school where I'd worked for more than fifteen years. I felt sick not going back there every day to offer my support to those mothers who craved a less wretched life for their children.

The last letter I received from Emmett contained some wonderful news: he told me he'd been awarded a scholarship from a Catholic university in the Southwest to continue the studies that he otherwise could never have afforded. In computer science, if my memory serves me right. The university undoubtedly needed his talent as a football player, and he must have accepted it as the only way to turn professional. It was a quid pro quo. Since he'd never been very good at math, I doubt he had much faith in his ability to tackle computer studies. Who knows, though, maybe in high school he'd had a teacher competent and patient enough to interest him in mathematics. Sometimes a wonderful human encounter with an instructor can work as a turning point for a student. Help him discover himself. The most touching part of this situation is that he'd remembered me and wanted to share his success with me. There's nothing more gratifying for a teacher.

Subsequently, I lost track of him. At times, I'd see something about him on TV. He'd become a huge sports star who was even mentioned in regular broadcasts. Like one of those people who distribute their money openly and publicly to stand out in the eyes of others. Did Christ not say: 'But when you give to the needy, do not let your left hand know what your right hand is doing'? That being so, I won't throw stones at them for anything. If they can reduce poverty in the world, that's already something for the unfortunate. So I knew that one day when turning on the television, I would hear them talking about my little Emmett.

But, I never expected it to be like this. I wasn't prepared for it. Will it never end? I can still see him, little kid, in the hallways at school, humming the lyrics of "Alabama Blues." Despite the weariness I feel inside, the sinner that I am is asking God to protect my heart from any anger, any desire for revenge, which belongs to Him alone as He says himself: 'Vengeance is mine, and recompense, for the time when their foot shall slip; for the day of their calamity is at hand, and their doom comes swiftly.' So be patient, until we see the new world where justice will be rendered and where all of us, White, Black, Asian, Native Americans, and Latinos will be able to live together. While I wait, may He guide me on the path to peace.

Through Mahalia, with whom I'd lost touch but managed to get on the phone, I found out that the funeral would take place in a church where the former prison warden, now a preacher, officiated. She told me that the burial would be followed by a peaceful march in Emmett's memory and to demand justice on his behalf. I will go very discreetly. To acknowledge his memory. To have the pleasure, too, of seeing Mahalia again after all these years. Will I recognize her? I know that I'll be attending the service with a bitter heart and feeling the pain of going back in time; not what I would have wanted, but to the tune of an old blues song hummed by a young boy named Emmett. In the meantime, as in the song, I can only sit and weep, while I think of the grievous and appalling conditions under which poor Emmett lost his life.

> *My brother was taken up for my mother,*
> *and a police officer shot him down*
> *I can't help but to sit down and cry sometime*
> *Think about how my poor brother lost his life.*

CHILDHOOD FRIEND

I RAN INTO HIM on the morning of that fateful day, and that was the last time. Emmett and I had known each other—I'm having a hard time speaking of him in the past—from way back. We were born in the same hospital, Saint Michael's, in the same month and the same year: the year the Vietnam War ended, where so many guys shed their blood for Uncle Sam who, at the same time, still treated them as second class citizens. We've come a long way since then, it would be bad faith to deny it, but the account still isn't settled. Emmett and I grew up all our life on the same street in the same Franklin Heights neighborhood in the north of Milwaukee, at least I did. Here, when you say you come from those neighborhoods, people look at you funny, are on their guard, ready to run off, to dial 911 like you're about to act weird or do something illegal. Emmett and I learned very early on how to detect that mistrust in the eyes of other folks. On Sundays our parents would take us to church together, looking for some fulfillment of hope I'm still waiting for. I keep going there and believing in it, it's one way to keep the spark alive that they bequeathed to us. What meaning would life have otherwise?

Apart from that, there's the difference in size between us. I'm smaller, true, but I was born a week before him. As a child he accepted it until he very quickly grew taller than me by a head, then two, then three. Even during my so-called growing period I didn't sprout very much. So I always looked up at him from below. Nature had given him his little revenge and he didn't hesitate to make it worse by calling me "Shorty" at every opportunity. At the time that really used to piss me off. Whatever he did, I'd tell him, I'd always be his elder. If that's what he wanted, he could grow as tall as the highest tower in Chicago, where I'd never even set foot. But, as everybody knows, where skyscrapers are concerned Chicago has no reason at all to be envious of New York.

'That's the way it is, nothing you can ever do about it. Anyway, sit down when I talk to you, you're giving me a stiff neck. It's a good thing I'm not your girlfriend, it would be a real pain to French kiss you.'

That's how we'd bicker with each other. The others called us 'the Siamese Twins'. And one of the teachers said we were 'the three musketeers', if you added Stokely, that other jerk. At Benjamin Franklin Elementary School the teacher had us change seats in every class so we wouldn't be glued to each other all the time. We'd catch up on the playground, on the street when we'd walk, then in the school bus when we were in high school, which was far away from Franklin Heights. He began to pull away from me when we were in eighth grade, I remember it well. Because of the girls who were madly in love with him. With his big body, his feline walk, and player's looks—though there wasn't anyone sweeter or more serious—they all had the hots for him, those little sluts. When we'd see each other in the hood again—we were still tight—he'd tell me about his love life, he couldn't help himself. With the success he reaped in spite of himself he'd become a real charmer. The more he told me, the more it got on my nerves. One day when I'd had enough, I finally asked him if I wasn't a girl, too.

'What do they have that I don't, those ho's of yours?'

It came out just like that. True, other than being a half-pint, I was rather well-endowed for my fourteen years. And all of a sudden, right there and then, he became aware that I existed. Other than as a buddy, I mean. With a face and a body that would have made quite a few others drool in his place. Even eighteen- or twenty-year olds. Still, he burst out laughing at my reaction: 'Yo, you're jealous.' Then he tried to make up for it: 'You, with you it's not the same. You're my sister. My *little* sister', he added, thinking he was cheering me up with his double joke. But that pissed me off me even more. 'Little sister, my ass, right.' Had I been at his house that day I would've slammed the door and left. But we were sitting on the stoop at my place. Even so, I left him high and dry and immediately went to join the others who were jabbering a few yards away. In the end, I made up my mind to assume the role of his confidante. One of whom he'd never let go, who would always be by his side against all odds. And vice versa.

Our teenage years flew by, long before we even realized it. Ultimately we lost track of each other when he left to try his luck at the university. Far from Milwaukee anyway, so far that he rarely came back here again. Less and less as time went on. That period without my *big* brother seemed so long to me. The one to whom I could say anything, tell anything, trying to understand men a little, assuming there's anything to understand, for where guys are concerned I was—and still am—completely confused. I would've liked to have been able to confide my rage and disgust to him when one of my boyfriends thought I was his doormat or, in the case of the guy I lived with, who didn't do shit at home until I kicked his ass out.

Don't mess with me. If I learned anything on the street from Emmett and the rest, it's not to let people walk all over me, or else they'll find out soon that I ain't fooling. On the other hand, how do you hang onto a guy, a good one, and keep him at home? It's something I've never managed. I'm not very tolerant. Even when I'm crazy about him. I wish Emmett was here to explain to me why I insist on collecting freeloaders and losers. It's not as if there aren't enough guys around. I just wanted to have had a shoulder to cry on or brotherly arms to hold me, without any misconstruing. With their 'sensible' advice, girlfriends all too often settle accounts through your problems, while they keep with their own man nice and warm in their bed for the long bone-chilling winter nights in Wisconsin.

When, after years on the road singing "Ain't Got No Home", he came back to our neighborhood to stay—perhaps he'd slept on the streets as if he were homeless, when

I would've been happy to take him in—those moments of tender complicity I used to dream about were no longer possible. Not because we were both adults now; he also had to face up to some other heavy responsibilities. No. For me he'd definitely changed; whatever he'd experienced while he was away had broken something inside him. He'd replaced his natural good mood with a fake, mechanical smile, as self-protection no doubt. As if he was playing himself in a show written by someone else. In fact, he covered it up so others would think he was the same as before. The kid whose mother used to yell from the porch at the first signs of dusk:

'Emmett, get your black ass home now if you don't want me to flatten it like a chimpanzee's.'

She had been so scared that her only son might find himself in bad company in Franklin Heights. And she wasn't wrong. That's how that moron Stokely landed in prison for dealing, even after he'd seen his own father go that way. He'd actually thought he could drag Emmett into his business. And that caused a gigantic fight between us. All of Franklin still talks about it, including the new generation. He knows perfectly well that I don't back down from anyone, despite my tiny body. And even less so when they touch my tall little brother. Since then, Stoke and I haven't spoken a word to each other, not until I heard the news on television.

So, Emmett's mother was damn right to be afraid he'd end up raising the statistics of Blacks behind bars. The highest percentage of every community in the country, in contrast to its representation relative to the total population. More or less the same ratio as for Vietnam from where my future father returned, out of his mind, his head screwed-up crammed with hallucinations that made him more and more violent with his family except when, roaring drunk, he'd begin to bawl like a kid who hasn't eaten in a week, then suddenly start howling: '*Vietnam, Vietnam, everybody cryin' about Vietnam...* ' He could run on like that for an entire morning, only to end up in a psychiatric hospital.

Emmett didn't return for the reasons most folks usually do when they come back home, to recharge their batteries, and recuperate before going somewhere else again. Or, why not, live out the rest of the time God gives you on this earth. He had come back to run aground on the streets of his childhood because he must have been tired of wandering and, more than anything else, had nowhere else to go.

He'd gone far, however. Farther than any of us. His athletic talent had opened the doors of a university while most of us had already started working at age sixteen, having at best, like me, struggled to finish high school. Whereas he'd become a star, gazed at by the girls at school and then, on the occasion of the regional championship, by those in Wisconsin and the whole Midwest, Wasps included. Those little white females, Protestant or not, were ready to defy the prejudices of their social class to have him. A risky bet, where there was a lot to lose but where they might also hit the jackpot. At stake: making a royal entrance into adulthood no matter what happens later—divorce, a child over whom they'd have sole custody—a meal ticket for life. In case Emmett were to be recruited by a major franchise, the chosen one would have been there from the beginning, you understand? The loyal one among the loyals, including family and friends. The one to lean on when you get into the upper ranks so fast that you can feed the illusion, which we all need, of being loved for who you are, and protected from the vultures that are always coming at you.

Getting a scholarship is the ticket, the only way for kids in our neighborhood, girls and boys alike, to even set foot in a university. You can only hope that God or nature endows you with a talent greater than the rest in one of the four major sports that serve as a showcase for these temples of knowledge. If you're born under a very lucky star, you might obtain the Holy Grail: be noticed by an established university. They have scouts all over the country looking to recruit young prodigies to apply to the university. There you are, from one day to the next, cast into the role of ambassador of a university that no one in your family has ever heard of even after five generations. Except maybe the obvious ones like Yale, Harvard, or MIT, without really knowing where they are, on the East Coast, the West Coast, or somewhere in the middle.

For Emmett it had always been football. His size and weight made him a natural first string defensive player. From the time he was little and until he left the neighborhood, I never saw him without that pigskin in his hand. Always doing something with it. He'd make believe that he was throwing the ball to an imaginary teammate at the end of an imaginary field, his body arched back so far that his hand would nearly touch the ground before his arm would catapult forward in a throwing motion. Sometimes, as a result of the force of his follow-through, he'd find himself flat on his belly, the ball still firmly gripped in his hand. At the same time, he could hear sports commentators touting his prowess to a stadium full of people on their feet wildly cheering him.

If he'd stumble upon an empty lot with some clumps of wild grass, he'd let go like a dog which has been kept on a leash for a whole day and finally has the chance to run around. He'd leap, fly in all directions, throw the ball in the air, then catch it in full flight. He'd let it fall to the ground and roll around before pouncing on it and freezing in place, his large frame wrapped around it in a protective posture. Even when he hung out with us, the ball it was in his hand; when he was sitting, he'd keep it between his legs stroking it constantly. Jesus, he treasured it more than if it was a girl. According to his mother, he took it to bed with him at night. Impossible to separate them. As if he'd always known that his future depended on it. I've never understood how he could love such a violent sport. But as long as it made him happy, I was happy for him.

Thanks to that damned ball, he was able to leave home for that university in a medium-sized town in the Southwest, whose name I don't remember anymore. We all pictured him getting drafted and becoming a star in the NFL. Then there was that awful accident during his last year. I only found out about it years later, I don't know who told me anymore. Whether it was he who told me after he came back, or his mother with whom I'd stayed in touch to get his news, and also because she was a good person. The coach had wanted him to repeat the year. I wouldn't say that Emmett worked very hard off the football field; in class he was no genius. Even at school he didn't exactly shine in that regard. But, in as much of a hurry to make money off his linebacker, his agent got it into his head that the university wanted to exploit his talent one more year for free. So Emmett didn't listen to his coach. Results: he failed to get into the NFL, as did so many before him. In any event, the university in question hadn't succeeded in putting many young people on that track. Whether it concerned football, basketball, baseball or hockey. The big four, in other words. But at the time he didn't know that. None of us knew. It's not like today when all you need to do is go on the internet and with one click you know everything about everything and everyone. Twenty-five, thirty years ago it wasn't like that.

In Franklin, we could already see him pulling his family out of poverty, which is to say moving them out of the 'hood, where he would've returned only to do charitable work, help those who were left on the margins waiting to get out of desperate trouble, too. All Emmett wanted was to get out of there. Not because he was ashamed of his roots, the place he'd left. Not at all. The truth? This neighborhood has too many bad associations for all of us, too much scarcity, too many deprivations. At night, sometimes during the day as well, it's practically like Baghdad here. Too much hassle. At the same time, these lousy streets reassure us. As soon as we move away a while, we feel we're at risk, unsafe, with all those eyes watching us.

That said, Emmett's mom would have never let the two of them clear out like thieves in the night, disregarding the others. Only Christ, and He says so himself, is allowed to arrive like a thief in the night. And that is so He can encourage us to stay awake and pray. 'We have no right to move up all by ourselves', she'd fling at him all the time. As if the others with whom, to put it mildly, we shared a lifetime of rough times had never even existed. 'We have no right.' I mean, sometimes you move up alone, so you won't have to lug the rest along like a millstone or have them drag you down, go back to where you started from. For this woman of faith and prayer, one has no right. Period. Otherwise, there will always be an eye fixed on you, the same eye that was already watching Cain in the grave where he'd buried himself alive, thinking he could escape from God's wrath after he'd slain his brother Abel.

In his Sunday sermons, the pastor—at that time Ma Robinson hadn't taken over yet by creating her own church—would often talk about the need to stand shoulder to shoulder; for the strongest to hold out their hand to the weakest. That is basic Christian charity, well-planned solidarity as well, which takes you back to your humanity. Without it, your people will see you as an upstart and won't forgive you for that, even if God might show you compassion. Others will make the most of your leaving your roots behind to exploit your frailty, lay you bare, and send you back to where you came from, as naked as on the first day of the Creation. A little like the careless lamb finding itself in the middle of nowhere before wolves devour it. High up in his pulpit, the pastor would point an accusing finger at the congregation to make very sure that if one of us were to cut loose by way of the Lotto, for example, which all the adults in the district played, and even some of the minors—because the Pakistani of the minimarket managed to turn a blind eye to such purchases—well then, that person wouldn't let the others down and the church even less.

And although she was a big woman, Emmett's mom would start flitting around like a hummingbird from her native South as soon as she heard the first notes of the music, eyes rolled back, already imagining herself among the saints called up high for the solemn meeting with the Almighty, as she sang: 'In the Sky, in the Sky, in the Sky/I will see Him one day'.

On the way home, my big little brother would get a diluted version of the sermon, the way that parents will cut a cup of coffee that's too strong with hot water for children who want to imitate the grown-ups. A review of the sermon would accompany him for the rest of the day until dinner, if there was any. Into his sleep, according to what he told me. In the end, it caused him nightmares. He'd see himself miraculously crossing the turbulent waters of a river, walking straight ahead without turning around, without listening to the screams that reached him from the other bank, until he couldn't hear them any longer. Then he'd wake up covered in sweat, his heart racing.

There are moments, nevertheless, his mother would moralize, when one even has the duty to look back despite the fear of being turned into a pillar of salt. Extending a hand to those less fortunate when you've managed to get away is part of that. In addition, she had already made up a list of people in need, once he'd signed on with a major NFL franchise. Under penalty of being rejected by her and all his people. First there were the neighborhood kids, before they'd follow in their father's, sometimes their mother's, footsteps on the road to sin and perdition. Those little angels hadn't asked to be born, but God and the errors of their mothers' ways had put them on our path in order to look into our own souls. They were her supreme priority.

'You have to pull evil out by its roots,' she'd say. 'It's the only way to break the ancient curse of the sons and daughters of Ham.'

Curse, my ass! You can have faith without believing in all that nonsense. It's like the story of Abishag, the Shulamite in the "Song of Songs". In the translation, white folks tossed in a 'but', coming out of nowhere, while Solomon sang nothing of the sort. That's what a pastor explained on television. As if being black and beautiful weren't naturally compatible. As if it had to be justified, almost apologized for.

In any case, for this pious woman the links with the practices of enslavement had to be cut, when Black males were used as studs to augment the master's chattle, their descendants sold to the other side of the country without them having any say in it. And the women they lusted after were like a fountain on the side of the road where every white predator who so desired would come to drink his fill. That emasculates a man. The Black man reaped the legacy without asking himself any questions. Treating his companion like an old rag is one thing, but abandoning your own kin! That really got Emmett's mom worked up. Only unfailing solidarity, she advocated, would help to create a new generation disconnected from our wounds. Disconnected from the scars that since time immemorial, since we set foot on this damned American soil, come with the communal march. She believed wholeheartedly in her theory. No need to have studied at a great university to understand that, is there?

After the little angels came the mothers, often single. They'd had them young, sometimes even before the age of consent. Because no one had taught them to protect themselves from smooth talkers with honeyed tongues.

To protect themselves period. She knew what she was talking about because she'd let herself be fooled by Emmett's father, who could sweet-talk anyone, as they say around here. And there you are, just barely out of your childhood and still dreaming of Prince Charming, having to exchange the Disney doll for one that's made of flesh and blood, to swaddle a little being who'd never asked to land in this valley of tears. To improvise something as a couple that resembles a good relationship with a guy—in a room at the in-laws, or better yet at one of the mothers-in-law of these often single-parent families—who's going to pack his bags at the first argument under the pretext that you're insufferable, while he's the irresponsible one. Then the educated folks won't hesitate to confine you to the image of the "Angry Black Woman", as they call this group of women with whom you've a hard time identifying. But they don't care about that.

In a nutshell, you very quickly find yourself playing the doting mother all by yourself, because in the meantime the bastard has split; solo or with someone else, whatever. Without a trace. Without giving a sign of life, even less any alimony. So, you start looking for someone else to help you bear the burden, that's only human. The expenses, keeping the pot boiling every day, the obligatory extras, all of it isn't cheap. You also tell yourself that the little angel will need a father figure. And you, you need 'body heat'—that, too, is only human—the nights when the Midwest winter holds your bones accountable and you've turned off the heat to reduce the bills. Excuses of that nature. And the guy takes advantage of it to plant one or two more seeds in your belly before he, too, clears out, leaving you no other alternative than to sign up for food stamps, a program for people like

Emmett's mom, and for a good portion of the women in Franklin and of the new arrivals who've come in search of their share of the American dream.

Fortunately, our men aren't all like that. But a Black woman in our situation must get up early to get hold of a good one. You're frequently outstripped by a sister who's gone to college and pulled herself up. Sometimes it's a little Latina—they're all the rage, those girls, Black athletes have turned them into their trophy, I don't know what they have that we don't—or even a White one, half loony, because you've got to be off your rocker to come pick up a guy in this ghetto. No wonder we're angry, right? There aren't enough of them as it is, so they have to come charging in from who knows where to steal the best ones from us. Well, the least bad ones. Like bats from their caves to come and binge on the finest fruits from a tree, leaving only the unripe or rotten ones for the locals.

But, back to the point, I ran into Emmett just this morning. Since that slut Angela—there's no other word for her—left, we've seen less of each other. And to think that I was the one who hooked her up with him, believing I was doing the right thing. When he came back to the neighborhood after all those years away, he didn't talk about it much, not even to me. I felt so bad for him with his two kids whose mother or mothers nobody knew anything about. I told myself that something had to be done. Look, I could have served as their stepmom, but Emmett had assigned me my role since we were teenagers, and I stuck to it. So then I thought of Angela, a longtime friend who was living in Madison. If I couldn't have him for myself, might as well have a sister have the benefit.

True, she had a reputation for running around, and not turning a blind eye to a man's smile even when she was already in someone else's arms. That's why I'd always kept them far apart from each other. But she also knew that Emmett was my brother, she would behave appropriately with him. And for herself, too. It was time for her to settle down. She scarcely pretended to resist when I introduced him to her. Very soon after she'd moved to Franklin. Emmett, who since his return was living with his mother and the kids, had rented a house to make her more welcome and all of that. In the time it took to produce a third child, she made the most of their going through a bad patch when he was a little down and out of work, to take off with someone else and leave him with the kid on his hands.

Since then Emmett and I saw less of each other. Not because he was angry with me, that wasn't his style. Or perhaps a little, who knows. It's just that he had his life and I had mine. Both of us struggling to make it to the end of the month. Holding our own, without damaging our dignity. But as soon as we would meet we'd be in a rush to tell each other our stories. A habit that dated back to our childhood. That morning I'd left my place as I did every morning when I had to work, six days out of seven that is. I help the middle class white folks pack up their items at a supermarket at the other end of town, which sells the organic products they've turned into a religion and that cost an arm and a leg. You put the purchases in the cart for them, and if it's not too busy, you take it to their car and help them put the bags in the trunk. Sometimes one of them slips you a dollar or two, not counting the twenty-five cents for the cart that you return on the way back, which allows you to have a better day.

These days, in addition to that lousy virus, you see the customers less. They prefer buying on the internet and having it delivered to the house. When I went out, the weather report announced radiant sunshine for this whole early springtime day. That was really something, for the winter had been rough, as it so often is in Wisconsin. I hadn't taken two steps when I ran into Emmett.

'How are you, sweetheart?' he said. He always had a kind word for everyone. In that regard he hadn't changed very much.

'Times are tough,' I told him. 'Are you going to kick me in the butt or lend me a hand?' I knew that would make him laugh. Indeed, he guffawed as he heard me use his own expression word for word.

'You're lucky to just have it tough, Shorty. Me, I don't even have a Kentucky Fried chicken wing.'

He always had a ready answer when he wanted. If not, he'd just keep quiet. Ah, yes, he would. He could spend an entire day without opening his mouth, not having anything to say to anyone. It all went on up there, inside his head. He would refer to his recent lay-off as the result of that filthy thing that the whole world had expected to stay in China. For them three or four million dead is just a drop in the water of Lake Michigan, they don't even notice it. In the worst case scenario it would have stayed in Europe without crossing the Atlantic. It seems they have everything there: free social security, unemployment insurance, extended paid leave, paternal leave for the guys who don't do jack, for it's us women who bring the children into the world, get up in the middle of the night to nurse them, wipe them, and all the rest of it. In the end, the covid virus came here, breeding grief and mourning among the families. Here, too, it's people like us who paid the highest price. It was almost the end of Emmett's mom, a saintly woman—may God welcome her into his Kingdom—had she not died of an embolism three months earlier. He hadn't stopped grieving yet when he was fired from his job.

Still, when he talked to me he was always in a good mood. At least, he'd try, even if his heart wasn't in it. He was—I'm having a hard time speaking about him in the past—one of those who always has a smile for other people. That's why he came out to me with his little joke about tough times and chicken wings. Except that it wasn't a joke, he had three kids to look after. All by himself. The two he brought back from his long absence and the third he'd had with Angela. But I couldn't afford to miss my bus, be late for work, and risk getting laid off as well. With the virus, bosses are taking advantage of the slightest irregularity to dismiss you. And at my age, it's hell trying to find another job. So I cut our conversation short. Without that, between the trials and tribulations of our own people, the mental case they put in the White House, the childhood memories, our lifelong worries, we'd be going on for hours. I had to rush to catch the bus, which even so I almost missed, because of the extra pounds I carry around with me since I was very little. My spleen was about to explode when I put my big black ass on the seat. Luckily the driver had seen me approach in his rear-view mirror and waited for me.

When I next heard about Emmett again it was on the "Evening News" when I got home. I recognized the street, the minimarket, everything. There was no doubt. And to think I'd run into him that very morning, my big little brother. That he'd teased me, which almost made me miss my bus. If I hadn't been sitting down, I would certainly have fallen to the floor, my legs were so wobbly. Fortunately, I had a glass of water and my hypertension medication within reach. When I'd composed myself, I called Ma Robinson, a longtime family friend who was so distraught at the news that she'd left it to Marie-Hélène, a young Haitian from Chicago who was close to her and very active in the community, to get me Stokely's telephone number. I had to talk to someone who'd known him as well as I did. Perhaps so I could believe that he was still of this world, that I would run into his big body again coming around the corner of some street in Franklin. To that end, there wasn't anyone better than that numbskull Stoke, with whom I hadn't exchanged a word since before Emmett left for college. I kept my cool, swallowed my pride and dialed his number.

THE DEALER

EMMETT AND I KNEW each other since Benjamin Franklin Elementary School, a big red brick building between 23rd and Nash Streets, where over the generations, a lot of the neighborhood's kids learned to read and write. It wasn't just about being local. Or about the quality of the education; for that you'd need to go to a private school. Parents with the money to send their kids there were rare, as were kids with the strength of character to handle being black sheep in these whitey schools, so disconnected from their natural environment. Some sixty years ago when the first members of today's Franklin Heights community arrived, the white folks fled as one. In this country, and in the Midwest even more so, you don't mix apples and oranges. As soon as one black family even manages to turn up in a white neighborhood, antennas go up like the heads of bewildered meerkats ready to sound the alarm. When a second one arrives they pack up and get out one after another at lightning speed, eventually leaving the area to the newcomers.

That's what happened in Franklin. When Emmett and I were born in the mid-70's, me a little before him, there were already hardly any white faces in the neighborhood. The few who live here today are such misfits that it's made them colorblind. Look, I don't know if it's good or bad not to see people's skin color. If it's supposed to stick you with a whole slew of cliches, it's better that the other be blind. Otherwise, I don't see the harm. In short, besides these destitute people, the rest are either cops coming to inflate their statistics and bonuses or else a stranger who has lost his way. And they're always in a car, ready to make an immediate getaway at the first sign of trouble. White locals never venture out into these parts. They're taught from very early on to stay far away from the Northside. Or, if they really don't have any choice, to put the pedal to the metal, even if it means being pulled over for speeding. From time to time, you can see junkies looking for their fix. Just poor bastards, completely spaced out, with nothing more to lose than a life that is no longer even of any use to them. Those with the most cash get their supplies on neutral ground, around the trendy bars in midtown, or have it delivered to the house.

That's the 'hood, now half deserted at the city's northern exit, where my buddy and I grew up. Partly by the grace of God, partly the hard way, like weeds that'll sprout anywhere against all odds. Once we'd outgrown the carefree years of childhood, our lives went in different directions. Something to do with his mother who stopped Emmett from hanging out on the street, to use her words. Truth be told, it was us she didn't like. As if poverty had turned us into lepers. She could boast all she wanted, but she couldn't lie. Not to us in the hood. At the height of what they called the crisis, when the other cowboy was ruling the roost in the White House, she was doing her shopping with food stamps given by the state, getting her supplies from foodbanks at the Protestant churches. Like all the single-mother heads of households in Franklin. True enough, she made sure that her Emmett was always dressed in his Sunday best. End result, our mothers didn't stop pestering us to take her son as an example: 'Emmett is so nice; Emmett is so serious. He doesn't rip the knee of his pants rolling on the ground. Emmett this, Emmett that.... ' It made you want to beat him up if he hadn't been your pal, and so big, too.

Other than that, we were all in the same boat. Which is to say, living in rotten dumps that were falling apart slat by slat, infested with cockroaches and rats. Surrounded by other equally dilapidated hovels with boarded-up windows that junkies would sometimes take over as long as Franklin's street muscles don't decide for one reason or another to kick them out, because the police don't get involved in the affairs of Blacks and degenerates. After all, just let them exterminate each other! That'll be one problem less for the community. The first thing anyone does here is clear out as soon as you've earned a little money or found a more or less decent job. No matter where, as long as it's away from Franklin. If only just to enjoy the feeling of having reached a milestone in your life. Without that you stay here, vegetating, like a tree that withers uncut. Waiting to disappear into the ground. Following a stroke, a heart that gives out, hypertension, diabetes—or a stray bullet.

For us kids there was plenty to keep us from being bored. If Emmett and I couldn't manage to get away from our parents' watchfulness to play hooky with the zombies of the Union Cemetery, we had to make do with the basketball hoop three blocks farther down. That was worse: the dreary games that brought boys and girls of all ages together, organized by a charity worker in the courtyard behind the church. On our lucky days a friendly adult might take us to play football on the wasteland beside the factory. That's when Emmett had a real blast, it was his favorite sport. His mom would have never let him go if there hadn't been an adult present, that's obvious. And besides, his father hadn't left them yet. She could count on him to set him straight. Our parents kept us alive thanks to little jobs that paid peanuts. Mind you, I can't say that's changed a whole lot. The mothers were cleaning women in hotels or in the huge homes with a view over Lake Michigan in the swanky suburbs. The luckiest ones plodded along at the A. O. Smith factory, which adjoins Franklin Heights over more than a hundred acres. Or at Harley-Davidson in Menomonee Falls Village on the other side of Milwaukee. As long as the Smith factory was standing, it wasn't exactly a fortune but it would do. It held on until the mid-eighties.

We must have been about eight or ten, Emmett and I, when deindustrialization began, as they call the curse that came down on the neighborhood, its claws out. Following the owners' logic, the factory became less competitive. New cars no longer needed the parts that were made there. Other, more modern ones were being made somewhere else, outside the United States, and at a lower cost. It had had its day. Something like that. Result: the Smiths sold everything to another capitalist who hurried to transfer its production to South America or Asia. Without ever wondering how the fathers and mothers who for a long time had worked twelve-hour shifts on the assembly line there, well, how they were going to manage to feed their kids. Capitalism can't be bothered with these feelings. For Franklin's families that was the beginning of the end. It hit very close to home and they were all affected. From one day to the next, parents found themselves twiddling their thumbs at home and then, as time went by, fathers began taking to drink, which led to their becoming violent because they felt powerless, before taking off altogether.

The crack epidemic descended in its wake. An even more brutal plague than unemployment, it would shatter the already shaky families. When you're responsible for children, you're not too attentive anymore, right? You have to fill the fridge. There's nothing more unbearable than the eyes of a hungry kid. In a case like that, you'd do anything to give him a chance to throw himself on some food with his little fists, like a famished dog, and see him smile again. The trouble is that this lousy crack didn't spare the community. Many who'd lost their jobs, and couldn't find anything else got into it. In the end, between dealers and consumers, unemployment and alcohol, the area began to look like Baghdad, once the boys who fought there came back and were treated like dogs.

That was the moment my father went into the business. He wasn't proud of it, but he didn't exactly make a secret of it either. And then one day he found himself forced to stick a knife into the guts of some junkie. In self-defense, I promise you. I saw it all, I had a front row seat. But the white cops and the judge didn't think there were any extenuating circumstances, any legitimate defense, stuff like that. And even less because the junkie was white, too. My father got fifteen years in the joint, all expenses paid. Well, in a manner of speaking. When it was my turn to go in, I realized you got to pay for lots of stuff in there, everything that in the eyes of the wardens and the administration is a luxury: soap, toothpaste, toothbrush, shampoo. So, fifteen years, to settle his business account for having knifed the other poor guy, and coming within a hair of a live interview with Lucifer.

From that moment on, with Emmett's old man running off at about the same time, his mom didn't want him hanging around with us anymore ever. Not with me, not with those whose parents and brothers she suspected of dabbling in the same business, or sisters involved in activities she deemed an abomination. She wasn't fond of us to begin with. She said we were bad seeds. As if her son had been a saint. Me, I can tell you that he wasn't exactly squeaky-clean, to put it mildly. Not to speak ill of him, he was my bro; and even more because he isn't here anymore to defend himself. His mother could afford to act pretentious, she had just one mouth to feed besides her own. But, when Dad got his long stay behind bars, we really had to be more careful.

There were three of us siblings, plus our mom who'd never really worked outside the house. Other than as a cleaning woman paid in cash and upon request, on the whim of her employers, needless to say. These were for the most part wannabes, one of them a former neighbor who'd managed to move up in life and had gone to live a few blocks farther down on the edge of the Latino quarter, who wanted to rub mom's face in her measly frail success and, while putting distance between Franklin and herself, still wanted to keep a connection so she wouldn't be completely lost. Besides that, mom did a huge amount of work at home. Thanks to her, we never lacked for anything, well, anything that matters. The unnecessary things we had to do without. There she was from one day to the next with rent to pay because the place wasn't ours, three kids on her hands to be fed, clothed, and all the rest of it, you can imagine. She tried to earn her living honestly but it wasn't the right moment. Nowhere in Milwaukee. Plus, some single mothers ditched it all and went to Chicago to try and make a new life. Others had to get by very soberly so their kids wouldn't starve.

To complicate matters, our father had left debts behind; his suppliers wanted to get their money back; if not money then the merchandise, but he'd already disposed of it. The retailers took advantage of his being in the slammer to disappear into the mist. It was his problem if he'd gotten screwed, he should just have been more sly, they said. We couldn't do anything other than face the music. These guys didn't hesitate to threaten our mother on the phone and all that sort of stuff. If she wasn't home, no problem, they'd leave freaky messages for her. They made no effort at all not to upset us, like they're just neighborhood kids who shouldn't get mixed up with this. They didn't give a damn. Got straight to the point. Since I'm the oldest, I had to step up, if you see what I mean.

I started as a lookout, early in the evening and on weekends, on the corner of 24th Street and Auer Avenue, not too far from Moody Park and Union Cemetery. A kid attracts less attention, you see. Unless, of course, he's Black and the cop is white. That's how it is here. In the eyes of the cops you're Black first, a kid second. They can bump you off if they see you playing with a dummy gun. Afterwards, all they have to do is tell the judge they felt threatened. On the whole I was up to it. Very much so, in fact. So much so that those above me started to give me a few grams to sell. I kept going to school not to arouse any suspicion. Otherwise social services and the pastor would get on your back. I managed to take them all for a ride until the beginning of high school, a feat in itself, because many here drop out after middle school. Having said that, I didn't do shit in class. Never was very skilled at all those exercises that just mess with your head.

Mom closed one eye, then both, when I brought home report cards that already weren't so great but gradually were becoming more terrible— and brought home groceries. You have to understand she had no choice. She didn't ask any questions, no doubt because she was afraid to hear me say out loud what she already knew. It was also a way of protecting the other two. She must have told herself that if they had food, a roof over their head to keep them warm in the winter, well, then they wouldn't have to hang around on the street, and they'd avoid bad influences. With a bit of luck, and if they worked hard at school, they might land a scholarship to go to college and make something of themselves. If that's the will of God, she'd say; she didn't pray as much as Emmett's mom, but she wasn't the last one to enter the church and sing gospel either. In a way she sacrificed the oldest one to save the younger two.

That's where Emmett comes in. He and Authie and me—we always called her Authie, even though her real name is Autherine, but we found that too old-fashioned and too long to say—were an inseparable trio all through school. I remember so well the day we sealed our pact of eternal friendship so well. I think we must have been in third grade. We had no school and we were hanging out on the empty lot next to the factory. Authie said: 'What if we swore friendship for life like the pirates do?' We'd watched *Swashbuckler* on TV the night before, an old Caribbean pirate movie from the sixties with the Trinidadian Geoffrey Holder, the only one in the story who looked like us. Authie had taken out the razor blade she kept in her pocket, to defend herself she said. Just at the sight of the blade and the thought of the blood that would squirt from our forearms, Emmett began to keel over. In spite of being built like Frankenstein he'd always been afraid of blood. To have everyone agree I suggested another solution.

I unzipped my fly and with my back turned to them I unpacked my gear and pissed on the sun-burnt grass, which bubbled and steamed. Then I spat on my urine before inviting them to do the same. They came forward and took turns spitting on my piss. Then Emmett unzipped his pants, pulled out his dick, urinated, and all three of us spat on it. Then it was Authie's turn but she lost her nerve. She didn't want us staring at her pussy. Emmett told her that all she had to do was turn her back like us. But she was afraid that we'd gawk at her ass. If she didn't want to, I said, she could just go like a boy: lift up your skirt on one side, open your legs like a cowboy, move your panties aside with your index finger and pee standing up. She told me I was just too stupid. She wasn't a guy or a giraffe. I never did get the giraffe part. So, maybe to impress us, she cut herself with her blade. We didn't even see it coming. I had to hold Emmett so he wouldn't faint. Authie asked us to suck on her forearm, one at a time, like a vampire. Her blood was bitter, like the wild berries we used to pick in the cemetery. That's how we became friends for life.

When I got started in the business, I didn't tell them right away. Look, it was to protect them, just as with my siblings. And I didn't want them to get to me either. Yeah, what you doin', kid? Stop screwing around. You're playing with fire, you'll follow your old man into prison, end up between four planks. These guys, they're no choir boys... Emmett was the first to catch on. Perhaps it was his mother who told him straight out to stop hanging out with me, I was bad news, kids are what they are. Just because you leave a piece of wood in a backwater doesn't mean it'll turn into a crocodile. Shit like that, to explain to him why and how he shouldn't be around me. She must have freaked out, that old lady of his.

Emmett's father had just left the house, more or less at the same time that mine got his fifteen years in prison. The guy just packed his bags without any warning, without leaving a trace. Like so many others who failed to provide. Better to run, right? In his case, the local rumor had it that the crisis could easily be blamed on something else. The truth was that he'd run off with a neighbor. And that she'd ditched her own man and two kids to follow him. That they were busy simply chilling in the middle of nowhere in Alabama. The things adults say, unaware that the kids are listening. For a large part of Franklin it was no surprise. Emmett's mom was a tight-ass whose single blessing was that she swore only by the Bible and other expressions of religiosity. If you don't know how to take care of your man, there's always another woman who'll be only too happy to do it in your place, as the women in the hood said. No matter what, there had to be some truth in all that gossip. Emmett spent his time singing an old blues that none of us knew. The song talked about a guy who didn't want to set foot in Alabama again because a cop had bumped off his brother and they'd let him off scot-free. Stories that have always been known in this country.

In short, Emmett's situation was no different than ours, except that his mom had an easier time putting food on the table, since he was an only child. Feeding two is easier than feeding four, right? Still, although his mom acted so proud, well, she had a hard time, too, like everyone else in this corner of Franklin. Even if she had more steady work then. Makes you wonder how she managed that, anyway, 'cause jobs weren't easy to come by and didn't come knocking at your door. And if ever you saw one it was always far away, getting away from you. She'd play goody-two-shoes, who knows what was behind that. In the end, she got a job at Harley-Davidson until she was laid off also because the economic crisis had gotten worse. After being brought to its knees first, the neighborhood found itself with its nose in the dirt. Like being struck down, spilling its last drop of blood. And for my brother that was the last straw.

How many times did I help him out with a Domino's

or a KFC menu, sometimes the only food for an entire day. Without that, we'd have downright starved. There was no Good Lord to throw manna from heaven, as they say in the Bible. There were days when we could have killed for a slice or a chicken wing. People don't believe you when you say that. They answer that you're in the United States of America, a great country. If you aren't lazy, well then, you can realize your dreams of money and everything else. But we, we were just goddamn kids. What could we do? Go back down into the mines, like a century before? Or go out on the street to shine white men's shoes for fifty cents, as in the era of segregation, saying yessah, thankya sah?

That's when Emmett joined my crew. Despite himself, I should add. We'd just finished 6th or 7th grade, I don't remember anymore. At the time Franklin Heights was a warzone for real. Luckily, the area was already teeming with innumerable churches of every Protestant denomination and their support networks. Thanks to them, we could eat once or twice a day. Before, there was the cafeteria with free breakfast and afternoon snacks, which they started at the end of elementary school, at Benjamin Franklin. On the initiative of two teachers: Ma'am Mahalia who lived in the neighborhood, and a white woman who'd strayed into the area and seemed to have made it her mission to rescue little Black children so she could enter the Kingdom of Heaven. Actually, I was wrong to see things that way, for she did a hell of a job. Together with her coworker she had a lot to do with the fact that we didn't die of hunger. That we didn't get involved in the business any sooner.

But hey, we have our dignity. In any case, it wasn't

enough to plug all the holes in the roof of our life. Like Emmett, always carrying the football around, that I had given him, laced up in the traditional way. I never understood where that passion of his came from. The city doesn't have an NFL team, while we do have the Bucks in basketball who are defending themselves super well lately, are in the play-offs and everything. At the time, 'Jesus'—as we used to call Ray Allen because of the ease with which he made three-point field goals, which made him the best shooter in all of the Christian world—and Kareem Abdul Jabbar before him, those guys, their triumphs spoke to everybody. In baseball we had the Brewers, and we could be proud of them until they went downhill in the Central Division. To find a football team to dream of you need to go to the Green Bay Packers, two hours from here. It's Wisconsin, no denying that, but it's not our town.

Emmett, he was so proud the day that I gave him that ball. Granted, at first I didn't tell him what was inside. But after he'd let it get 'stolen' two or three times and found it again as if by accident, I finally told him. He was my pal, I couldn't keep lying to him all the time. I explained there was no risk. It would never enter a cop's mind. And besides, he didn't have to do anything, just 'forget' it somewhere and the trick was done. No one would be any the wiser. It would put peanut butter on his bread and help his mom. If your father isn't there when you're thirteen, it's up to you to take over.

Since he was the youngest of the group, I think he was intent on showing he had the guts. In fact, he didn't have any at all, because he quit after only two or three months, telling me that I, too, should stop since it was bound to end badly. Perhaps he was afraid of being beaten or of his mom's tears, he'd always been a mama's boy, Perhaps it was Authie who also got worked up over it. She's great at that little game. Besides, from the day that Emmett quit she never talked to me again. He did, but distantly, when Shorty or his mother weren't hanging around. That's to say, not very much anymore, 'cause he was always tied to the apron strings of one or the other.

In those years there was a sort of cold war going on between us, as we used to say during that time. Until he got the scholarship and left for college. Meanwhile, I'd dropped out of school before I got nabbed. A detention center for delinquent minors, I wasn't sixteen yet. When I came out, I got caught over a brawl between dealers that I wasn't even involved in. I'd come back from the two years in juvie full of good intentions, and run into a teacher there, a secular boy scout, who saw the real me inside. He gave me back my self-confidence, explained that I had to show them that their statistics were wrong. That if I continued this way I'd be going straight to where they'd been planning to send me all along. In short, I'd be proving them right. That would be stupid, because they'd have won twice and me, I would have lost everything. His speech did something to me. But not even a week went by before I got caught red-handed.

It was the week I turned eighteen. I was older than the other two, by two years I believe. Meanwhile I couldn't even talk with Emmett; he was working like a dog to try to secure his scholarship. I also suspect Authie and his mother of putting up barriers. In their eyes I'd become an example to stay away from. I can just imagine the whole scenario: Emmett with hanging head while the two bitches tell him off.

Authie: 'Little bro, don't be stupid. You've got a golden opportunity waiting for you. You can't make an omelet without breaking any eggs. And the rotten ones, even if it's just one, you throw them out if you don't want to ruin the taste of the whole thing. You're not going to keep me from putting my hands together at the stadium, are you? In a VIP seat, obviously.'

His mother, preaching like Ma Robinson: 'You'd better keep Stokely at a distance if you want to realize the goal that the Almighty has assigned to you in life: to be the beacon of Franklin Heights. It's written in Matthew 5:29–30: "And if thy right eye offend thee, pluck it out and cast it from thee [. . .]. And if thy right hand offend thee, cut it off and cast it from thee: for it is profitable for thee that one of thy members should perish, and not that thy whole body should be cast into hell."' She'd all but quote the entire New Testament to him.

That's how she talked, Emmett's mom, so full of proverbs and parables that you'd think the good woman was Christ himself. Long story short, the two cops, both white, the same ones who'd already sent me to the reformatory, caught me again. This time they were flanked by a Black one, too. One of them, his face covered with pockmarks, exulted: 'I told you we'd see each other again. I know your type. There's not much to be done with you.' And he ratcheted the handcuffs as tightly as he could. Since I was on probation, the judge, who was also White, didn't waste any time on me. Ten years to do my time for the crime. I don't want to make any excuses, I gambled and lost. But my question is: how's any of this fair? I hear people say: 'Yeah, he acts the victim and all that as if it hasn't happened to anyone else.' My answer: 'The justice of those in power is that might makes right. Better not to have anything to do with it.'

When I got out, the neighborhood had changed for the worse. Everything had become more expensive, because of the constantly rising inflation, the repeated financial crises, the stock market's yoyo that shocks even nature, the virtual economy—all the things that the experts talk about on television. Emmett, who hadn't succeeded in joining the NFL, took a lot more time to come back home. With two kids on his hands. After going all over the place from California to North Carolina, via Louisiana, maybe in search of his father. Actually, he never talked to me about it but I know that his absence really hit him hard. Like me, he came back to the house he'd left. Back to his mother who hadn't left the neighborhood. She could have afforded it. From time to time we'd greet each other, have a little chat. Once we even had a beer together. He realized that I was clean now. I became a mediator between the cops, social services, to try to keep the neighborhood kids from screwing up the way I had. It's a job of permanent acrobatics. Sometimes it works. Sometimes it doesn't. Brothers accuse you of betrayal. Cops suspect you of not really having kicked the habit. Always caught in the crossfire, trying to convince both sides of your good faith. That's life let's face it.

Emmett was still as chill as always, a sweet guy. But something inside him had broken, it was clear. He had lost his fire. The system had reduced him to a zombie. He did lots of little jobs to feed the three children that he'd been stuck with after the mother of the last little one, a girl, had walked out on him to find out if the grass was any greener somewhere else. He should have had a mission like mine, that would have given his life some meaning. He did try to interest the Franklin Heights youth in football, but that idea didn't take. Those kids grew up in the glory years of Sam Cassell, alias 'Sam I Am', of 'Big Dog' Robinson, and of the other stars of the Milwaukee Bucks. For them there was only basketball, or dealing. In their eyes, the only means to get away. He was crushed that he couldn't communicate his passion for football to them.

On the other hand, Authie and I never spoke again, didn't even greet each other. As if she didn't believe I'd turned the page. She really holds a grudge, Shorty does. Only Emmett could call her by that name, which he'd given her. If anyone else dared to go there, she'd go into hurricane mode. She must have thought I'd drag her Emmett back onto the wrong path. She was always in love with him, ever since she was very young. Even if nothing ever happened between them, and it hadn't as Emmett swore to me on the head of his mother. She would have wanted it. She must think I was the one who kept Emmett from letting her play substitute mother to his girls.

Everyone, or almost everyone, knows the rest. The homicide filmed live and broadcast worldwide via satellite. His slow dying agony that kept the entire planet breathless. That's how we made up, Authie and me. She phoned me that very evening. Her call surprised me but I knew. She needed to talk about Emmett. The man that only we had known, she and I. Together with him we'd been 'the three musketeers'. I think it did her good. Me, too.

And then there was the march in honor of Emmett

that we'd organized right after the funeral. Men, women, children of all colors had come rushing down from every corner of the land to participate. Among them were two former teachers from Benjamin Franklin whom I hadn't seen since then, and others who were new to me: Emmett's ex-football coach at the university, his fiancée at the time, an NFL star....

At the end we weren't far from the municipal building when someone, I don't remember who exactly, came up with the idea. And with good reason. In fact, there was no real leader of this event despite the good will of Ma Robinson and her two collaborators, a young Haitian-American woman from Chicago and her white Rasta fiancé. Like in the era of the Reverend Martin Luther King, Malcolm X, Angela Davis, and Stokely Carmichael. With today's social networks they draw from all over and in all directions. There's no single discourse, no single action that could bring the system to its knees for good. Everyone improvises as a leader, says any old thing and its opposite. Mind you, the good will is there. But it's not enough. You need unity, someone to take control, right? Otherwise it goes down the tubes.

The idea was launched at the end of the march when we weren't too far from the municipal building. I wouldn't know who came up with it. Perhaps someone from another movement who'd slipped in among us. One of the women from Black Lives Matter—I'm not sure, because those girls don't seem violent—or from some other group maybe. It was a woman's voice. Yes, that I remember very clearly. A clear voice, packed with suppressed rage that carries and knows how to make itself heard. She didn't have to say very much.

Even so, everyone was up for it. Had to go to battle with the supremacists on the other side, those of the Aryan Nation and the rest who wouldn't stop giving us trouble. Had to shove their arrogance and prejudices down their throat, damn it. Had to make them understand that we weren't sheep heading for the slaughterhouse without saying a word. If they wanted a fight, they'd get one. All the more because there were a hundred times more of us. And there they were, facing us, coming toward us gesturing like angry apes. That's how it went down, that's the story.

II

THE UNIVERSITY OF FOOTBALL AND OF LIFE

Millions of stars separate us
Millions of trees and animals.
Millions of human faces
Are unknown to you and me.
So many boundaries, my beloved!
So many boundaries for a love!
RENÉ DEPESTRE
"Boundaries", from *Journal of a sea animal*

THE COACH

Coming to our university on an athletic scholarship was a last-chance opportunity for Emmett. Right from the start he put tremendous pressure on himself, even more so than other student-athletes entering under the same conditions. Unprecedented in my whole career as a coach, and I'm close to retirement. From the beginning his primary adversary, if not his worst enemy, was fear of failure. The more time went by the more that fear took over. In comparison—and I'm hardly exaggerating—a professional player is far less stressed the night before he plays in the Super Bowl, the NFL championship, which is watched worldwide, the one that is every player's dream to play in. The overexposure of the sport in the media, the challenge to meet expectations, the entourage, it all contributed enormously to Emmet's fear.

In a way I understood it, even if it was my job to put him in the best possible position to succeed. Like all young men in his situation, Emmett had known pressure since high school, from the moment he decided to land a scholarship so that he could play football at the university level. Due to the ferocious competition more than nine out of ten athletes won't make it. Once that milestone has been achieved, the ultracompetitive system adds an even more intimidating layer, for, after all these sacrifices, less than two percent will finally become professionals.

Emmett had another major handicap to overcome before he could even hope to be counted among the fortunate few. In addition to not being very good academically, he came from a more than underprivileged Black family, with a single parent in the bargain. I know what I'm talking about, my experience was very similar; I could have traced his trajectory without even having seen his file. He didn't have the luck of having a father at home. From one day to the next there's this kid from a black ghetto in Milwaukee, raised by a mother in the Pentecostal faith, catapulted into a universe of affluent white middle-class Catholics. It was obvious that he felt like a fish out of water. He didn't know the codes, he seemed on guard all the time, like an animal set loose in a hostile environment.

Many others in his place would have chosen aggressiveness as a defense. The best defense in life and on the field is to attack, isn't it? He did the exact opposite. In the early days he withdrew into himself. He took no initiative. He settled for answering his teammates when they addressed him. He tried to overcompensate with extreme kindness. As if he didn't feel legitimate and was apologizing for just being there. In short, the impostor syndrome. And his playing suffered because of it. He was hesitant, he brought no assertiveness at all to his game. Which is a shame, for a linebacker's role is to disrupt the offense. He was anything but the hulk whose talent the scouts had bragged to me about and whose videotapes I'd viewed. We had to find a way to free up all that energy. How to manage that without coming at him head-on and risk seeing him get his back up?

In view of the boy's potential, I decided to take him under my wing. Since he knew no one in town and didn't go home during breaks, I used to invite him to our house on weekends in the hope that he'd relax a little. My wife, my two daughters, and I were one of the three all-Black families at the college. We lived at some distance from the campus in a very comfortable home with an unobstructed view, an open veranda and a front lawn, surrounded in the back and on the sides by a hedge that I maintained both summer and winter under my wife's iron rule. As a good Southerner, she has a warm, maternal side and is also an outstanding cook. As for me, the rare times that I'm in the kitchen I can say in all modesty that I don't acquit myself badly at all.

All of it immediately put Emmett at ease. He didn't have to be begged to do justice to the table and honor the lady of the house as well. In my day I've seen some athletes who were big eaters—one has to recoup the energy spent on the field—but hardly ever anyone like him. He fell under the spell of the girls, too, seven and nine years old, real chatterboxes, who quickly turned him into their pet. He was all too happy to oblige. Being an only son he'd now found two little sisters. You had to see the three of them rolling around like puppies in the back yard before they'd come back inside all covered with dust, sometimes with mud.

My wife, who hated cleaning up after them, didn't su-
garcoat things when she told him off. 'Emmett, you're the
oldest one here; you need to set the right example. If that's a
problem for you, the vacuum and the mop are in the broom
closet next to the toilet.' His mother must have dealt with
him the same way because he'd answer very sheepishly: 'Yes,
ma'am.' And in a flash my wife would say: 'Stop calling me
ma'am, I'm not your grandmother.' She couldn't stand the all
too formal 'ma'am' that made her seem older than she really was, although it simply attested to Emmett having been
raised properly.

This cozy family atmosphere allowed for the high-
ly satisfying discussions we had together. The boy had an
encyclopedic knowledge of football in general, and of his
position in particular. Quite surprising at a time when the
internet was in its infancy and when the young kids weren't
yet walking around with their heads down and noses glued
to their smartphones. He told me he'd spent hours and hours
at his high school's library reading the sports magazines and
articles, and listening to those adults in his neighborhood
who were crazy about football, always talking about it at
the local barbershop where his father used to take him and,
once his dad had disappeared, where he continued going
without his mother's knowledge. As is so often the case, his
expertise didn't stop with just the players who'd marked his
generation, like Lawrence Taylor, who was the key to the
success of the New York Giants, or Mike Singletary of the
Chicago Bears. Once he got started, he was peerless talking
about guys like Willie Lanier or Bobby Bell whose feats were
accomplished long before Emmett had come into the world.

He'd speak with such passion that even those least enthusiastic about football would sometimes stop what they were doing for a moment just to listen to him.

Without playing the veteran I'd tell him my story. I wanted him to know how I'd come to be a coach at a private Catholic institution whose team was preparing to join an NCAA conference. I didn't hide from him that I'd gladly have forgone this position for a professional career before then becoming an NFL trainer or a TV football commentator. That being the case, it would be rude of me to complain. I landed the job and was very well paid at that. And it didn't come falling from the sky for me. 'Hell no!' They didn't offer it to me for my beautiful eyes or my Colgate smile. 'Hell no!' my wife would echo each time, like a gospel response; she'd been a choir member in New Jersey before she followed me for my work. I explained to him how even at this level I had to fight like a starving man, be serious, lead a healthy lifestyle. 'Oh yeah!' my wife would add.

Truthfully, I wanted to suggest a model to him with whom he could identify without carrying on about Malcolm X, Martin Luther King, Rosa Parks, Mary Louise Smith, or Angela Davis. I wanted to show him that he could get there if he found the way to achieve his goal. In the meantime he should remember one thing: he was where he was because he deserved it. Life never gives anything for free, 'Hell no!'. Neither does Uncle Sam. 'Hell no!' Everyone's fate is in his own hands. 'Oh yeah!' Plain words he could figure out by himself and make his own. One night when the five of us were together at the house, I arranged for the girls to recite their favorite poem for me. 'Mother to Son', a poem by Langston Hughes that my wife used to repeat to them before they fell asleep. As a result they knew it by heart and we would say it together. That night they wanted to show off to Emmett and their hearts were really in it. Standing before their big 'brother', they began as soon as my wife had spoken the first line: 'Well, son, I'll tell you:'

> *Life for me ain't been no crystal stair.*
> *It's had tacks in it,*
> *And splinters,*
> *And boards torn up,*
> *And places with no carpet on the floor—*
> *Bare;*
> *But all the time*
> *I'se been a'climbin' on,*
> *And reachin' landin's,*
> *And turnin' corners,*
> *And sometimes goin' in the dark,*
> *Where there ain't been no light.*
> *So boy, don't you turn back;*
> *Don't you sit down on the steps,*
> *'Cause you finds it's kinder hard;*
> *Don't you fall now—*
> *For I'se still goin', honey,*
> *I'se still climbin',*
> *And life for me ain't been no crystal stair.*

That night I saw tears running down the cheeks of this strong young man who had, after all, been through the mill on the much more corrupt streets of Franklin Heights. A simple poem had laid bare the sensitivity that was concealed beneath his shell. He tried to hide them from our eyes by opening his arms to embrace the girls, burying his head between their shoulders. Maybe he was thinking of his mother whom he hadn't seen since his arrival almost two months before. Maybe the warm atmosphere of the early fall made him think of the family he would have wanted but that life hadn't given him. No matter. It still added to activating the trigger that would get him to validate the hope placed in him.

The following week I already didn't recognize him on the field. At last I saw the jewel the scouts had described to me. He no longer hesitated smashing into the players who were mostly white, but without the slightest personal animosity. To him, they were adversaries identifiable only by the color of their T-shirt. Day after day, he managed to release the negative energy amassed from the moment he was born in a Milwaukee ghetto, by the father's desertion, and by the discrimination he'd suffered along the way. I never broached the matter with him, it wasn't necessary. I knew it and he knew that I knew. All the injustice that fate had dealt him, which hindered the progress of those who didn't come from a well-to-do family and that quite a few turned against themselves through the use of drugs, violence, and the self-destruction so common among the youth in our neighborhoods—took form in Emmett as excessive timidity that he was going to have to manage to convert into positive energy.

He wasn't just a solid hunk who settled for beating up on the dancers as they like to mockingly refer to their opponents, svelte, swift and slippery like eels. Or a mountain at 6 foot 3 and 243 pounds of muscle that the attackers repeatedly came up against, whom his teammates soon nicknamed 'The Steel Mountain'. In addition to his huge build and weight, he also possessed versatility and speed. His flexibility allowed him to go beyond his role, changing any attempts at short notice if other players weren't in position. He could sprint like the finest quarterbacks. His natural talent was such that, with less muscular mass, had he devoted himself to track, he would have been equally successful in the one or two hundred meter dash. He told me that he'd briefly hesitated between football and basketball, which he played with equal success in high school. Before he decided on football he'd even been approached by Marquette, a Catholic university in Milwaukee, that played NCAA Division One basketball. To round out the whole picture, he'd add the determination he drew from his social background and the discipline he gained from my daily coaching. Thereafter, nothing could stop him anymore, I was convinced of it.

However, after reaching a certain peak he began to level off, almost as if he'd attained his limits. It was predictable. We then had to avoid the doubt beginning to creep in that he could reach the next level. He seemed to accept the role of perpetual promise, powerless to go beyond where he was. As long as it was a matter of technical or athletic progress, I knew how to help him overcome this obstacle of self-doubt. The task proved difficult, though, all the more so because a player from the rival state university team had been drafted at the end of his second year. Of course, the news reached us. The campus felt it was an affront, would we have a player drafted? It intensified the pressure on Emmett. When all is said and done, these stimulating rivalries show whether an athlete truly has what it takes.

There are much harder things for a coach. Timid as Emmett was at the beginning, as the weeks and the months went by he took on the role of a charismatic player, the natural captain that teammates, sometimes one or even two years ahead of him, would turn to. His fame began to surpass the photos posted around the campus. The local radio and television called on him for interviews. They saw a rising star in him, whose trajectory was sure to break him into the NFL. And it definitely whetted the appetite of agents whom I tried to keep at a distance as long as he wasn't a senior yet, just so he could get out of there with a diploma, should the NFL not recruit him. From then on those sharks converged on the campus to watch him in training, dangling the stars and the moon before him, while he was barely able to look up at the sky.

That wasn't all I was worried about. Sometimes, even outside game days, I'd see him being followed by a slew of little white girls—normal, one might say, since the university counted less than four-percent Blacks of both sexes. I was afraid that he already imagined himself at the top and that his performance on the field would suffer from it. The desire to squander his energy on one-night stands was strong, it had happened to others before him. In either case, he was at risk of overrating himself and missing out on his dream. But I have to admit that I was wrong. That wasn't his style. Despite the temptations, the kid kept his eyes riveted on his goals, solid as a rock, better yet, solid as a linebacker.

Even so, I was relieved when at the end of his sophomore year or the start of his junior year, I don't really remember any more, he began to seriously date a girl who was a year ahead of him. As a coach, other than prohibiting any liaison—which was briefly a fashionable fantasy—I have always encouraged this type of regular relationship. It brings the man some stability and keeps the athlete from running around. It's also an inexpensive way of having a bodyguard prone to controlling his comings and goings. In case of trouble with the guy in question, I know who to turn to. That being the case and without being cynical, I had no illusions about the true feelings of those naïve young women, who at a very tender age are taught to go after a 'meal ticket', as student-athletes are referred to here. And who better than a potential professional football player to provide them with greens, butter, and caviar all on the same tray and on a silver plate at that? In Emmett's case, wealth and fame could compensate for a lot of shortcomings, erase many faults, in the eyes of any future parents-in-law.

The girls were the first to get me thinking. I remember that day very well. My wife and I had invited him for Thanksgiving, knowing that he wouldn't go home to Milwaukee because of the distance, the money, and a lack of facilities available to him that would let him keep practicing during the break. The turkey, golden-brown and stuffed to perfection, was accompanied by cornbread, sweet potatoes, and many other delicious dishes. As for me, I'd finished the tasks that the lady of the house had entrusted to me: bring the turkey and the wine home from the supermarket the night before; set the table on the day itself; make sure the girls would be ready on time, things like that. At one point toward the end of the meal, the girls started whispering together. Then the little one turned to Emmett and asked him point blank if he had a fiancée. The poor guy was utterly embarrassed. If Blacks could blush he would have turned pure crimson. Unable of lying to his little 'sisters' he finally stammered, 'She's not really a fiancée.'

'Then what is she?' the youngest and sassiest of the two, asked.

'Eh, let's say she's a good friend.'

'Is she in your class?' the older one asked.

'No, she's not.'

'You kiss each other on the mouth?'

'That's enough, girls. Stop those questions of yours.' My wife intervened to get him out of trouble. 'Just clear the table instead.'

But when Emmett joined her to rinse the dishes and put them in the dishwasher, she grilled him, too. That's how I found out about the 'fiancée', and that she was studying anthropology at the university. Still, I very unobtrusively did my own little investigation with two colleagues, a couple of practicing Catholics, to find out more about her. Without a single word about it to Emmett, of course. Had he known, he might have blamed me for interfering in his private life. Like myself, these colleagues insisted that the boys on campus conduct themselves beyond reproach and simultaneously be able to give the very best of themselves on the field. For several years now, our institution, more accustomed to shining on the basketball court like so many Catholic universities, was determined to make a name for itself in football as well. It was out of the question that a sex scandal should impede these efforts.

Personally, I was torn over the relationship. Even if, I admit, it was giving Emmett some emotional stability. Oh, not because the girl was white, let's be clear. I think that with its past, not to mention our present, it's a good sign that this society is able to give itself the opportunity to do a little blending. It'll take time, I know. A lot of time even. Human beings rarely rush to run away from their screw-ups, or their fears if you prefer. What bothered me about this story was to find out that she intended to specialize in Black or African-American Studies, I don't recall which. Besides, I don't see the difference. That's what I was unsure about. The interest in our community certainly showed that she wasn't merely after someone with strong financial prospects. On the other hand, it was hard to take that she saw us as an object of study. I've never seen a Black person take up White or European-American Studies. I'm not even sure that such fields exist. I consoled myself thinking: 'After all, that's for Emmett to worry about.' He was old enough to know what he wanted. Ultimately, this relationship would perhaps help him to grow as a human being. And since the girl had the reputation of being serious, that was something, at least.

The following months would confirm this when Emmett was forced to face his first serious injury: three broken ribs and a fractured collarbone if I remember correctly. Every athlete lives in dread of this and does his utmost to eliminate the risk. But when that day does come you realize you weren't really prepared to handle it. Once the shock is over and the surgery behind you—in the event you needed surgery—the only question running through your head is whether and when you can play again. No matter how much the doctor reassures you, as he did with Emmett, until you've gotten back on the field, felt the strength again that you thought you'd lost, you're not sure of anything. At moments like that, when you keep mulling things over and over again inside your head and come up with the darkest ideas, your immediate circle plays a significant role.

Far from Milwaukee, away from his mother, his friends, this girl turned out to be a veritable guardian angel for Emmett. From what I understood, she made him spend the time of his convalescence at her studio downtown where she could pamper him as much as she wanted and cook him healthy meals every day. If not, he would have stayed in his dormitory room, down in the dumps, surrounded by the noisy comings and goings of the other students. Although she had her own classes to attend, the time that she could be by his side must have helped him get through the ordeal without too much damage, helped him overcome the obsessive fear that everything would come to an end, which was already eating him up inside.

In the early days I went to see him at the hospital. Once I brought him home for dinner, without his girlfriend. He'd worked it out so that I'd pick him up at the dormitory. He must have thought it was too soon for us to meet her. Or maybe he wanted me to believe he was convalescing in all innocence without any distraction at all. When we got to the house my wife had to intervene to make sure the girls wouldn't throw themselves at him and hug him tightly because, since they'd gotten wind of the accident, they were dying to see their brother. Still, he couldn't get away from having to lift his T-shirt to show his 'war injury'. The girls used that moment to put their first name on his bandage with a red marker and a whole bunch of hearts around it.

Their way of marking their territory. Until he went back on the field, I only got his news by phone and from the reports of the doctor who was treating him, so I wouldn't create the impression I was favoring him over the other players. In any case, it would have been difficult for me to ignore him. His three accomplices at my house wouldn't have allowed it.

Once he'd fully recovered we were all immensely happy to see him step out on the field again. His teammates welcomed him like the disciples greeted the Messiah the day after the Resurrection. They wanted to touch him everywhere as if to assure themselves he really was alive and well, was ready to get back to work with them. During the recovery training they tried to protect him, steering clear of any contact that was too rough. I had to intervene and tell them not to shy away from hitting him. The doctor had pro-mised me that they could use physical force once he was out of the period he'd spent training by himself. Emmett would provoke the others, seeking contact, no doubt to reassure himself that he could take the beating.

And then the big day arrived. An official game. He didn't have full strength for a complete game yet, so we had to convince him to stay put on the bench. But when he finally rose to warm up on the edge of the field, a huge roar burst from the jam-packed stadium, from the spectators who had been waiting so long for his return. More than eighty thousand people, including the supporters of the opposing team, began to chant: '*We want Em-mett! We want Em-mett!*' The public was in a trance. Without exaggeration, the only time I'd ever been present for such widespread excitement was at a meeting with Barack Obama before his first election when people realized he'd have a chance to beat John Mc-

Cain. The stands were shaking in a riot of sound and color. It still gives me gooseflesh. He didn't disappoint us that day. When he came in for the third quarter, he delivered a true show, putting on display the whole array of his skills, his tackling, the way he covered the field, and even intercepting the ball several times. It was the Emmett Show, which led the press to announce that day that he was headed straight for the NFL.

Unlike other athletes, Emmett never considered a future outside of football. The question 'What would I do if it all came to an end tomorrow?' seemed not to enter his mind. As if there were no other salvation besides being recruited by a professional team. This all or nothing approach can be the lever to press to realize one's objective. But beware of the backlash. It was my duty to have him ask himself that question. That's one of the difficulties of being a coach, especially at this level, when you have to wear the coat of an educator. How do you make a player aware of that possibility and at the same time encourage him to keep believing in it? After the first accident, at the end of his junior year, I tried to broach the subject with him more than once. Maybe I was wrong to insist too much on needing a backup plan should he not be picked by the NFL. He'd close up every time like a clam that smells lemon. I felt like I was crying in the wilderness; worse, like I was speaking to a wall that would fling my own words back at my face with cold indifference.

The last time we had this conversation, at least when I spoke to him about it, he got me all tangled up in a monolog I never wanted to get into in the first place. I had to remind him that I, too, had been there. I had dreamed of it, like thousands of others, without managing to join the NFL.

Fortunately, I'd anticipated the possibility and had a Plan B. Without that, God only knows where I might have ended up: in crime? behind bars? at the morgue? In this country, I essentially told him, men like us, more so than the rest, have to deal with such threats constantly. You must never lose sight of that. 'That's what I did. Today I'm a coach, I have a family whose future I can assure.' I was expecting him to spit back at me: 'I'm not you, I have more talent. I don't need to realize my dreams through other people.' The way an angry and vindictive adolescent would have done with his father. But the only answer he gave me:

'You don't believe in me, Coach Larry.'

It was the first time he used my first name. Usually he just called me 'Coach'. It wasn't a question, just a statement. Pure and simple disappointment, mixed with a profound sadness first reflected in his eyes, then his head bowed down over a long silence before he stood up and left my office, his footsteps heavy. That day I blamed myself, feeling that I hadn't been up to it. Worse, that I had betrayed his trust after having embraced him, if not as a son at least as a member of my family. That is without any doubt why he didn't listen to me after his second injury, when I recommended that he repeat his last year so he could take the time he needed to come back. Then he could try for the draft a year later. He must have told himself that I wanted to benefit from his talent for my own interest as coach and for that of the university. And yet, I was only warning him as a wise mentor, as a Black man who knew all the difficulty it implied for those like us to make it in areas other than sport and music in this damned country; as a man who'd walked the same path without making it to the end. I'd gone through the disease, I knew the remedy to help him stay away from missing out on a fine professional career.

I feel that he cut the cord the day he left my office, silent, head down. At that time I didn't know that he was already in advanced contact with an agent who kept pushing him to declare himself eligible for the draft, even before finishing his Bachelor's. It happens every so often that the most talented, or the luckiest—depending on the vintage— are drafted in their third or even their second year. But that's rare. And once you have declared but aren't selected, you can't go back anymore. It also means that you abandon your scholarship and by the same token your studies, too. Finished, game over. Today I still blame myself for not having recognized this rupture. Even when the girls were complaining about not seeing him anymore. And yet my wife pressured me, asking whether anything had happened between us, an argument, a misunderstanding.

'I know you, you men with your testosterone and your grand airs of fighting cocks. I hope you haven't ruined your relationship over some foolishness. If that's the case, you're the adult and it's up to you to take the first step.'

I reassured her then and there that everything was fine. Between his last year as a senior, the university championship in full swing, and his girlfriend, poor Emmett had a lot on his plate. I wasn't lying to my wife, I was convinced of this. Not long after, the second accident occurred, a double fracture in several places of the tibia. Pretty nasty. Standing at the edge of the field, I could hear his bones crack at the moment of impact. It was the second time I saw him cry. Added to the pain, he must have already started wondering if he was going to be able to come back or not. And all of it because of that damned agent who saw him as the goose that would lay the golden egg. Also because of the pressure he'd put on himself from the moment he'd arrived at the university. For fear of ending up at the factory, like so many of Franklin Heights's youth. Of being forced to hold down some shitty job just to make ends meet. Of struggling along and signing up for welfare or begging for food stamps. Of depending on public charity.

But, for once, I didn't drop him for a moment. I was there from the beginning to the end. My wife and the girls visited him at the hospital three times, bringing him the sweet potato pie he loved. The day I realized he wanted to come back quickly, too quickly, I tried to dissuade him. I almost begged him. I tried everything to warn him against a hasty return. Other athletes before him had made the same mistake and thereby ruined an opportunity that doesn't come around twice in one lifetime. I suggested that he repeat the year with the goal of having every chance on his side: 'What is one year in the life of a young man your age?' I asked the surgeon who had operated on him to intervene, as well as the physical therapist who worked with him afterward. Perhaps he'd listen to them. He didn't want to hear any of it. I even went so far as to meet with his fiancée to explain the situation to her. My words seemed to convince her and she joined my crusade. It was my last card. I played it. We played it, she and I. We lost.

Meanwhile, I'd approached the university administration, the president, the dean, the provost, the athletic director, all those who could tip the scales in his favor, to renew his scholarship for an additional year. They heard my plea.

Except that, urged on by the agent, Emmett had already made his decision on his own. Determined and stubborn as a mule as he could be at times. In retrospect, I assume he used drugs to control the pain and pull the wool over everyone's eyes. For him there was no other solution, no contingency plan of any kind. Against all advice, whether wise or not, he came back after signing a release to clear the doctors and the university of any responsibility. It was three months before the draft. He didn't make it. And that isn't all. Having overburdened and put too much force on the leg, he came out of it with a limp that made him definitively unfit for playing any sport at a high level.

And since he'd dropped everything for the trap and delusion of the draft with, what's worse, very mediocre academic results, the administration could not or would not renew the scholarship that would have let him finish with a diploma. I insisted on telling him this myself before he'd received the letter with the bad news. He accepted it with a disturbing detachment, as if it concerned someone else. Or as if he were already gone. Gone to where those who're crushed by the huge illusion machine find themselves, those who are the losers of the American dream. When I wanted to know what he was planning on doing, or if he even had any plans, he told me he'd go back to Milwaukee or else to Alabama where he had family as well. He hadn't made up his mind yet. I didn't dare ask him what would become of his girlfriend. In any event, he didn't give me the chance. He was in a hurry to tell me not to worry, he would send us news, to the girls, to my wife, and to me.

'Why don't you come for dinner before you leave?

That way you can say goodbye to them.'

'Good idea, Coach. I'll call and let you know.'

It was a phrase he tossed out just to avoid me, because after the last conversation in my office I never saw him again. Well, yes, maybe once. I was about to enter the downtown grocery store when I saw a large limping silhouette towering in the distance. By the time I got there he had vanished. I immediately thought I was mistaken. It had been three months since he'd promised he would come to say goodbye. I still thought about him often. The girls couldn't stop asking me why he wasn't coming to the house anymore, and I couldn't give them a satisfactory answer. In bed that night I couldn't fall asleep until very late. If it was him, I told myself, perhaps he didn't want to see us, have contact again with anything or anyone that reminded him in any way of his broken dream. Perhaps he needed time before he could turn the page.

After that 'sighting' I didn't hear anyone speak of Emmett anymore. Many years have passed since then, I left my job at the university to go back to New Jersey with the family. Until I received a call from a lady who said her name was Nancy. It took me a while to recognize in this adult female voice the one that belonged to his girlfriend all those years before. I have no idea how she had managed to get my phone number. I don't spend time on social media. When I finally made the connection, she asked me if I'd seen the news. I told her I hadn't. I don't watch anything but sports on television anymore. Too much bad news. All the world's hatred exploding in your face. As if the planet were nothing more than an immense valley of catastrophes. I'm close to retirement, I want to protect myself so I can enjoy that to the fullest.

There was a long silence on the other end of the line. After a moment, with a suppressed sob she announced Emmett's death 'under the most horrible circumstances', she added. She wanted to make sure I knew, and to share my sorrow. Or hers with me, it was the same. She knew how much Emmett had meant to my family, who'd made him welcome as one of its own. He, too, had a great deal of respect and affection for us, especially for me, in whom he saw a model, as he'd admitted to his girlfriend. In some way I was the father he'd never had. He regretted for a long time that he hadn't sent any news. But for him it had been the only way to explain the loss of his dream. 'I paid for it, too,' she added.

During the conversation I found out that she lived in Manhattan and was teaching in the department of African Studies at New York University. She also informed me that she would take part in the funeral service to be held in the Franklin Heights neighborhood in Milwaukee the following Sunday. There would be a demonstration in honor of Emmett afterwards. She didn't know who had initiated it: a spontaneous movement of simple citizens who were sick of all this hatred? Black Lives Matter? Another group? Politicians who were trying to capitalize on the tragedy in this election year? To be frank, it didn't matter to her. What did matter was to demand justice for Emmett. In the name of the three girls he left behind as orphans. I told her that my wife and I would gladly go with her, if she'd like. I would alert my oldest one who lived in New York State as well. The younger one was abroad and wouldn't be able to come back in time. In spite of the circumstances it would be a pleasure to see her again. And, along with her, restore the memory of Emmett.

THE FIANCÉE

I COULDN'T TELL YOU exactly when my relationship with Emmett began. All I know is that it was a very lovely one, perhaps the loveliest I've ever had so far. Lovely, but far from easy. Far from it. We met in the mid-nineties, in a university town in the south-west where I was studying anthropology. 'A useless subject,' my younger brother, a mathematician, would tease me. Countless children dream of becoming doctors, paleontologists, firemen, adventurers. But to me, ever since I was very little, the cultural evolution of human groups has always been fascinating. Even more so in our country where so many communities interact with each other at their workplace but almost nowhere else. The rare times that they do, it's often difficult, not to say painful. That was the case for Emmett and me as well.

To be honest, I 'knew' him long before we were introduced. His reputation had preceded him to our private, ninety percent white, Catholic university, a stronghold of the region's wealthy middle class, and even beyond it. Months before his arrival, with a mixture of excitement and hope, the entire campus was talking about this treasure the coach had discovered in Milwaukee—the largest town in the State of Wisconsin. Even I had heard of Emmett, although I wasn't one of those groupie girls who'd rush off to the stadium when our university was playing an opposing team. The town would be buzzing with the noise of supporters; bars, restaurants, hotels, and guesthouses would overflow with patrons all weekend long.

Courtney, my best friend and one of my sorority sisters, had gone so far as to become a cheerleader. By joining the pompom girls she was hoping to get noticed by the boys, be among the first to be invited to the 5th Quarter, in the bars that is, after the games so she could focus on her favorite sport: chasing after potential suitors with the most popular in her sight. In spite of myself, I'd often let her drag me along without having the same success. Although no Cindy Crawford, I wasn't unattractive either and men didn't turn their eyes away at first glance. Slender, light brown hair down to my shoulders, fairly graceful for anyone who'd take the trouble to look. However, I didn't have Courtney's facility to simper, entice, or take control of things, depending on the situation. To score, as she put it. All of it with disconcerting speed and ease.

It's in this context that Emmett first set foot in our institution. I was in my second year, without a boyfriend after a failed first attempt, to use the football lexicon. He was coming in as a rookie on two accounts: both as a student and as part of the football team. Or the other way around, since it was only the sport that mattered to him. In the early days—until his departure in a way– he seemed somewhat out of sorts. Certainly, he wasn't used to being surrounded by so many white people. Being Black from a modest background, and a Protestant in a Catholic institution attended by the upper crust of the white middle class, Emmett faced multiple stumbling blocks. He was unfamiliar with the vernacular: body language, dress code, vocabulary, intonation, humor, and other specific signs of belonging. His Wisconsin working class accent, which he persisted in hiding while bolstering his reticent character, seemed to bother him as much as his huge body; his giant wings, in the image of the poet as albatross.

Then again, on the field he was a totally different man. Even someone wholly ignorant of football like me—I'm not sure Courtney was any better informed—could tell it was he who controlled the game, his teammates constantly looking to him. He exuded such charisma. In his first year we beat the town's public university, which had become accustomed to handing us one defeat after another. In addition to shutting down the opponents' offense almost single-handedly—maybe I'm not being very objective—he was responsible for two touchdowns and managed one turnover. That was the day he entered the university's pantheon of rookies with all the popularity and glory this implied. The following year, flanked by three other talented rookies, he helped the team become a member of an elite group, as he'd later explain to me, by joining an NCAA Conference.

That was the year we began seeing each other. Emmett

was already a star on campus and attracting girls like a bee-hive to bears. He'd smile shyly at them all without granting any favors to anyone in particular. In his position that would have become public very quickly. Someone would have seen them holding hands, kissing in the bushes, caught them glancing at each other languorously, and would have spread the news in a flash. Or the girl would have confided in her most talkative friend to mark her territory in a roundabout way. Was this unyielding distancing intended to keep him from being distracted from his goal? Or because the girls were white? One of them, most likely because she'd been turned away, spread the rumor that he was gay, to the great disappointment of many of us. Emmett was a tall, handsome man, with a short curly Afro shaved on the sides—his only idiosyncrasy—whose stunning smile ended up consuming girls already under his spell.

'What a waste,' a peeved Courtney said when she heard the gossip. The whole thing didn't concern me any more than that until she hauled me off to a club to celebrate the team's making it to the play-offs. In spite of the exceptional cold that year, the girls were dressed like sex workers, without any jacket or tights, hoisted on such high heels that they were clutching each other to move along, or hanging on to the boys' arms who were themselves encased in suits that robbed them of all that was natural and made them walk as stiffly as royal palace guards. After an hour and an impressive number of shots to bolster their courage, the atmosphere relaxed and everyone was smooching with everyone else.

Courtney was bubbling with excitement, ready to plunge into her chase of the night when Emmett happened by, followed by a horde of exhilarated female students.

Perhaps these practicing Catholics had gotten it into their heads to 'cure' him of his alleged homosexuality with their passion in the space of a night or two, behind some shrubbery or in the privacy of their room for those who had one in town. I couldn't quite see them taking him home on the weekend and saying: 'Mom, Dad, guess who's coming to dinner?' Long story short, that evening Courtney didn't hesitate to collar Emmett as if they'd known each other forever, thereby snatching him away from the whiffs of fantasy of those little sluts. He raised grateful eyes to my 'sister' and friend when she grabbed him by the arm and pulled him over to us:

'Hey, Emmett, come here. Did I introduce you to my friend Nancy yet?'

Unnerved, the girls who were following him didn't seem to want to let go of their prey. But Courtney, dauntless, faced them down until they understood they were dealing with a much stronger force, and cleared the floor on their own. Let them go hunting somewhere else! Once the girls were gone Courtney withdrew as well, in pursuit of a consenting victim with whom to end, not the night as usual, but at least the rest of the academic year. Her reputation as an easy lay after a few drinks was starting to hurt her. We were in our third year and she'd sworn to complete her degree with an official fiancé in tow.

We found ourselves alone, Emmett and I, without knowing what to say or do, as awkward beneath our shell of shyness as sea turtles moving along the sand. The mood thawed out a bit when, after a long moment of silence that seemed to have lasted for hours, he saw fit to introduce himself. I couldn't help but burst out laughing. Coming from such a frail body type like mine my raucous laughter has always impressed people who don't know me. Poor Emmett looked at me dumbfounded:

'What did I say that's so funny?' he stammered with the sheepish look of someone who had just made a monumental blunder.

'Stop acting so modest. Everyone knows who you are, even I do.'

'Why even you?' he pulled himself together.
'Because my friend Courtney, the one who pulled you away from your pack of scantily clad fans, thinks that all I'm interested in are my anthropology books. To tell you the truth, she's not far off in her thinking.

'You're exaggerating, there were guys there, too.'

'Mostly girls though, no?'

'Doesn't matter. I'd be glad not to have any fans. But apparently you need them if you want to be noticed. It's part of the price you have to pay to reach your goal.'

'Which is what?' asked the ignoramus I still was.

'To be drafted into the NFL,' he answered taken aback. 'The more attention you attract the more the recruiters are interested in you.'

After a short silence he added:

'If it's true none of this is your thing, then how do you know who I am?'

'Because you'd have to be blind not to see your pictures on campus, or deaf not to hear them talk about the immense, the monumental Emmett, the savior of our football team (my irony helped me compensate for my nerves). You're everywhere, even when you're not.'

My comment got a smile out of him, which helped me

relax. Once the first moments of embarrassment were over, the conversation took place so naturally that I was delighted. He, too, looked as if he appreciated my company in that crowded place, he who despised moving around in a group the way the other students did. We quickly found refuge in our bubble, impervious to the ambient hubbub. Our physical proximity seemed to make him uncomfortable—sometimes we brushed against each other, sometimes jostled by the crowd we inadvertently squeezed each other in spite of ourselves. Fortunately, I didn't have Courtney's protruding chest, which would have embarrassed us both. After half an hour, maybe more—I didn't feel time go by—we found two stools in a less congested corner and settled down with our back against the wall where I could discreetly observe him as much as I wanted.

Besides his smile and the harmony of his features, he had a sharp look in his eyes that, when not lowering them in a flash of timidity or by pure reflex to protect his privacy, moved eagerly across people and things, in clear contrast to his delivery that was so slow it could make a dog weep. He told me he came from Milwaukee, Wisconsin, a city renowned for its widespread racism and sanctioned segregation. Sensing my self-control slipping away from me, I was asking myself a thousand questions throughout the conversation. Had he gone out with a white woman before? If not, had he not had the opportunity or had he told himself not to? Maybe the rumors about his sexuality were true.

However, that was not the impression I had when we separated deep in the night when the bar closed, the others having already left the place and I'd lost all trace of Courtney, and he fixed his burning gaze on me. It was my turn to feel uncomfortable. I was perspiring all over. Except my face, just imagine the shame if I were. The sweat was dripping under my armpits, between my breasts, transforming my crotch into a moist, tingling swamp. Had he been more adventurous that night, I would have happily returned his kiss. And even more. But he didn't dare. Afraid to be refused? To seem too bold? Wanting to avoid disapproval? He would often persist in trying to explain the complexity of race relations in this country, particularly between Blacks and whites, and why this situation causes Black men to constantly need to protect themselves to the point of living on the margins of society—all this without drawing a breath.

Whatever the case, my frustration that night was the same.

Even with our class schedules and his countless long practice sessions we made time to meet. To have a drink in one of the town's many bars, preferably not too popular with the other students so we could enjoy a minimum of peace, to go for a walk or go jogging in the nearby park without overstepping the limits of a growing curiosity about one another. Over the weeks, I had the impression it was a gentle glide into a black and white relationship, from another century to be honest, while in a single evening Courtney would rate and wrap up an encounter she'd have already forgotten by the next morning. I became a regular at the football games whose rules and regulations continued to escape me, under the quizzical look of my friend who refused to believe that nothing had happened between Emmett and me. Not even the hint of a caress, of our lips touching.

'You realize you've managed to convert a gay man into a hetero? Hallelujah!'

'Stop your blasphemy.'

'You, the agnostic, are saying that?'

'It doesn't keep me from respecting someone else's faith.'

Basically, despite the obvious pleasure of getting together, these hesitant beginnings revealed a more profound discomfort that kept Emmett from clutching at my clumsy attempts at seducing him. And the discomfort had to do with that damned question of color, the invisible line that defines human relations in the United States, which prohibited us from living together rather than separately. Over time the country had been established on compartmentalized, fragmented relationships, the memory of which we have transmitted from generation to generation. And we've all become so inured to it that it has become normal.

I grew up in a family of liberals, in a privileged environment where the only Blacks we dealt with were service personnel, delivery people, or those we saw on television. In his Franklin Heights neighborhood in Milwaukee, on the other hand, Emmett had little contact with whites, other than the principal of his elementary school, and one or two idealistic teachers who must have asked to be placed in that unsafe area, a few individuals with shattered lives who found themselves trapped there without anywhere else to go, and some police officers.

Perhaps that's what was at the root of his sarcastic reaction the day he finally understood what my studies consisted of and my desire to specialize in African-American Studies. I saw his face change into a mask of mistrust and disappointment. 'So you're getting closer to the topic of your studies?' he flung at me. 'You'll have to learn to talk like a nigger.' That cheap and offensive provocation hit me in the face like a thick gob of spit. It hurt me even more because our relationship had seemed to be taking a positive turn.

We finally kissed one night, on my initiative, when he'd taken me back to the entrance of the girls' dormitory. Without pushing his back to the wall, I didn't leave him any choice that evening. When we were about to separate, I took his hands, held them in mine for a moment, then the kiss meant for his cheek landed inadvertently on the corner of his lips. The whole thing in a clever ambiguity that left the door open for him and provided me with an honorable emergency exit. In case he declined my advances, I could always hide behind a misunderstanding on his part. I was using Courtney's coaching here who, if ultimately she'd actually believed that our flirtation was completely platonic, refused to admit it might not go any farther:

'It ju-st is-n't nor-mal, Nan-cy,' she said taking the syllables apart, 'You need to close the deal now. If need be, put your hand on his fly. That way you'll know once and for all if he's gay or not.'

'You think it's easy? The guy is closed shut like a clam. Surely I've shown him my interest enough, haven't I?'

'Not enough, from what you're telling me.'

'If he didn't grab the chance it means he's not interested in me. Period.'

'If you want, I'll make a date with him and show you what to do...'

'Eh, no, I'd rather not, you know? On the other hand, if you have any more sensible advice, I'll take it.'

That first night we kissed each other on the lips. It's all we did. Neither he nor I dared to touch any other part of each other's body. A more audacious man would have put a hand on my breasts, let the other one casually stray down to my bottom. He didn't go any farther. There was a mixture of fear and respect in him, a lack of preparedness in me. I'd only had one experience, after a drunken evening in my first year. The only memory I was left with is that it went very badly. Since then I'd stuck to a more or less innocent flirtation that would last about a month without knowing which one of us had grown tired of it first.

Thinking back, I see us as so naïve, Emmett and me. Having taken the first step, we were just looking forward to one thing, to seeing each other the next day, and then the next, and the next. Meetings where our bodies felt the urgent need for something other than endless fondling. But our hunger for each other ran into a considerable obstacle. The dormitories of this Catholic institution, besides being strictly non-coed, were located at two opposite ends of the campus. Any offense was punished, which could go all the way to expulsion from the university. With arrangements like these, it was difficult for a straight person to sneak around unobtrusively into a partner's bed. Emmett would not have followed me. In addition to being expelled, he'd risk the pure and simple burial of his dream: his reputation would have preceded him to other universities that would certainly have been in no hurry to offer him a new scholarship.

If I didn't see us in a dark corner of the library for our first time together, neither did I see us imitating those couples on campus who, without a nest for their amorous encounters, would slip away into an open classroom at the end of the day, even if it meant getting locked in for the whole night. Such audacity hardly suited us. The solution to our logistics problem could only come from Courtney who, in her second year had rented a room in town, so she'd have a place to take her one-night stands without having to get permission from anyone or ask a housemate to make herself scarce for an hour or two. Still, I hesitated to seek her help because I didn't want to have to deal with her 'So? Tell me. How did it go?' and her right to a detailed account in exchange for the favor she'd done us. For several days I turned the matter over and over in my head before I made my decision.

All that time Emmett, who had no alternative solution, showed no sign of impatience whatsoever. In the end, I took advantage of Courtney's leaving to spend a weekend with her family to ask her at the very last minute and in my most guileless way to leave me her keys; right at the moment she was about to get on the bus heading for the bus station. She burst out laughing. She rummaged around in her purse, finally got them out and dangled them for a few seconds at the tip of her outstretched arm before handing them to me with a peremptory, 'You'll tell me when I get back.'

'It's not what you think.'

'Of course not. You want a quiet spot to study, the campus library isn't open on weekends. You think I'm an idiot?'

We'd already come a long way together when he flung those harsh words at me, about learning to talk like a negro. I thought it was the end of our relationship. The end, too, of my plan for the next school year to swap my room at the university residence for a studio in town where we would have some privacy. After all, such a choice would make no sense without him. That night I left him standing on the doorstep to the girls' dormitory and went to my room, hurt and angry. Besides, I didn't want him to see me cry my eyes out.

I let him stew for a whole week before I could let it go. I needed to make the point. Even if I missed our daily encounters, our affectionate looks. How I suffered from not hearing the enfolding warmth of his voice, his hesitant words when he broached a serious subject. I wanted him and his obstinate head to understand and his heart to feel what had been so hurtful in what he'd said. Thanks to our coming back together, which we sealed with an insatiable night of love— there, too, he had quite an appetite—we swore to each other we'd move ahead in complete transparency in our relationship, whose intertwining was already consuming us, though we weren't aware of it; we'd tell each other things in all their naked truth to avoid feeding any harmful bitterness in one another. We believed in it with all our youthful intensity and naïveté.

It was that night of the almost solemn pact that our interminable discussions around questions of color and race began. They continued in the rather basic studio downtown where I moved at the end of the summer and where Emmett would join me at every opportunity, although officially he continued to live on campus. The next three to six months were a true fairytale. Until today I have no more beautiful memories of love, in spite of the passing clouds that would occasionally darken above our heads but were good for sunny reconciliations anyway.

Then Emmett had his first serious accident. It happened during practice where, as I sat in the bleachers near the field, I heard him howl at the moment of impact before I saw him twist in pain, his hand clutching his helmet as if he wanted to keep from crying in front of so many people, he, the tough neighborhood warrior who'd been through plenty of other struggles, the steel mountain who showed his teammates the way. His worst nightmare was taking place right before my eyes: 'Just imagine me having an accident', he repeated incessantly, as if to ward off the possibility. That day he suffered a crack in his right collarbone and three broken ribs. Luckily, the ribs hadn't punctured the lungs, which according to the attending physician would have made matters much worse.

Three days later, when he came to my house to convalesce, he finally allowed himself to cry in my arms. At the moment of the impact he'd been so scared, scared to see the dream of his whole life turn to dust. On the other hand, I was completely overcome to see how helpless and diminished he felt. As I rocked the flood of his grief against my chest that day, I would've given anything to watch him again putting on his armor of fearless knight beyond reproach. Fortunately, the university's hospital was outstanding. The doctors managed to get him back on his feet very quickly, which gave him renewed hope.

Conversely, it would have been hard to find anyone who could have exorcised the evil spirits that were progressively taking control of his mind and mounting an insidious assault on us as a couple. Like a malevolent spider weaving the web in which she would catch her prey one thread at a time. More than once he'd mention the eyes of others on us, similar to those people who swear they're hearing voices that only they're able to hear. I admit I didn't really believe this at first. To reassure him, I contributed this to his ever-increasing fame. At the same time, I used it to establish my position. The others, I argued—with a shrewdness I didn't know I had—were curious to find out more about the exact nature of our relationship. Was it a flirtation? a passing fancy without any future? a brief affair as they say, a friendship with extra benefits? one of the trophies of a star football player? a relationship meant to last? And since he refused to hold my hand in public, I took this with a bit of jealousy as a sign that his refusal to have us be seen together as a couple was one way for him to leave the door open to other adventures. To get back to his fears, I went on, I'd not caught wind of any nasty gossip on our account. Courtney, who always heard everything, would have told me. He insisted that one night at a bar he'd picked up some snatches of a conversation between two half-tipsy, half-jealous Black women:

'That guy, can't he just stick with us sisters? As soon as they're a bit successful they have to have their little snowflake... '

It was a unique experience for me, as opposed to Emmett for whom this wasn't just an academic exercise. From the time I was born until I went off to college I'd never been in a situation where hostile looks were directed at me, except perhaps at some student evenings where usually bashful boys, emboldened under the influence of alcohol, would undress you with a predator's lustful eyes.

And it left a peculiar taste that first time. Shortly after he'd recovered, for his birthday present I'd given him a lovers' weekend at a theme park with a marvelous hotel complex, having reluctantly dropped an earlier idea of our going to a mountain resort to discover the joys of skiing—a suggestion he'd vehemently rejected.

'Hell no!' Besides risking breaking my leg and seeing

my dreams go up in thin air, have you ever seen a Black ski champion where you're from? The only Blacks who've ever participated in the winter games were the Jamaican bobsled team, they made a film of it. I love you very much, sweetie, but you'd be going there by yourself.'

Ultimately, after making sure that he had no practice schedule for that weekend, I opted for the theme park. I knew for sure that it would please him since he'd never had a chance to go before, while my parents used to take my brother and me there often when we were kids. On the phone everything was fine. When we arrived after five hours on the bus, exhausted but happy at the idea we'd be alone, far from the campus in a place where Emmett could take my hand without worrying about his star status, the white male receptionist asked us twice with a scrutinizing look whether we had actually reserved one king-size bed, especially since the reservation was in my name and the credit card was mine as well.

'It's the minimum for a big guy like me, no?' Emmett cleverly slipped in.

Yet, the idiot spent an inordinate amount of time finishing our check-in before he gave us the room that had the worst view in the entire hotel. I was so sickened that I wanted to turn right around and demand a different room; or else, speak to the supervisor. Emmett convinced me not to take that route.

'Perhaps there isn't any room available at our price level,' he argued, ' or no room available at all. At any rate, it's not worth ruining our weekend over.'

'No, but did you see how he looked at us? Almost as if he took me for a prostitute.'

'Just drop it, sweetie. You realize this is the first time anyone's ever given me such a beautiful birthday cake, I won't let that guy keep me from enjoying the cherry that comes with it.'

'And what might that cherry be?'

I was so beside myself that I didn't even get the double meaning.

'You mean who,' he said, bending over to lift me off the ground—I was a feather in his arms. He gave me a kiss that was anything but chaste.

'You have a bit of a dirty mind, stop seeing evil everywhere, Madam Anthropologist,' he added jokingly. It was his way of defusing the tension.

'What should I see in it then?'

'Maybe the guy had a fight with his missus before he went to work this morning and he's in a bad mood.'

'It's easy to blame it on the wife.'

'Let's just say he was surprised to see someone built like me with such a wisp of a woman. What he doesn't know is that you're the one leading the dance here.'

He didn't believe in this nonsense himself but preferred to keep a low profile, as I would often see him do. In this specific case, his main concern was to protect me from the quiet aggression of that creep. In Emmett's eyes, this little white girl from one of the ultra-privileged residential areas, albeit overflowing with well-meaning sentiments, didn't know much about the real world. Much less about the racial hatred destroying the country, and the unshakable repercussions of centuries of slavery—the original sin that President Obama spoke about. That paternalistic side of him drove me up the wall. At the same time, his maturity at an age when anger can flare up suddenly at the slightest hint of injustice would never cease to amaze me. Perhaps this was a sign of a conditioning that came from a much deeper place. 'Better avoid any aggravation,' he concluded as if to justify himself. Luckily, that dolt must've had the weekend off and we didn't see him again, so I was able to let go of my anger and enjoy our stay.

Once we began to settle into a lasting relationship as a couple, the reactions like the one we'd experienced at the theme park multiplied. My close circle of friends was not the most supportive, starting with Courtney, that shallow one who changed lovers the way she changed her underwear. One night, when Emmett was playing a game in another city and I wanted to find her to apologize for having neglected her a little, too busy with my love and my studies, she asked me point-blank if I wasn't thinking about finding myself a fiancé one day. As if my involvement with Emmett wasn't a real relationship.

'Time doesn't stand still, girl. If you don't shop around on campus,' she insisted, 'you've no idea what nutcase or loser you may run into outside.'

True. Big, handsome, charismatic Emmett had helped me get over the failure of my first relationship with that clod. Now it was time to move on to serious things. Listening to Courtney, you'd think our affair was just a passing fancy of a little rich white girl. It was just the response of an ignorant, privileged college girl whose political consciousness didn't extend beyond her own instinct for survival, her hunger for success within her own social class. Seeing my bewildered look, which shielded my hidden frustration at her narrow-mindedness that she'd experienced reluctantly—she tried to smooth things over.

'It's good that your anthropology studies push you to link theory to practice. But in this country it just isn't done, my little Nancy. In any case, for people like us it's very complicated. Those who've tried have only gotten burned.'

'Perhaps they simply weren't meant to be together. Mixed couples have a right to fail, too, just like everyone else.'

'That's not all there is, and you know it.'

'But that's where it stops for you? No need at all to tear down these walls?'

'What do you think? You're the only one up against the wall? I started long before you, girl. You know I've got nothing against getting laid but campus fun stays on campus. I'm not cut out to be a heroine.'

'Unless the guy is loaded, right? Money has no color, we know that.'

'Look, it might be an investment,' she replied cynically. 'You can only hope the guy hits the jackpot by getting into the NFL. There are plenty of girls who look for that at the university. But's it's a risky bet. What if he doesn't make it? You'll have lost everything.'

That a girl our age, my best friend besides, would think this way early in the twenty-first century drove me to despair. And, as if she hadn't grasped the irony of my words, Courtney added yet another layer.

'Really, girl, what crime did you commit? You're not responsible for what happened in the last century. Or segregation, which disappeared thirty years ago. You weren't even born yet. You and your need for redemption,' she mocked. "for someone who claims not to be Catholic, I think you flagellate yourself a little too much.'

'You're kidding, right?'

'Stop repenting, girl, or the guy will take advantage of it. Would you have the same attitude if he were white? I bet then you'd be a lot more realistic and focused on your own interests.'

When I finally broached the subject with my parents, their disappointment was even greater. A great debater, my father found some weighty arguments to avoid attacking me head-on and risk getting my back up even more. He couldn't have threatened to cut off my allowance since I was about to get a substantial grant for my master's, and the little money that the family would continue to pay could be made up for with a student job. He also tried to explain the importance of my aiming for one of the most prominent institutions in the country where I could combine master's and doctorate degrees.

'With your major, you'll need a doctorate from an excellent university if you want to have any hope of getting a job in higher education and pursuing your research.' Which amounted to distancing me from Emmett.

In order to understand how deeply disillusioned I felt at his response, I should point out that it was my father who first awakened in me a consciousness of equality and humanism. I was somewhere between thirteen and fifteen when together as a family we watched the movie *Cry Freedom*, whose story takes place in South Africa during the long dry white season of Apartheid. Denzel Washington plays the role of the activist Steve Biko, who was imprisoned, tortured, and then assassinated by the Pretoria regime. My parents were as outraged by this as I was. Bolstered by these memories, I was convinced they would have no trouble understanding my relationship with Emmett. They themselves would say: 'Nothing to understand, Nancy. You can be in love with whomever you want. It's your life.' To my great dismay, that's not the way it went down.

That day I left my childhood home as distressed as I'd been when that stupid Emmett advised me to learn to speak like a negro. It felt like a ghastly laceration inside me and, though I hadn't made the decision, I had the desire to never set foot there again. I was completely stunned. I felt as if I had aged ten years overnight. I didn't mention it to Emmett when I returned to campus, not wanting to feed the demon that was already eating away at him on the inside. He wouldn't have missed the chance to almost jubilantly point out: 'You see, I knew your parents wouldn't approve.' Still, I really needed to open my heart to someone and that someone couldn't be him. I'd never felt so alone before.

His second accident occurred early in the fall semester. It delivered a death blow to our love affair; even if it took another two years to finally succumb. The team was playing yet another game against the state university team. The old rivalry between our two institutions had once again divided the town into two opposing camps, who spent the week sparring good-naturedly, in spite of a few intense booze-fueled moments at night in some of the bars. On D-day the cheerleaders' performance lived up to its name. The two teams entered the field with a wild ovation, encouraged by the sportscaster who did his utmost to rouse the jam-packed stadium.

When the game finally got started, I only had eyes for my fiancé—it was my weakness to consider him as such. I thought he was handsome, powerful, fast. A stadium god, all muscle, and with a total grasp of the game. It was toward the end of the first quarter when the accident happened. Emmett suffered a double fracture of the tibia and fibula. Seen from the bleachers the incredibly violent blow was even more dramatic than the previous one. The stadium let out an 'ooooh' of shock. I would have fainted were it not for Courtney, who had the presence of mind to throw her glass of soda in my face. Emmett was put on the stretcher in tears—this time he couldn't stop himself—whereupon an ambulance took him to the hospital where he would stay for at least a week.

After being immobilized for three months, he was finally discharged. Although he hadn't even started his physical therapy yet, he was already thinking of getting back onto the field. As a result of all the pressure he'd been putting on himself since the day he arrived. The coach was placating him, however, and advised him to take his time. He met with me to almost beg me to support him in this. If my fiancé would agree to repeat the year, he would intervene with the president, the dean, the provost, and anyone else who mattered in the administration to ask them to renew his scholarship for the following year. Emmett would hear none of it. Against expert opinion, he was convinced that by doubling down he'd speed up his physical therapy and could come back in time for the draft. How to deter him from that goal? He could be so stubborn when he insisted on going one way and someone tried to cross his path. And I loved him so much that I was ready to follow him to the end of the earth. He made his bet—and lost. He came out of it with a limp that made him unfit to play the sport at the next level.

As was to be expected, the university did not renew

his scholarship and he no longer had an income, other than the few hundred dollars he'd managed to save. In addition to our relationship, which he now needed to reckon with, under these conditions going back to Milwaukee would have felt like a failure to him. His natural sense of restraint kept him from stating this in such clear-cut terms. Since he had nowhere to go, I suggested that he move into my studio with me. A decision I made unbeknownst to my parents, as I had no wish whatsoever to confront them at a time when Emmett needed me so much. He accepted, though not without reluctance, on the condition, he decided, that he would share the cost of food while waiting to find work and then take on all of it. This precondition wasn't merely an explanation for his giant appetite. As I grew older I learned that it was typical of people who'd gone hungry as children to hate seeing an empty refrigerator.

After this setback, we made our one and only trip to Milwaukee, the second trip after our weekend at the theme park. He dreamed of taking me to the Caribbean and to Europe. That was his fantasy. He'd continued talking about it even after he could no longer be drafted and had lost the chance to play in the NFL. With him, the hope to fall asleep a poor man and wake up rich in the morning was never far off, like a tenacious dream of which he couldn't rid himself. I saw him try his luck at Lotto, as if wealth, material comfort at least, couldn't come from a regular well-paid job and from savings. No doubt, a legacy from the conditions under which he'd started life, the place he'd come from, where he'd seen families who struggled all their lives without ever managing to get beyond the corner minimarket.

His mother welcomed me with immense warmth.

She was a very affectionate woman, who often took me to her bosom. I wasn't used to such effusiveness. Once I was grown, my mother never gave me more than a quick hug and even then only on special occasions, like when I left for college or when I came home on vacation. With Emmett's mom it was an open bar, a self-serve buffet, at all hours of the day or night. She called me 'my daughter', 'sweetheart'. She gave me the feeling that I'd always been a part of the family.

'If that knucklehead Emmett gives you any trouble,' she told me, 'you let me know, alright? Me, I know how to set him straight. Above all, don't let him even try to behave like the bastard his father was.'

At night, in the beautiful, pink-draped bed his mother had prepared for us—it was hers, in fact, for in Emmett's room there was only the single bed from his adolescence—I wanted to know more about that father of his, a man he'd told me almost nothing about. Instead, grand master of evasion that he could be, he explained the origin of his first name to me: 'If you want to know the whole story, it was my father's idea. Which didn't stop him from clearing out once things began to go bad and leaving us to fend for ourselves, mom and me. The worst is that she still loves him, that bastard.' I wasn't going to find out anything more. He immediately withdrew into himself before I had a chance to delve further into this glimpse of his vulnerable side that he'd exposed with this remark.

In view of the distance, we'd planned at first to be in Milwaukee for a week. Since Emmett refused to do the trip by Greyhound bus as I'd suggested, we rented a car for the occasion. It would have been cheaper and we weren't exactly rolling in money. But, he'd insisted on taking a car, defending his arguments tooth and nail: it would save time, give us the possibility to stop wherever we wanted, be easier to get around once we were there as his mother wouldn't have a car to lend us and he wanted to show me around Milwaukee, and so on. Arriving in a rental car helped him to keep the truth to himself. I understood this when I realized he hadn't said a word to his mother about his dismissal from the university.

To be honest, it was the first time I'd ever set foot in a Black neighborhood, and not just your typical 'hood either. The poverty in the streets, the dilapidated fronts of the abandoned houses, and the clothes worn by people whom I furtively observed, troubled me even more. In some places there was a certain electric spark as I passed, something like 'What the hell is that white girl doing here?' Then the tension in Emmett would go up a notch, I could feel he was ready to jump at the throat of the first person who might direct a misplaced comment at me. It was no doubt the reason why we didn't visit anybody in the neighborhood other than his mother, even though he had been born there and had lived there all his life before going to college. During a one-on-one that she insisted on having with me without Emmett present, his mother divulged that Stokely, his childhood friend, was serving a long prison sentence. She'd always warned her son against "consorting with his type", as she put it. For some reason I'm still not clear about, Emmett didn't want me to meet his great friend Authie either, of whom he'd spoken so often. Perhaps she'd moved, but I preferred not to bring the matter up with him. His mother seemed to soar high above all the decay. She'd planned to take me to the church on Sunday morning to introduce her daughter-in-law to the community. But circumstances and Emmett didn't leave her any time.

Two days after we arrived, we were driving around town. Night was beginning to fall. Emmett was at the wheel, calmly cruising around the Whitefish Bay area to have me admire the sun's reddish glow on the lake, the façades of the luxurious homes that overlooked the view, when we heard the sound of a patrol car's siren. Emmett parked along the sidewalk and instantly put his hands flat on the dashboard. A reflex I wasn't familiar with and unconsciously imitated. Two white cops presented themselves. One of them shone a flashlight in Emmett's face while the other kept his hand on the butt of his gun. They asked him to get out of the car under the pretext that he'd been going fifty in a forty-five mph zone. He was thoroughly frisked while the other officer held him at gunpoint.

I was so petrified I couldn't utter a word. The cops wanted to check the car's documents, the rental contract, his identity papers, but not mine. Throughout the entire scene Emmett kept a composure that was beyond admirable. When they finally left, he had a hard time starting the car again, he was shaking so much. With the fear, of course, that had caught up with him. With rage as well. He felt he'd been humiliated in front of me, as he admitted the next day. At the time he didn't want to talk about it. Maybe if I hadn't been there, things would have gone badly. The cops would have goaded him further until he'd fly off the handle. And only God knows what might have happened then. After a restless night we left Milwaukee early the next morning, without his mother having had a chance to introduce me to her church.

On the way back Emmett drove a good hour without opening his mouth. I sensed I had to leave him alone inside his universe and not appear too intrusive. He was driving with his eyes riveted on the blacktop in front of him, his hands clenching the steering wheel, sticking to the speed limit, a sign that he was in control of his nerves. I felt safe. And I didn't suggest that I could take a turn driving. After an hour, he finally spoke. The police stop the previous night had rekindled an old wound. The story he told me went back to the end of elementary school.

His mother and he had accepted an invitation from a teacher who had devoted a lot of her time and energy pushing him in his studies. The woman lived in East Side, a white neighborhood. They had visited her one summer Sunday, dressed in their finest clothes. Dressed to kill, as he put it. When they got off the bus they had almost another mile to go on foot. They had barely walked a hundred yards before the police stopped them and asked them underhandedly if they were lost, if they needed directions to find their way. His mother had thanked the two cops for their kindness, God bless you, before mentioning the address they were going to. Whereupon they let them go. At that moment his mother hadn't commented to him on what happened and they continued on their way. But none of it compared to what awaited them when they arrived. He still remembered the silence that accompanied their footsteps and the burning looks on their backs when they showed up in the street under the watchful eyes of the residents who were outside taking advantage of the nice weather.

'Did you ever, if only for an instant, experience being forced to hug the walls?' he asked. 'Not because they order you to do it with words, but with their look. With every glance they make you feel you have no right to be there. So, to avoid those murderous eyes you hug the walls. You don't demand anything, you don't lay claim on anything. You make it a habit to be transparent, to be a shadow. Not to make any waves so they won't notice you, 'cause you're not in your place.'

It's the lesson his mother taught him later that afternoon when he came home: 'Don't make any waves so you can avoid trouble.' No matter what you do, you'll be wrong. It's the old story of unequal contest. Subsequently he would suffer other baseless police stops. As teenagers together with Authie and Stokely, if they happened to wander off into the posh neighborhoods of Fox Point or Whitefish Bay, they'd routinely be stopped under some pretext or other. Even here in this university town, where his status as the football team's star should have entitled him to some consideration, he was stopped twice. For no particular reason. As if the cops were just bored or wanted to exercise their power.

But none of it measured up to that first humiliation, which he recounted with clenched jaws, his eyes brimming with tears. The child he was had wanted to wipe away the affront that had been done to his mother. Never, he confessed to me, had he felt the absence of a father as much as he did that day, who could have explained and told him what attitude to take. How to restore his and his mother's honor. Stand up for himself other than by keeping a low profile: his mother's gospel. He thought he'd forgotten that story until the questioning from the night before.

Since the trip to Milwaukee, the slightest tension—as

happens with any couple—gave way to endless discussions that inevitably drifted toward the small chance that in such a toxic environment our relationship would be able to last for the long term. At moments like that he was so tense that no caress could relax him. My lack of experience being in a relationship didn't make the task any easier for either of us. Sometimes I tell myself that with a little more maturity I might have handled it better. And that we'd be together today, as a family. In New York, Chicago, Los Angeles; a big city anyway, more likely to embrace a mixed-race relationship like ours. When we were full of love, nestled in each other's arms, fantasizing about everything and nothing, the place where we'd like to build our nest, the first names of our children, he'd answer dryly:

'And where will we raise those children? In case you haven't noticed, if you want to rent or buy in certain places, it's the whole community that decides whether they'll accept you or not.'

'So? We're bound to find one that'll want us... '

'... that we certainly wouldn't have picked ourselves if we had the choice. And if by chance they'd accept us in some white neighborhood, our children will be stopped at every streetcorner. In addition to being stigmatized, they'll always be the Black friend that the parents of their pals will show off to prove how progressive they are.'

'We don't have to live in a white neighborhood you know.'

'You, you don't have any idea what you're talking about. We'll already have broken up as a couple before we'd have the means to live in a middle-class Black neighborhood, which you don't find in every town anyway. And while we're waiting you wouldn't last six months in a place like Franklin Heights.'

'You think I'm that much of a wimp?'

'As for me, I've no desire whatever to drag you there or to raise my children there.'

Since he no longer had to stick to a strict, healthy lifestyle and long periods of sleep, our discussions would go on for entire nights about all sorts of things. To keep from hurting his feelings during these times, I wouldn't remind him that I had to work the next day. It would have sent him back to his own precarious situation as well as signal to him that I was breaking our agreement of telling each other things openly, and that our relationship no longer mattered to me. As a result of all this talk about imaginary problems before we were actually living them, we were, without even realizing it, sawing off the branch on which we as a couple were sitting. Maybe that's the destructive power of the system: it prevents you from living the life the way you want, with whom you want; but it does so in a way that makes it seem like it was your own choice.

Having to depend on my scholarship, and worse, in the town where he'd suffered his failure, didn't help the situation either. Emmett, however, did the best he could. He brought home what he could, managing to get little jobs he carefully chose outside town so he wouldn't run into students who'd known him in his fleeting glory days. He compensated by doing household chores, cooking—he did quite well in the kitchen in a rather irresistible mother-hen-like way—to give me time to devote to my thesis. Despite it all, he felt he was sponging off me. We had to find a solution, but what? He doubted his ability to return to any university to pursue an academic field. By his own admission, he hadn't accomplished much in the three preceding years. The fact remains that neither he nor I had the means to finance any such studies. And no serious bank would have loaned us the money.

Despite our ever more frequent arguments, we held on as best we could. One year, then two. Each week, then each hour that went by without a fight made me very proud. But the cord was unraveling without my knowing it. One day when I came home from the library I found an envelope on the table where we used to eat. First I thought it was an apology from him. The night before we'd shouted at each other again and he'd been particularly unfair to me. He wanted me to forgive him, I thought. I was not in the least concerned before I opened the envelope. The letter began 'Dear Nancy' instead of 'Sweetie'. It was a first sign. Two lines later I felt my legs buckle; I had to hold onto the table for a moment before finding the strength to take three steps to the chair where I dropped down with my full weight. I understood that he was ending the four years of love that had given me so much. As a woman. As a human being.

He said he loved me very much but that our relationship was unlivable. It was better to stop here so we wouldn't hurt each other anymore. And it would protect a marvelous memory of our relationship. After him, I'd often hear that same refrain from men who didn't have the courage to face life's difficulties as a couple. He asked me not to try to look for him. Without realizing it perhaps, he was putting me in the same mold his father had created with his mother and him: he vanished without a trace. For months I would call his mom to get news about him. Either that lady, who continued to call me her daughter, was a very good liar—which I doubt—or he intentionally wasn't giving her any clue about his life either so I wouldn't be able to track him down. Whatever the case may be, I never heard from him again. It took years before I finally was able to stop thinking about him every single day.

After I defended my thesis, I became an assistant professor, then associate professor in several universities across the country before becoming Professor of African-American Studies at New York University. In that cosmopolitan city where women and men from all over the world are living, I spent some time with a Haitian diplomat, then with a musician from Trinidad. I was involved with a white colleague at a private Catholic university in Chicago, whom I'd met during a colloquium before he moved on to other things: he didn't want to leave the cozy comfort of his family and saw in me nothing but an ordinary bit of enjoyment. Is it because of the impossible love with Emmett that I never married and have no children? Who knows.

The day I heard the news on television I couldn't prevent myself from contacting his onetime coach through our former university, which had kept his information. Although I'd lost track of his mother by now, I dialed her old number, but it rang and rang for a long time into empty space. I needed to talk about him. To bring him back with someone who'd known him. The conversation was very trying for me. Coach Larry may have sensed it. Before hanging up he suggested that we go to the funeral together for a final tribute to one of the most promising players he'd ever had and with whom his family and he had maintained a very warm relationship.

Before returning to Milwaukee, I spent days in tears. Undoubtedly, it was my way of dealing with the grief I hadn't been able to express over my loss the first time. I still hear him saying to me: 'Let's avoid any arguments.' As for me, I remain convinced that all of us, women and men, can rise above our social and ethnic condition to adopt a full and complete humanity that goes beyond these criteria. Otherwise what's the sense of life? Especially for someone who, far from breaking with her agnostic education like me, is moving more and more toward an atheism that has no name.

THE EX

IT WASN'T A MAN I shared my life with for three years but a rush of air. Emmett was never home. To be clear, he wasn't chasing after other women. No, that thought never entered my mind. In that case he would've been a great actor, like Denzel Washington, Morgan Freeman, Samuel Jackson, and the other one, that handsome kid who played in *Twelve Years a Slave*. He's so cute that every time I mention him to someone, I get emotional and forget his name. It'll come back to me. Anyway, if Emmett had been that good an actor I wouldn't have taken off with the other guy. We'd be living the good life in Hollywood today, in a villa with a swimming pool hidden by the dry vegetation of California, filled with the cries of children, his and our own. Like a real family. Everything we'd do or say would be on social media: how the family mourned when our Yorkshire died, my stretch marks after the diet that would make me lose twenty pounds—except from my butt, that magnet for men—a daughter's heartache—all the things people post to keep from being bored.

You've got to understand. With a guy like that, always off somewhere going after jobs that paid a quarter or fifty cents an hour, coming home every night so beat you wouldn't believe it, and letting my youth fade away in bed like that, life wasn't exactly a piece of pecan pie with maple syrup, like my mother used to make—it makes my mouth water just to think about it. True enough, without those little jobs we could've never made it through the month. But I deserved better. I was young and, quite frankly, pretty well built. They still tell me that, by the way, and not only men, who just want to flatter you, who know exactly how to say what you want to hear just to have their little business. No, women, too, tell me I'm thick. Even if you can tell it's not easy for them to say so. For a girl who isn't LGBT to say something like that to you, you have to be well above average. Because us women aren't always very generous. Women's solidarity is only for those who have an image to protect—politicians, activists, artists, intellectuals. In reality, sister, my ass, yeah. Excuse my language. They try to trip you up, just like men do. At the end of the day we practice sisterhood without all the talk. And when we have to call somebody out, we get straight to the point. We openly lock horns.

What I'm saying is that at my age I needed to dream. Not stay at home, in some neighborhood that sucks, wipe the kids' bottoms when the two older ones weren't even mine. Having to move in with a mother-in-law who only cared about Jesus and his father, because we had no money.

It was one woman too many under the same roof. You can't say I didn't show any empathy. No woman as well-equipped as me would've gotten involved with a single father of two. Unless it was to have a good time while waiting for something better. Or if the guy was loaded. But Emmett, he didn't have a cent. *Nada de nada.* So I really have nothing to blame myself for. No one else to blame either.

Truth is I was in love with him. Really crazy about him. At least in the beginning. I love being in love, can't help it. I need to love someone to feel alive. When he showed up with that big lanky body of his and then gave me his totally unpretentious smile, it was impossible to resist. Or I wasn't a flesh and blood woman. Or one of those dolls inflated with silicone everywhere. Which isn't my case. I have everything I need, where I need it. Natural. And besides, I'm far from being indifferent to handsome men who know how to talk to women. And he was a smooth talker. Why wouldn't I melt when, the first time Authie introduced us, the guy looked at me as if he was facing Naomi Campbell in the glory of her thirty years and said: 'Blessings on the mother who gave birth to you, baby!' And he seemed really sincere, too. He got that from his father, I guess. I said it before, he didn't spend his time whispering sweet nothings in the ear of every woman who crossed his path. But when there was someone like me he was interested in he knew exactly what to say. So I challenge any normal woman not to fall for that. And yet, I've been around. Even if you're still not supposed to shout it from the rooftops today, at the risk of having people think your morals are beyond salvation. Of being blasted by the goody-goodies or solicited by the first dickhead that shows up and thinks he has a chance with you because you've been

labeled an easy lay. In short, I had my little involvements before I met him. Which just goes to show...

But I wasn't ready to take on a family with three kids,
and what's more, to deal with dust and clutter every day just
to get them fed. I saw my youth disappear, pass me by, without being able to do anything about it. And he, always running around from one place to another, going after jobs at
starvation wages. Still, we'd gotten off to a promising start.
Even if he'd forgotten to tell me he had two kids at home
whose mother had ditched him to go make a new life in
Georgia. It makes me laugh to think about how he'd turn the
radio off in a rage as soon as Ray Charles started crooning
the song that has the same name. That's why I had a hard
time leaving him under those conditions. But we all have
our own karma in life, as they say. His was to let women re-
ject him. Maybe because he was too attached to his mother.

We met at my friend Authie's when I came to spend
Thanksgiving weekend. Authie knew about Emmett and his
two kids but had been careful not to mention them. Basically, she's always had a thing for her childhood friend. As a
teenager she would spend an entire night talking about him
without even once getting up to go to the bathroom. She
finally admitted that she'd never have him, that he saw her
more as a sister than a lover, she'd rather see him and me get
together. Looking at it more carefully now, what may have
seemed like generosity on her end was perhaps a strategy to
keep some little bitch from coming out of nowhere and sep-
arating them. Keeping them from meeting in her absence, or
not meeting at all. Or worse yet, taking him far away from
her. When I realized that, I was a little hesitant at first. But
not for long, he was too irresistible. With me, she had two

for the price of one. She was pulling off a double coup. She had her girlfriend and she kept her Emmett nearby. Except that I didn't know anything about the kids.

I'm originally from Madison, a two-hour drive from Milwaukee going nice and slow. It doesn't seem far but it's two different worlds. They can boast all they want about being the metropolis of Wisconsin but we're the state capital. And that changes many things, the air is different there. As if created by an offshore wind that makes you want to go somewhere else. You're open to the rest of the world in spite of yourself. Even with a larger population, Milwaukee is closed in on itself and closes you in. Authie and I became friends through our parents. My father is from Franklin Heights, too. Initially he came to Madison for work at a time when there was absolutely nothing to be found in his hometown. That would've been in the late seventies. He told himself: 'We'll see'. Maybe after six months or a year he'd get tired of it and go back to Milwaukee. He just needed a change of scenery.

That's what he told me when I was old enough to have a real conversation with him; I was going on twelve, or maybe thirteen. He must have been getting sick and tired of answering one of my countless questions. Besides wanting to understand, it was also my way to have him to myself, without my brother and sister there, without mom. Dad's still a good-looking man even now. When he saw I was becoming seriously involved with Emmett he brought the subject up again. Without ever going into any details. He knew about my affairs. He must've felt powerless to reason with me, so he let mom play the prude. With Emmett he sensed it was serious and he stepped up. He told me to be careful. That it wasn't right for a Black man, who'd marched for civil rights during the difficult years of segregation as well, to tell his daughter not to get involved with another Black man. 'But Franklin Heights is different, places sometimes rub off on the people who live there.' A very fatherly word of caution. Nothing more. When I saw Franklin up closer, I understood. But it was too late.

So, having gone to work in Madison, my father met my mother there. And decided to stay and start a family. Trapped, like me with Emmett. That's how I came into the world, then my brother and sister. But he hadn't burnt his bridges with his hometown. Authie's parents used to visit us several times a year, at Thanksgiving, Christmas, or Easter. They even came in the summer once, giving them a change from Milwaukee. In Madison we lived in a fairly quiet neighborhood, without all the problems that tear Franklin apart. On the other hand, we must have gone down there only two or three times in all. Authie and I developed a very strong relationship over the years, even if she was older than me. Each time they visited, she'd stay in my room with me, which meant that my sister had to share our brother's room and that put them both in a very bad mood. In those days, Authie could talk about Emmett all night long, even waking me up sometimes and forcing me to listen to her. She's four or five years older than me, I don't really remember anymore, and always saw me as her little sister. Until I broke up with Emmett, that is.

We hadn't seen each other in a while when she decided that I should spend Thanksgiving with her. It wasn't right that she always had to make the trip. 'Friendship is like love, it's not a one-way street. Otherwise you get frustrated and go look somewhere else.' And, while we were on the subject, it would give her a chance to introduce me to someone. I was used to the fact that my girlfriends were always trying to marry me off. They didn't think it was normal that being over thirty I still hadn't started a family. Or they were envious of my freedom. Or, since I was attractive, they saw me as a threat to their own relationship. In short, I went to see her so she'd stop making me feel guilty. She was something else once she got started! And then she introduced her Emmett to me. As illogical as it may seem, I'd never met him before. She told me he was her beloved brother, the apple of her eye, and I'd better take good care of him. 'If you ever hurt him, Angela, I'll scratch your eyes out,' she added when the relationship began to come together as more than a flirtation.

At first he said nothing about the kids who were left with his mother that night. She only lived two blocks away. It didn't occur to me for a moment that at his age he could be a mama's boy. Thanksgiving fell on a cold but sunny Thursday. We had a long weekend to get to know each other. He pulled out all the stops: a stroll downtown, which I actually didn't know very well; a walk along the lake before taking me to a restaurant that serves slammin' spareribs with mashed potatoes and a nice beer, made in Milwaukee. They learned how to brew it from the German immigrants who arrived in a continuous flow from the middle of the nineteenth century on. I tasted it for the first time and it took me a while to really appreciate it. Even though he wasn't a basketball fan, he took me to a Bucks game. He'd bought tickets just so he could take me out. He was so proud to have me visit the Harley-Davidson Museum that you would've thought he was one of its primary shareholders. Authie told me that his mom had worked there.

That first dreamlike weekend made me want to go back. Each time he left the children with his mother. I didn't know this then. We'd see each other at Authie's who lived by herself and arranged it so we could be alone together. He waited three months to talk about his daughters. Noticing my dubious look, he told me it wouldn't change anything for us. 'We love each other, that's what matters, baby. I'd have a hard time spending the rest of my life without you next to me. It wouldn't be the same. A little like a barbecue without any meat.' He knew how to talk, the old guy. And since everyone, Authie in the lead, was putting pressure on me because of my age, I finally gave in and went to live in Franklin. But, I told him, not before he'd found us a house. 'I'm not the kind of woman who'll live under someone else's roof. And at my age even less so.' So then he found us a two-bedroom place halfway between his mother's and Authie's.

I admit it was a shock to see the neighborhood in full daylight, beyond the weekend honeymoons. Later on I got used to it. Human beings adapt themselves to anything no matter what. Even more so a year and a half later when our daughter came. I hadn't wanted to get pregnant right away, just so I could see how things were going. Having said that, it wasn't as if Emmett had the energy for things like every night. Wiped out as he was once he came home. Render unto God the things that are God's. When he got down to it he made you touch the heavens above; it made you want to start right up again as soon as you came near the bed. And then, Authie and the others wouldn't stop making allusions. Even his Bible-thumping mother. Each time we'd run into each other they'd say:

'You'd make some beautiful babies together.'

When it finally did happen they all seemed happier than I was. The fact that there was a fifth member in the family didn't seem to concern anybody. Large families were common here. One mouth more or less to feed wasn't going to make them lose any sleep. His mother now had a ready-made excuse to impose her presence on us; help me a little with the three girls, she said, while her son blew in and out like a gust of air.

Oddly, Emmett himself didn't exactly jump for joy either. You can't say he didn't love me. Perhaps that was the moment he realized what it would mean financially. (As long as they're not holding it in their arms, men sometimes find it difficult to imagine the reality of having a child.) Also, I was among the forty percent of Milwaukee's unemployed Blacks and couldn't be much help to him on that front. Still he told me: 'Don't worry, baby. We'll find a way. I'll work twice as hard.' I didn't know then that it meant I wouldn't see him anymore at all, or only very little. And find myself at home alone with three kids, and a mother-in-law getting under my feet, especially since we lived only three blocks apart from each other. So, mother in the house. I who liked nothing better than taking care of myself, never being the last one to party, I was watching my youth pass me by, drift away, unable to do anything to hold onto it, even less to catch up with it.

I can't say he didn't make certain we weren't lacking for anything. He was working like hell, three jobs at the same time: two during the week and one on the weekend. He came home only to go right back out again. A true rush of air, I'd say to his friend Authie who, instead of feeling sorry for me, accused me of being a princess. 'There are women who'd pay good money to be in your place.' But her 'brother' was leaving me alone more and more in this area that is no place to raise children. Fortunately, there are support networks, churches, the mother-in-law, the non-profits that provide precious material assistance, and sometimes a listening ear. Without that, I would've fallen apart sooner. That said, all of it was still only a bandage on a wooden leg. Too many problems. A hydra with a thousand heads. The more you cut off the more it grows back. You don't know which end to tackle to eliminate it from the face of the earth once and for all. When Emmett lost the first job I told myself: that's a win, being able to spend more time together will compensate for it. Then he lost the second job, only hanging on to a lousy security guard gig. And then the world fell apart.

Since he was freer now, he got it into his head to help local youth find a way out instead of spending it with me to make up a little for lost time. That was how he phrased it: 'find a way out'. He applied it to everything. As if he, I, all the neighborhood's residents were stuck in a damned swamp that we had to drag ourselves out of at all costs. He certainly was influenced by Stokely, the other one of his childhood's partners in crime, who'd spent ten years in jail and came out with the mentality and the goals of a boy scout. One of the rare cases, I must admit, where being locked up didn't make the person even stranger. For him everything was a pretext to try and redeem himself. Emmett would've done better looking for work, because the young folks didn't seem all that interested in the game of football that he wanted to teach them. When they weren't involved in the drug business, directly or via their parents, it was only the NBA they

dreamt about. And one guy they called 'Jesus', a former player for the Bucks, who'd drain consecutive three-pointers as if
he were peeing 'em, all while chewing gum.

The rest of the time, when Emmett was home, he no
longer had the same light in him. He was snuffed out. Like
when he came back to the 'hood after failing to make the
NFL and slogging away for years before coming back to
square one. I didn't know him then, Authie and Stoke told
me about it. It was the same story it seems. Something in
him was broken. He could spend a whole chunk of the night
telling you how everyone in the stadium would be on their
feet during the college football championship games. How,
if he hadn't suffered that nasty injury, he would surely have
more to offer us today, to the children and me. He didn't
say that we clearly wouldn't have met, that he would've
been busy swimming in vaster and deeper waters where we
wouldn't have known each other. The rest of the night, he'd
stay eyes wide open in the dark replaying the film of his failure, so close to his goal. I knew he wasn't sleeping because as
soon as I got up to go to the bathroom he'd say: 'You alright,
baby?' In the morning, he'd drag himself around like a zombie before planting his big security guard frame in front of
the Whole Foods on Prospect Avenue, a supermarket for the
trendy middle-class, where nobody from Franklin would
have ever been able to shop.

The last straw came when we'd spent every last cent of
his savings and we were forced to move in with his mother,
who'd been waiting just for that ever since she'd invited us to
live with her, 'there's space, it'll save you money'. No more
privacy at all. Finished. The end. It was more than I could
take. Don't get me wrong, in the meantime I'd helped as best

I could. I was taking responsibility. I wasn't complaining, no matter what Authie thinks. Many women wouldn't have deprived themselves. Especially when they're as well-built as I am. In spite of the pregnancy and delivery I was still a fine piece. Out of necessity I'd become expert at supermarket promotions and clothing stores sales. Besides Emmett's hair, I cut the ends of the girls' hair myself, though they'd grumble about not going to the salon to get those weird braids that were in style. All of it to save on the price of a haircut and spend it on something more basic. Never having experienced this at home with my parents, I was relying on food stamps to improve the everyday fare, along with the rest of the city's poor. On the other hand, I avoided the support networks managed by the district's bountiful ladies: too ostentatious, too much gossip. What's more, having to move in with a mother-in-law who was interested only in her big baby and her granddaughters, was already more than I could bear.

One day I went to see my parents in Madison. Mercifully, I'd gone by myself and run into an old flame who still remembered me. He was over forty and I was worrying about approaching my own forties. He wasn't married, had never even lived with anyone. It set me thinking right away. If after a certain age a man is still alone, you don't have to look very far: either it's a manufacturing defect, or he's a pain in the ass that no woman wants anything to do with, or he's gay and hasn't admitted it to himself. In all three cases, it smells like trouble. Otherwise, the sisters wouldn't have let him walk off all alone into the wild blue yonder. As for me, where trials and tribulations were concerned, I'd been there already. But you should never test fate.

I went back two or three times to make sure, to sound out his feelings in case he wasn't part of one of the three mentioned categories. He'd just gotten a job as foreman of a construction site in South Carolina. He suggested I come with him. It was too tempting. I couldn't stay any longer watching my youth go down the drain. It goes by fast for us women. After that it's not easy. Men begin to look at you like an expired product, just barely good enough to be consumed so they won't die of abstinence if there's nothing else around to open their fly for. I had to take advantage of this while there was still time. All the more because he wasn't bad at all, this one. My weakness for good-looking guys will be the death of me yet.

Truthfully, it made me sick to take off like a thief in the night, leaving our daughter behind with Emmett. But I knew he'd take care of her. He was a good man. I promised myself I'd reclaim her once I'd settled down somewhere. But I soon realized that stability wasn't possible with my new companion. He might stay a year at one site, six months at the next. We were going from one state to another, following the work. And then, kids weren't his thing, he didn't have any paternal fiber in him. In addition, I didn't really see him taking care of someone else's child. I must admit that I, too, liked not having any kids around. Being able to come and go as I wanted. Totally free. Time went by, I fell in love with another man. I'm on my third one since I left Franklin Heights. All without being aware of it. It isn't my fault that I'm a serial lover.

Then I heard the television news. It crushed me, I must confess. Not only because I'd lived with Emmett. No human being should ever find death this way. Period. I called Authie to offer my condolences. As luck had it, she still had the same phone number. I hadn't heard her voice in years. She'd written me a nasty letter via my parents in which she sided with her Emmett. And she called herself my sister. I asked her for news about my daughter, just like that. To let her know I hadn't forgotten about her. Like a dog left by the side of the road, to go on vacation. I knew her grandmother would take care of her. Then Authie told me that she'd died three months before. That it would be a good idea to get my ass back right away if I didn't want social services to take my daughter. That I shouldn't count on her to play surrogate mother. Poor Emmett didn't deserve this. I didn't really understand if she was talking about his meeting me, which had been her doing, or about what had happened to him. I told her she had to give me some time to get back. I was at the other end of the country. I also had to talk about it with my man first so he wouldn't be completely bewildered, poor guy. Anyway, Authie would never abandon Emmett's daughter to the street.

III

THE MARCH

Not everything that is faced can be changed.
But nothing can be changed until it is faced.

JAMES BALDWIN

True peace is apolitical, it consists of
having the other inside your skin
without reciprocity.
[La véritable paix est apolitique, elle
consiste à avoir l'autre dans sa peau,
sans réciprocité.]

EMMANUEL LEVINAS

THE PRODIGAL SON

LIVE-STREAMED OVER the internet, then picked up by every television channel on the planet, Emmett's assassination unleashed an unprecedented tidal wave of outrage in a country that you would have guessed was exhausted by a situation that, since the vigorous struggles of the sixties to end it, continued to be bogged down by, if not actually backsliding into, segregation. Hurriedly organized over social media, telephone (cordless or not), and word of mouth, spontaneous demonstrations erupted, sending millions of women and men into the streets. Employees of American embassies overseas barricaded themselves in shame as angry demonstrators jeered, waving accusatory placards at the Marines, hiding behind the barricades, their jaws clenched, their fingers trigger-ready on their weapons, prepared to defend the superpower image of their country.

Milwaukee, and the neighborhood of Franklin Heights in particular, was not to be outdone. Ma Robinson, former prison guard and now pastor, told herself that ideally this fury should be channeled toward something constructive, to instill some optimism where there was now only rage, without yielding to detractors and populists of every political persuasion. Wisconsin's largest city, since that's where it had all happened, was duty-bound to lead by example. By organizing a huge march that would make a real impression and at the same time be a sign of hope and brotherhood the city would be a beacon in the darkness of hatred in the funeral's wake. But how to go about it? What energies to draw together and in which direction to go now that ever since that puppet with his toupee arrived at the White House, the country had become even more divided?

Ma Robinson knew she could count on the willingness, the unfailing enthusiasm, and the technological expertise of her digital assistants: Marie-Hélène, a young Haitian from Chicago, and her boyfriend Dan, a dyed-in-the-wool Milwaukeean, both of them students at the University of Wisconsin-Milwaukee. Thanks to social media, they were able to reach an audience with whom the pastor generally was not able to connect. By providing the march with greater publicity and seek justice on behalf of Emmett's daughters, they might even succeed in replacing the journalists.

She could also count on the help of Stokely and Authie, Emmet's two childhood friends, who'd been gracious enough to put aside their old disagreements to shake up the apathy of Franklin's residents whom she'd been having trouble mobilizing these past few years—crushed as they had been under the weight of everyday life. All the tremors she'd been feeling for two days excited her. Things seemed to be in motion. Babylon would finally expunge the wrath of the divine. Even if the death of poor Emmett—to whose mother she had always been very close—was a price to be paid that tasted more like bitter gall. The whiff of the battle for civil rights reinvigorated her, proof being she hadn't felt her rheumatism in two days.

Ma Robinson still had that speech in mind from the previous evening's debate, in which an elected Republican senator, when questioned by a young woman in the audience sitting in the front row, ornately adorned with tattoos from her knuckles to her neck and with facial piercings, who wanted to know what the senator had done so far, or intended to do, on behalf of the rights of minorities, which were all too often trampled in this country that prided itself on being the land of liberty. 'Words aren't enough anymore. We want action. My generation wants action,' declared the girl whose soft voice clashed with her provocative appearance as she was making an attempt to angrily drive home her point. Rather than answering her, this elected official seized the opportunity to settle the accounts of a whole series of citizens' movements that in his opinion were harmful, and to address himself to those he considered his electoral base.

'Minorities' rights, you say. I suppose by that you mean the rights of Blacks, women, LGBTQQIAAP—those initials that don't seem to care how ridiculous they are—drag queens, queers, trans, little monkeys, big apes, wildlife, elephants, dolphins, birds, ants—preferably black ones—the Amazon Forest, the sun that will soon be gone... and I forget the rest. I've nothing against any of this but who will take care of the little White straight people of our country? Tell me, don't their lives matter?' slipping in underhandedly a double allusion to the #MeToo and Black Lives Matter movements. 'Or do they only come after everything else I've mentioned?'

This lively exchange had reminded Ma Robinson that if she wanted to carry out her ministry she needed to get closer to the young through their preferred means of communication: social media. An unfamiliar universe for the former prison warden who was used to direct contact, to the frank look in the eyes of the other that made any evasive answer impossible. How many crises hadn't she managed to defuse that way, both behind the prison walls and on the streets of Franklin Heights! More than adrenaline, it was this physical contact that she missed with the so-called social networks. Observing every gesture, even the involuntary ones, of the other person. Getting a whiff of their smell, knowing whether they were sweating fear, challenge, as in hand-to-hand combat. Mistrust or trust in the middle of a negotiation. Hence her preference for street activism, for word of mouth, for real words exchanged face to face, even if they come with sparks.

Today's young claimed to be saving the world from behind the screen of their smartphone, whose production furthermore never stopped draining the planet's resources. The rare few who showed just a bit of interest in the sacred insisted on attending Sunday services while sprawled on their sofa, or even in bed, their bodies still sullied from the wafts of last night's sin, barely covered in pajamas or a jogging suit. The weekly appointment with the Almighty should require a minimum of decorum, after all. Well, you had to change with the times as they say, in order to give the cause, whose protection was taking all her energy, a chance to succeed. And then, she really should pass on the baton one day. She had three quarters of a century behind her, much more than her parents put together—may the Eternal One welcome them in His Kingdom. From this perspective, her assistant Marie-Hélène and her slightly crazy fiancé were more than precious to her. They were an enormous help in all sorts of ways, among other things with those damn new technologies about which Ma Robinson didn't understand shit. It was the Savior who'd sent those two her way.

The time was long gone when she and Mary Louise, Emmett's mother—may God protect her soul—would spend hours getting ready for church, with, as a final touch, the hat worn to one side so it wouldn't over-shadow their hair style. To get all dolled up like that for Sunday service was not just a habit from childhood. Nor was it intended to go hunting after a suitor, a serious one if possible, whom Mary Louise was convinced she'd find at church. About which she was wrong. 'Don't you believe it. Philistines always manage to slip in among even the most pious of congregants,' her saintly mother used to say. The evil spirit could take on a thousand faces to deceive the young women they were, even though they didn't ask for much. Like any good Christian woman, they were aspiring merely to a life worthy of the name, with a hardworking husband who loved and respect-ed them, under the benevolent eye of the Lord and in com-pliance with His laws.

Ma Robinson would never make it. 'Because of that nasty character of yours,' Mary Louise used to tell her at the time. They had become chummy when she arrived in Franklin Heights in the mid-60's, escaping from the all-too venomous segregation of the deep South. Strengthened by her network of friends and extended family in Baton Rouge, she knew she'd be able to find work here in Milwaukee. She was barely twenty years old and the future awaited her with open arms. From her life in the South she'd inherited a character forged in steel and a passion for living. So she'd never known how to try to keep a man by cooing as so many women do, accepting small and great humiliations if not actual beatings. In any event, men always ended up heeding the malicious spirit in their head that advised them to pack their bag, most often on the sly, without taking responsibility for their actions, leaving you with two or three children on your hands; before another one of their type shows up, materializing from the Devil's lair and planting a new seed in your belly, then disappears without even giving you time to find a nickname for him—*honey, sweetheart,* or *dummy* just to tease him. Of course people said that Ma Robinson exaggerated, that she was creating grist for the mill to slanderers, but it was the plight of large numbers of Franklin's women for whom she had to patch things up every day, just with her words, the same ones that Providence had put in the stammering mouth of Moses to free the Hebrews from slavery.

So, when Sunday came and it was time for church she didn't dress to please a potential suitor. Not even Christ who, by the way, was a man as well—may the good Lord forgive her! At the time her faith wasn't that strong. If she was dressing up that much it was to get rid of the persistent smell of the prison that clung to her all week long. That job, which she found soon after her arrival, had turned into a true calling; the road that the Lord had provided her so she'd try to bring back to the right path a few of the thousands of young women who'd lost their way in sinfulness. She hadn't taken up this profession for the salary alone or for job security. Far from it. Despite her youth, she made a point of saving these sinners. It was where she drew the energy to get up in the morning—even in the winter at five degrees below zero, the Midwestern climate being the worst enemy for a Baton Rouge native—even at the risk of letting that segregationist scum and other allies of the Klan pass for altar boys. She was a fisher for souls. That's what she was doing, until upon retirement, she founded her own church. Emmett's mom attended it until her death just three months earlier; a premature demise as she was five years her junior.

Mary Louise was over the moon when her Emmett left for college with the help of a scholarship that the Almighty in His infinite goodness had been willing to provide him. Both women had prayed for that day and night. Unable stand the wait for a reply any longer, Emmett's mother had reached the point of setting an ultimatum for the Creator. 'Three weeks, not one more. Far be it for me to be rude. You alone are God, and there is no other. I have glorified You all my life without ever asking You for anything and I'll continue to do so for as long as I live. But this concerns my only son, and You know something about that. So, I beg You, put an end to this torture, I can't stand the waiting anymore. Three weeks, not one more.' When the mailman finally delivered the envelope and she opened it in Emmett's absence since he'd gone who knows where, she burst into tears before phoning Ma Robinson to tell her the good news. She had proof that the good Lord was indeed a man. Like any man, you had to shake him from time to time to get anything out of him. As she had done. The two friends and accomplices had laughed uproariously.

After four years of not hearing any news from the neighborhood kids about Emmett entering the NFL, of which they would certainly have been very proud, Ma Robinson concluded that Mary Louise's son must have failed in his quest for glory and wealth. Despite their intimacy, her friend never uttered a single word about it to her. As for her, she never spoke to Mary Louise about it either. It wasn't out of hypocrisy. There are subjects that are too painful to broach without being asked, it would be like needlessly rubbing salt in a wound. Then the years passed, as time does, with their share of problems and the small pleasures of finding a solution for these when possible. The years passed, with the strange machine of our body creaking ever more regularly and with our memory taking a nasty pleasure in messing around with us.

Emmett, the lost sheep with the shattered dream, had yet to return to the fold. From time to time he'd show some sign of life, almost as if he wanted to follow in the footsteps of his degenerate father. At least that's what his mother had believed, thinking she'd raised him at a good distance from these acts of cowardice. From time to time she'd speak to Ma Robinson about it—one really has to confide in someone to soothe one's soul—in an attempt to persuade herself with whatever ews she'd pass on to her, that she sometimes would spontaneously make up. The pastor pretended to believe her stories if merely out of Christian charity.

God only knows, however, whether Ma Robinson had warned her against the smooth talker who appeared at the church one Sunday rigged out like Don Cornelius, the host of 'Soul Train'. The rest of the week, when he went back to work at the auto factory, he'd dress even more extravagantly: shirt unbuttoned to the navel both summer and winter, flared black and white striped pants that hugged his spindly thighs. No matter how much junk food he ate he never gained an ounce. The whole was topped by a huge Afro that devoured his bony face with its indelible smile. He spent his time arranging it with a metal Afro pick that he carried in the right back pocket of his pants, whose horn handle ended in a clenched fist with a *peace and love* sign in the center. That is what in the end had fooled Mary Louise. He moved about perched on varnished boots with wedged heels at least four inches high, his chest pushed forward as if his spinal column were incapable of holding him straight up. His head was permanently ahead of his body, which people said behind his back that he was pecking as he walked.

Dropped from one day to the next by that good-for-nothing, Mary Louise lived only for her son, even after he left for college and even more so when he, too, evaporated into thin air without leaving any address while he went chasing after the mirage of the American dream. A rather heavyset woman under normal circumstances, she would flap around inside her clothes when she didn't have any news from her Emmett for an extended period of time. Which last months or even a year. Until, weary from wandering, and clearly not knowing where to go anymore, he eventually came back to settle down in the small house his mother had been renting ever since the 1980's. More than a decade and a half had gone by.

She'd welcomed him like the prodigal son, covered him with kisses, killed the fatted calf she didn't have, opened her door and her heart to him. He showed up with his own progeny, two little girls from an earlier relationship which Ma Robinson could swear he'd never said a word about to his mother before. Later on he showed up with another stuck-up girl who'd give him a third child before disappearing into the wind. A desertion that rang like a curse on mother and son. Mary Louise couldn't have endured seeing the death live on TV before the eyes of the whole world. She wouldn't have survived it. She would have followed him with a bitter heart. You had to understand, she'd devoted her entire life to her only son. Thank God she went before he did. At the time everyone, including Ma Robinson, thought the death was unjust because of its brutality and because he was so young. But the Almighty always works judiciously even when His plan seems obscure to us mortals.

In a way the so-called modern communications technology had its good side. It's thanks to this, one might hope, that justice has been provided for Emmett today. After Providence itself, of course, had put witnesses on the scene to video the ghastly crime. Who knows what false report the villainous police officers would have otherwise concocted to justify their deed? Marie-Hélène and her fiancé's vigilance should also be praised. Ma Robinson could tell that the boy didn't believe much in her religion. Not because he was Jewish, no. He didn't seem to believe in any religion. Nor in God or the devil either. He'd really come for Marie-Hélène's beautiful almond-shaped eyes and her prominent cheekbones to make sure he'd have a place in her heart. Had she been a Buddhist, a Muslim, or a non-believer, it wouldn't have made any difference at all. But it was fine this way. His joy in living was a pleasure to behold. Above all, he spared neither his strength nor time for the support network. And he was incredibly effective. In Ma Robinson's eyes that was the most important thing.

The minute they heard about Emmett's murder they had both relayed the information on their numerous accounts under all sorts of colorful names. The news had spread like wildfire throughout the country, spontaneous demonstrations began to take place pretty much everywhere. Ma Robinson had strongly urged her two 'assistants' to temper the fervor of their followers. She would do the same on the streets of Franklin, with every parishioner, every neighborhood resident that Jesus had put in her path. She would also pray to the Almighty to ask for protection for them—because the opposition wasn't disposed to sentimentality. This was exactly what they were waiting for. Waiting for the situation to degenerate, to beat them up, if not to wipe them off the face of the earth, one by one. Waiting for the situation to degenerate so that they could then discredit their right to be outraged. Waiting for the situation to turn ugly to nip the legitimacy of their struggle in the bud. 'Of our struggle,' she insisted on specifying. 'For there's only one struggle and it is a common struggle. There are no Whites on one side and Blacks on the other. Asians on one side and Latinos on yet another. Be smarter than your enemies. Be smart and be careful. You are the future of the cause, the salt of the earth. Better yet, you are humanity's future.'

That, in essence, is what Ma Robinson told them. In her now long life, from her native South that she'd fled to Milwaukee, she'd seen too many get lost on the way, carried away by their emotions. She'd never forgive herself if something were to happen to them, no matter what it was. 'And besides,' she'd added, 'if you're no longer here, who will connect with your generation? Who will serve as an interface, as you say?' Thanks to the actual church that they administered, and failing to round up the neighborhood's youth, the two young lovers had contributed by attracting tourists who were passing through Milwaukee. They could be seen in Franklin on Sunday, descending in clusters attracted by the gospel choir that had a rich repertoire of classics, which they'd all passionately join in on at moments of collective communion: "Go Down, Moses", "When the Saints Go Marchin' In", "Swing Low, Sweet Chariot", not to mention "Oh, Happy Day" that ended the service and sent all those beautiful people off in a good mood.

Ma Robinson wasn't bothered by these tourists of faith. Were they coming for the show? Fine, they'd have one. She added lots to her sermon. Since she still had some energy left—if she were to lose any, since her fickle body was taking malicious pleasure in playing tricks on her, the Almighty would give her the dew of His grace—she'd strut around, walk in front of the pulpit, pace the platform in a trance, modulate her voice, address the mesmerized congregation as beloved sisters and brothers, prompting responses of 'Amen', 'Yes, Lord', and 'Hallelujah'. She gave them their money's worth, which she was careful not to ask for when they entered, as her colleagues in Harlem did, nor would she park them in a wing of the church reserved strictly for them. Doing so would have reminded her of the dark times of segregation when 'Colored' and 'White' were forced to walk through life in two separate lanes. Two parallel paths without a single intersection where they could meet and share a bit of humanity. In her space in Franklin everyone mingled: faithful and visitors, rich and poor, gentile and pagan, the poorly dressed and the elegant. It didn't matter.

Still, it wasn't a show even if it looked like one. She demanded respect for the place, and people should be decently dressed. No question of coming into this sacred place with flip-flops or tank tops for men; boobs showing and in sinfully brief shorts for young women. None of that in her church. At collection time, which was held to the beat of a gospel song that could pass for frenzied were it not for the context, the visitors understood instinctively that they had to contribute their share to the Lord's cause. Green bills would lavishly rain down like manna for the children of Israel stranded in the desert. Among other things, the collection served to help families in trouble, women abandoned by their partners, children whose fathers were behind bars or had vanished without warning; to pay off some of the hospital costs of those who tended to avoid medical care because they had no social security. If in passing, Ma Robinson told herself, she could bring some lost sheep back to Christ's herd, it would always be a plus.

Marie-Hélène and her nutty fiancé had much to do in creating the reputation of the retired warden-turned-pastor that had reached beyond the boundary first of Franklin Heights, then Milwaukee, and conquered the United States and even reached the sky, as they said. It was thanks to them that, following the day of Emmett's death, journalists arrived from New York, Los Angeles, and even the ends of the earth, to interview her, ask her if she'd known him, and so on. And, did she ever know him! She'd wiped his bottom, swaddled him, that little guy who as an adolescent had grown to be a six-foot-five giant towering over her. Together with his deceased mother, they'd played hooky, dreamed up dozens of fantasies, shared bread and had some good laughs. But she was careful not to mention what she thought of his good-for-nothing father, over whom his mom had briefly sacrificed her friendship with Ma Robinson. That was well outside of her role as a woman of the church. As a child, Emmett hung out with two other rascals, a neighborhood boy and girl from whom he was inseparable, apart only when he went home to sleep, for if there was enough to eat for a kid at any home around there'd be enough for everyone; therefore, the little devils wouldn't leave the place where they happened to be. When his father left, Emmett had grown even closer to them. Stokely, the boy, was a true black sheep, the evil twin to Mary Louise's son. He ended up doing ten years dabbling in the drug business, following in the footsteps of his own father, like so many young people in Franklin. When all that happened, Emmett was, thank God, already possessed by the demon of football and saw less and less of him. That's what saved him. For a while, Stokely was incarcerated in the prison where Ma Robinson was holding down the fort as warden before she was transferred at her request to the women's penitentiary on the other side of Wisconsin. When Stokely came out, he'd gone straight, and taken up his place in Franklin Heights again without ever backsliding. From time to time he'd help out with the young, motivate them to find a sport as an alternative to the drug business. It wasn't always obvious, but he held on, even if he hardly ever came to church on Sundays.

Authie, the girl, had never had any problems with the police. Although the temptations were rife in the area, especially for a single woman who'd always lived from hand to mouth. She, too, had held on. She'd come to church intermittently. Sometimes she helped with collecting and distributing basic needs to the most disadvantaged, which she'd almost become a part of due to her job that paid less than minimum wage. But Ma Robinson had a knack for such things. On days when she sensed Authie was in bad shape, she'd encourage her to go home with a filled bag and a few dollars that would give her a little break for a week or two. Despite it all, Authie never faltered, praise the name of the Lord!

When the news was announced, the trio's two survivors were devastated. At the first meeting the pastor called on the day itself, Stokely had spontaneously suggested that a fund be created online to finance the funeral and meet the future needs of Emmett's daughters since, for lack of money, he didn't have any life insurance. He knew this for a fact because his childhood friend had mentioned it to him, even though they hadn't seen each other very often since Emmett's return. It was as if he'd wanted to give him a message, that is: 'I'm counting on you to take care of them should anything ever happen to me.' That's how Stokely interpreted it. The idea appealed to the pastor and to her 'assistants', who agreed with the rest of the group they'd refuse any donations from political personalities. It was a matter of avoiding any hijacking of their approach and to potential donors indicating its humanist character above any party.

Examples like that, miracles if you want, given the social context, were what Ma Robinson presented to the journalists who'd come swarming in from everywhere. Who wanted to see Franklin Heights as a place of perdition, a kind of Sodom and Gomorrah where no single resident could save another. Nevertheless, it was from there that justice for Emmett would come. From there that the salvation of the city, of the land, would come. From that area neglected by those in power but not by God, where the humblest of the humble languished. The more the hours passed, the more Ma Robinson was convinced of it. She was dreaming of a demonstration on a scale that would leave its mark. Three days had already gone by since Mary Louise's son had died under the cop's vengeful knee. Asphyxiated the way a piglet is killed, under the blank eyes of the police accomplices, who were more concerned with keeping the suppressed anger of the onlookers at bay.

It was time to strike a blow. That's the intention she revealed to her two webmasters, and also to Stoke and Authie who were eager to seek justice for their fallen friend. She began to set that good old word of mouth in motion. There was much to be done elsewhere: photocopying and putting up posters all over the city that she herself had written. Everyone contributed their own small piece. She was already envisioning the route of the march, which would leave from Franklin Heights, go through other neighborhoods less concerned with this kind of problem, picking up along the way all those of good-will, like a tree feeding itself on the vital energy of each of its roots to grow tall and solid toward heaven, before it would end up in front of City Hall. 'Milwaukee will be the light in the darkness', Ma Robinson rejoiced, feeling as if she'd gone back fifty years. Back to the time of the great marches for equality.

WOUNDS THAT ARE SLOW TO HEAL

ALTHOUGH THE REVERSE path was more common, coming from Chicago, Marie-Hélène had landed in this city thanks to a scholarship for her master's at the University of Wisconsin-Milwaukee. Normally it was the students from Milwaukee who moved on to the prestigious universities of Chicago, the largest city in the Midwest and third largest in the United States. To be honest, it hadn't been a very difficult choice. Of the different institutions to which she had applied, UWM was the quickest to respond. Her qualifications and excellent academic record had attracted the attention of its scholarship department. Once she'd initiated the registration process, she couldn't see herself reconsidering except by a miracle, for instance an offer from an elite university, such as an Ivy League school, whose ultra-selective image had deterred her from applying anyway.

What's more, the proximity of the two cities, an hour-and-a-half apart by car, offered the major advantage of re-assuring her Haitian parents who were having a hard time cutting the umbilical cord. 'Why go so far away?' her mother had wondered uneasily, although she herself had spent an entire day on a bus, slept one night in Port-au-Prince, and continued the following day for six hours on a plane to come to Chicago from Jérémie, a town in the south of Haiti. 'Can't you take the same courses here?' After bringing her to Milwaukee by taxi to get her settled, her father suggested in passing that he'd pick her up every weekend and take her back on Sunday if she'd like to come home to see her brother and sister. Then he added: 'They'll miss you a lot, you know.' An emotional blackmail of sorts. Marie-Hélène was aware of it but chose not to react. Basically, she understood, she'd only lived with them since she was thirteen years old.

To find her bearings in the city where she knew nobody, Marie-Hélène had gone to the community networks for which she'd obtained valuable information on Twitter, TikTok, and Instagram. An activist at heart, she was recruited for school tutoring sessions in Franklin Heights as soon as she arrived. Considered to be a tough area, it was a half-hour walk from Lindsay where she shared a place with three other students: a French girl originally from North Africa and a practicing hypersensitive Muslim, with whom every detail of their cohabitation created a daily ordeal, every word—if you had mistakenly started a discussion with her—requiring grueling gymnastics; a young man from the Ivory Coast, son of a good family, and a white New

York LGBTQ activist who spoke French, and had knocked around a bit in Canada and Europe.

For the first tutoring session in Franklin Heights, Marie-Hélène was sent to the family of a single father with three little girls who turned out to be this Emmett whom she had heard about for the first time from the girls' grandmother, and from Ma Robinson, a famous neighborhood figure. Not a week would go by that these two women didn't get together. The pastor had the habit of stopping by unannounced at the house of her longtime friend to evoke bygone times and complain about their old creaky bodies. 'But they won't get us, will they, sister?' she'd hasten to point out without anyone knowing to which old complicity that 'they' referred. And the two old ladies would clap their hands, bursting with laughter like schoolgirls. Marie-Hélène was impressed with Ma Robinson, the former warden who had founded her own church in order to, among other things, help the frailest get off the street and away from its dangers. She reminded Marie-Hélène of her own grandmother, who had looked after her as a child in her parents' absence: the same combination of severity and sweetness, generosity and determination. The pastor in turn took her under her wing, won over by her devotion to others and the sharp political consciousness evinced by the young Haitian-American.

The other person in Milwaukee who was going to mean even more for Marie-Hélène than Ma Robinson was a young history student, Daniel, whom she'd met at the university's Golda Meir Library about a year after her arrival. Dan thought Marie-Hélène's life was extraordinary, although she herself believed it was no different from that of hundreds of thousands of immigrant children with parents who had entered illegally or on a tourist visa. They lived here for years in secret before obtaining a work permit, then would get their green card thanks to an administrative or political decision, and finally they'd be able to submit an application for family unification with their sons and daughters whom they had sometimes not embraced in more than a decade. As it had been now about ten years since Marie-Hélène had seen her grandmother.

Her story did have a slightly more incredible touch, though. One day, her father had boarded a boat that regularly ran from Port-au-Prince to Jérémie, when it was hijacked by five armed men who forced the captain to set course for Florida. That's how, in spite of himself, her father found himself heading to the United States, unable to alert either his lover, who'd just given birth to Marie-Hélène in Jérémie, any family member, or even a friend. (At the time the cell phone epidemic hadn't yet engulfed the planet.) Emigrating to the land of Uncle Sam or anywhere else had not been part of his immediate plan. But, since he had been struggling to make ends meet in Haiti, he'd told himself that maybe, one day, why not? Of course, he had not expected this change of plans to happen under such circumstances. Wedged in between other surprised, helpless passengers, he'd come to the following conclusion: if they were accepted upon arrival, why refuse what destiny was handing him on a platter?

In a manner of speaking. For, between the overcrowded boat that was by no means prepared for such a long voyage, and the fear inspired by the presence of the pirates, hunger twisting their guts, and an incompetent captain whose few years of navigational experience was solely based on the Port-au-Prince/Jérémie round-trip, combined with the vehement mood swings of the Caribbean Sea, the crossing was anything but a pleasurable cruise. On top of everything else they even ran out of gas, and were three days adrift during which the passengers' pleas to heaven, the saints and the angels poured forth from every heart, until the voices died down and the boat was finally towed by an American coastguard patrol. No one, not even the captain, dared to betray the pirates. Like all the rest, Marie-Hélène's father ended up in Florida, in the Krome refugee camp near Miami.

He had to wait several months before some human rights activists were able to get him out of the camp. They'd procured him 'temporary protected status' that allowed him to stay in the country and work for a period of time that was filled with uncertainties, and dependent on the goodwill of successive administrations. However, this status didn't allow for any family reunion, especially since he and Marie-Hélène's mother weren't married. After five years, through toil and tenacity, he sent for her mother, after sending her money every month that she deposited in an account, enabling her to apply for and obtain a tourist visa. Marie-Hélène had to stay with her maternal grandmother until her parents, who by this point were married, had managed to get their green cards. A year and a half later, with the help of a good lawyer who had cost them an arm and a leg, Marie-Hélène finally joined them. She was thirteen and was entrusted to a good soul traveling on the same plane. A phantom awaited her upon arrival—her mother, and three unfamiliar figures: her father and her two younger siblings, by that time seven and five years old.

The most painful thing, her father admitted to her later, was not being there to see her grow up. All those years had been stolen from them, and they would never get them back. The photos he'd kept of her and would sometimes look at with tear-filled eyes would never make up for this deprivation, not for him, not for her. Maybe he should have given up on what fate had offered him and gone back to Haiti to be with her and her mother. 'Forgive me, daughter, forgive me.' Every time, Marie-Hélène who'd grown into a courageous young woman aware of the social inequalities around her and in the world, reassured him: 'You did it for our good, Papa, and you were right. Here we are, back together again.' And she'd take him into her arms. Dan simply couldn't believe she'd spent more than half her life away from her parents.

'I can't imagine how I would have managed all that time without mine,' he said.

'You would have survived, like all the others who had to,' Marie-Hélène replied.

When she arrived in Evanston, a suburb in northern Chicago, she hadn't felt too out of place—save for the brick buildings on the main arteries and all the paved roads that contrasted with Jérémie—because of the Latino neighbors whose loud Spanish she heard all day long. Countless Haitians and their descendants had been living there since the '60's. She never set foot on the street without hearing Creole spoken at one point or another. It had helped her adapt to the place, to her father whom she was getting to know, to her mother whom she was rediscovering after eight years away from her, her brother and sister whom she only knew from photos and whom she very quickly had to help take care of. Her father, a taxi driver, and her mother, a nurse's aide, spared no efforts to offer them the best.

'Otherwise,' her father said, 'we would've made the sacrifice of leaving our country for nothing. I would have missed seeing you grow up for no reason,' he'd repeat.

'There's no question you'd end up in crime,' her mother would add. 'This country gives nothing for free, even less to Black people. You have to work and walk the straight and narrow. Marie-Hélène, you're the oldest, it's up to you to set the example for the little ones.'

At school she worked diligently, while always keeping a close eye on her younger siblings. She helped them with their homework, made sure they were always clean and well-dressed, ate properly and went to bed on time on days that her parents came home late, and that was often. It hadn't kept her from making straight A's at school. One B and she'd be frantic. After high school, her parents, already imagining her in a doctor's coat, had a hard time grasping the point of her studying literature and what concrete job opportunities it would lead to. All things considered, though, she was going to college, her father thought, which they hadn't been able to do. It was enough to comfort him. 'She'll manage better than we have, with the help of God and the *lwa*,' her mother told herself, taking her children to the Haitian church on Elmwood Avenue every Sunday. But at Halloween she never forgot to pour a little water and rum in honor of the saints, while her father chose to crisscross the streets of Chicago in his cab, so that his family wouldn't lack for anything, before picking them up when the service ended.

At first, Marie-Hélène hadn't paid much attention to the guy with braids bound together in a Rasta cap. He had to be one of those Whites with a serious identity crisis who's trying to look blacker than any Black, walking around displaying their worst faults without realizing it. In other words, he was to be shunned. She didn't see how she could bring home a boy with dreads either. In her parents' eyes he could only be a drug addict. She was aware she was building castles in the air because nothing had happened between them, and she had no inkling what his intentions were. And if he had any, it was up to him to declare himself.

'No way,' her mother told her the day she turned eighteen, 'will you show your feelings to a boy just like that. He'll take what he came looking for and then won't respect you anymore.'

Anyway, it had started off very badly between the two of them. Using their wait in line to check out books from the library, Dan had asked her point blank if she was going to the screening of the documentary *I Am Not Your Negro* by the Haitian filmmaker Raoul Peck. Without saying hello or introducing himself. 'Hi, I'm Dan Bronstein, I'm a history student, and you?' Something like that. Nothing! Last she heard they hadn't been hanging out together. Perhaps in his mind a Black woman should automatically be interested in films like that. Later on, once she'd gotten to know him a little, she would understand that it was simply a matter of clumsiness on his part, one of his prime qualities, as she kept thinking with some irony. His way of being cool had shocked Marie-Hélène to the core who, at the time, chose not to say anything.

'The screening,' he pushed on, 'will be followed by a discussion with the director. There may even be a dialogue that day with a former French Minister of Justice. That hasn't been confirmed yet but it would be super in a city like Milwaukee. Can you imagine! She's the first Black female Minister of Justice in France, you don't want to miss that.'

'Would you have specified her pigmentation if she was White?' she'd answered dryly. She would have blamed herself for letting such nonsense go by.

'You may not be wrong, sister. But I've made some inquiries,' he went raising his index finger deliberately. 'If there were other female Ministers of Justice in France before her, none of them, not even any male, were Black.'

'Still, you should have just said the first female.'

'You're absolutely right, sis. A white man's old reflex, which I'll be getting rid of. I'm working on it.'

'I didn't ask you for anything.'

'In any case, I think it's brilliant,' he concluded with a smile that lit up his baby face.

'As long as we're on the subject, stop calling me sis just so I'll think you're cool. Do I call you bro?'

Dan's enthusiasm was genuine. His gentle gaze and shy smile soon managed to touch, then disconcert, Marie-Hélène who let herself be persuaded, and so began seeing him at the library now and again, then have tea or carrot juice with him between classes. She was starting the second year of her Master's in Comparative Literature, a discipline she'd chosen because of the credits in Francophone Literature where she discovered authors like Jacques Roumain, Marie Vieux-Chauvet, and Jacques Stephen Alexis. Dan himself was in the first year of his Doctorate in Contemporary History, doing research in 'Intersectionality and Post-Colonialism'. When he found out that Marie-Hélène came from Chicago and was furthermore of Haitian origin—'a shit country' the young woman said alluding to a remark by the puppet with the toupee—he asked her if she knew that the Windy City had been founded by a Haitian of mixed race, named Jean-Baptiste Point du Sable. It was the first time she'd heard the term mixed race mentioned by an American and it had taken her by surprise.

Since she was never at a loss for words, Marie-Hélène then asked him what a petty bourgeois from the East Side, who was studying a subject that was of no concern to him either as someone White or male, was doing with those rags on his head. This time Dan laughed heartily before he explained the meaning of it all to her. He was a vegetarian like many true Rastas, and an Ashkenazi Jew. His Ukrainian grandparents had fled Nazi Europe with their respective families before coming to Milwaukee's East Side after a short stay in Chicago. The Illinois metropolis had been too large for them. They were looking for a city of human proportions where they could lick their wounds and start a new life. Although in the meantime his own parents had become middle-class, his grandparents had remained staunch civil rights activists and become early members of the local NAACP. They'd participated in every demonstration during the bitter years of the civil rights movement. And never stopped marching on behalf of human dignity, taking up in chorus the words of Bob Dylan's song:

> How many roads must a man walk down
> Before you call him a man?

'We Jews,' his maternal grandfather told him not long before he died—Dan must have been eleven years old —'we've known too much discrimination throughout our history not to be united in solidarity with struggles for human rights. Don't ever forget that, my boy. That, by the way, is one of my problems with the State of Israel. If I'd been in South Africa, I would have done the same thing and joined the ranks of the ANC, like Ruth First and her husband Joe Slovo, or Harold Wolpe who spent time in prison because of their egalitarian ideals.' Ever since, Dan had been part of every fight for equality, at the risk of sometimes getting lost in the struggle.

Marie-Hélène's gradual entry into his life contributed to his becoming more down-to-earth while still retaining the energy they had in common. For her 'wanting to stand out too much, you end up by locking yourself in, by becoming a community of one, and then forgetting the collective struggles from which we gather our strength. And the system takes advantage of that. Divide and conquer, it's as old as the hills. Having said that, every individual has a right to be respected for what he or she is. If it's right to pursue this tolerance for everyone, we shouldn't lose sight of our own place in the larger human community.' She shared this view with Ma Robinson whose words and experience were an inspiration to her. It's what she'd been fighting for since her adolescence, since she'd set foot on American soil and had grown aware of the enormous distance that separated people from each other. When only eighteen she'd joined the ranks of the Haitian-American women of the Midwest, whose mission it was to fight for 'the inalienable right of women and affirm their contribution through an active presence in society'.

Over the course of their endless discussions Dan had replaced the early "sister" with "babe" to address Marie-Hélène, and she much preferred that. She came from a country where even the street vendors whom you don't know from Adam call you "darling". In Dan's mind, switching from one term to another was much more meaningful, which he confessed to Marie-Hélène one evening on the phone. She responded with a long silence—her favorite defense when she was taken aback—before claiming an emergency and hanging up. In reality, she didn't know how to react and for an entire week stopped answering his calls. He left her interminable text messages, then lengthy ones on her voice mail in which he apologized, he hadn't meant to offend her and was so sorry if that was the case; or he said that he couldn't live without having her in his life, without their endless discussions, that he missed all of it, it was pretty wild.

Despite her inexperience with men she'd seen it coming though. She'd even dreamed of it. But she was going on twenty-four and had never kissed a boy in her life. The previous ten years she'd been too preoccupied with her studies and with helping at home to be interested in such things. And if the relationship were to take shape, how would Dan's parents react, they who had voted republican and, as he confided to her later, were dreaming of a spoiled Jewish American Princess for him or, failing that, of a Christian girl acceptable in all other respects. And what would her own parents say when they saw this novice descend on them with 'a pile of rags on his head'? That's how her mother referred to the dreads of a neighbor who, she was sure of it, was Jamaican but after Marie-Hélène's investigation turned out to be from Trinidad.

'They don't have the same accent, Mama.'

'Doesn't matter,' answered her mother who didn't want to lose face, 'one of those Caribbeans who speak English.'

Two days before the film's screening, Marie-Hélène decided she'd go, knowing full well that she would see Dan there. That's how their relationship began. A Milwaukee native, Dan knew the city inside out. He'd attended the Golda Meir School from elementary through high school. His grandparents had moved heaven and earth for him to go to this public school instead of the private one his parents dreamed of to nurture their self-segregation. As Jews, they'd argued, it should be a reason of pride for them to send their son to a school like that, which was one of the finest in the city, although it was a public school.

'Not to mention the fact that Golda,' the grandfather had emphasized, 'was a hell of a great woman of conviction. Nothing like those fascist wheeler-dealers leading Israel today.'

His parents finally gave in without making any further concessions after that. In short, the city held no secrets for Dan, except for Franklin Heights where he'd never set foot and which under Marie-Hélène's guidance he would get to know. She didn't hesitate to point out to him that in fact he wasn't as cool as he thought.

'No, but that's because of the dreads. The tough guys on the corner may think I'm making fun of Blacks while the White people will suspect I'm going to get my fix.'

'So for you Franklin Heights is just that? The majority aren't just regular citizens who live here making an honest living?'

'I didn't say that.'

'I don't see what else it could mean.'

Marie-Hélène wasn't the kind of woman who'd let things go, always pushing him into a corner. Not giving the other a way out. Always in conflict, whether consciously or not, was basically a way of reassuring herself. Since Dan had a tendency to feel guilty, she was lucky. Besides her penchant for debates, she was glad to have a local on call to guide her through the city. A great lover of jazz and blues, Dan took advantage of the slightest opportunity to take her to unlikely places where she would have never gone on her own, certainly not at night. She had a hard time with jazz, which she described as music for intellectuals.

'Don't complain.' Dan said caustically. 'All my mother listens to is classical music. Everything else gives her a migraine, she says with a sneer.'

Marie-Hélène preferred country music, which to her ears was more exotic and more catchy. Just to prove it, she'd begin leaping around like a mountain goat and laughing to the boisterous sounds of "Cotton Eye Joe" or "Milwaukee Blues", pretending to play the violin or the banjo. She began to change her mind the night Dan took her to the Jazz Estate, a small, cramped spot in the East Side where, pressed against each other, patrons literally stepped on the feet of other customers, a mugs of beer in their hands that they'd intermittently spill on each other when for the umpteenth time they were jostled. That night, Dan asked the quartet, whose drummer seemed to be someone he knew, to play "Sweet Home Chicago" in honor of Marie-Hélène. It made her cry, while as it was played, Dan wouldn't let go of her hand.

Recognizable for miles, and with the passing of time, Dan had also become a figure in Franklin Heights. Those who didn't greet him left him very much alone, knowing that he enjoyed the sacred protection of Ma Robinson and that, besides, he was no informer. He was overjoyed when a neighborhood youth gave him a 'brother' without appearing to notice the color of his skin, or when an elderly lady called him 'my son'. That's how he, too, became part of the huge demonstration that followed Emmett's funeral, to demand justice for Black victims of the police, of which there were already more than a hundred even though the year wasn't half over yet.

In their private moments, when Ma Robinson, Stokely, and Authie weren't around, Marie-Hélène insisted that Dan take color out of the plan. They should just say 'victims', period. Otherwise it might bring grist to the mill to those who, in bad faith, wanted to have people believe it was only for Blacks, to the detriment of everyone else. All too happy to ask in a voice filled with innuendo whether the lives of Asians, Whites, Latinos, and the police didn't count. As a politician had recently said on TV, who'd been called out by a LGBTQ activist whom she'd run into a few times on campus, and who'd given the impression of being at the university more for the political struggle than to study.

How many times didn't they have this discussion until all hours of the morning in Marie-Hélène's room where Dan joined her on weekends. He still lived with his parents, as his mother didn't see the point of paying rent for him when there was plenty of room at the house. According to Dan, this was a way for a good Jewish mother to keep him close to her. He'd often insist on examining the historical roots of the problem in the United States, and the rather recent end, officially at least, of segregation that had left wounds which would take time to heal.

'A parameter that must be taken into account,' he argued heatedly. 'It explains the excessive racialization of our society, hard to understand sometimes when seen from the outside. It doesn't all fade away overnight. Unless you're in denial as may happen in other countries. Here we're accustomed to tackling things head-on, for better or worse.'

Once Dan got started he'd go on with all his passion and all the goodness of his soul as well. As if all by himself he could find a remedy for the evil. Still, he'd listened to Marie-Hélène—he didn't have much choice —who was adamant not to shame others if they were to win them over to the cause. 'Most people are part of what they call the silent majority, they have no feelings of hostility toward anyone. They just want their peace and quiet, that's all. If you rush them too much you'll make them put their back up.' Dan made sure to heed his girlfriend's advice when it came to inviting the friends of his childhood and adolescence to the march in homage to Emmett, although they weren't particularly involved in this sort of struggle. Quite the contrary.

THE SHACKLE OF SHAME

ONE OF THE STUDENTS in Franklin Heights being tutored by Marie-Hélène was a thirteen-year old girl with the lovely name of Abigail. Her thin face with its very gentle look clashed with her strapping figure and her five-foot-six height. Marie-Hélène soon met the grandmother, Granny Mary Louise as she would respectfully address her, who was none other than Emmett's mother. Approaching the age of seventy-two, she was friendly and always well-groomed. She would get even more dressed up for Sunday services and, despite her age and heavy build, wouldn't hesitate to wear two-inch heels, all of it embellished with a hat the same color as her dress, set sideways on a head held high by a very straight neck. From the very first day on she spoke to Marie-Hélène about the pastor of her church, a certain Ma Robinson who was also a childhood friend.

'I'm sure you two would have things to talk about and do together,' she slipped in affably, in a voice that contrasted with the harsh tone of her longtime friend, a former smoker.

Three generations: the grandmother, Emmett the father, and his three daughters, all living under the same roof, on the floor of a rundown house a few blocks from the A. O. Smith factory, or what was left of it, which now specialized in the production of residential water heaters. Once inside, you came upon a staircase next to the wall with a hallway on the right side that led to the ground floor apartment of another family. At the top of the stairs a door opened onto a single space that served as kitchen, dining room, and living-room. It contained a faded leather couch against the wall, just below the window looking out over the street, and a television set stuck in a corner on top of a small coffee table on wheels. There were three different doors, two of which led to the bedrooms and the third to the bathroom.

When Marie-Hélène started her tutoring sessions, some eighteen months before the drama that would shake the country, she had to make do with the available space: the dining table in the middle of the room also served as Abigail's desk. She had trouble concentrating because of the incessant comings-and-goings of her sisters, seven and three years old, who needed to be constantly reminded to go play in their room. The girl's struggles with focus surely were caused by things other than the bustling around of her younger siblings and the constricted area. Perhaps the problem also lay with a mother who was part of the group of absconders but whose name was never uttered in Marie-Hélène's presence, whether good or bad. As if Abigail had been adopted at birth or conceived by surrogacy, which seemed quite unlikely considering the family's financial situation. In any case, she was very motivated and Marie-Hélène had high hopes of bringing her up to the proper grade level.

She didn't have time to get to know the grandmother very well, simply known to her granddaughters as Granny. It wasn't for lack of interest. Other than the first day when it took some time to get acquainted, by the time Marie-Hélène arrived, Granny Mary Louise had already left, sometimes to do a few hours of domestic work on the East Side, paid under the table, to supplement her meager pension, sometimes to lend a hand to her old friend Ma Robinson. She didn't know how to be idle, always looking for something to do to keep busy or make herself useful. So much so that the two of them hardly saw each other, or only very rarely and always in a rush. Nevertheless, at every one of their rare encounters, whether at home or at church, Granny Mary Louise never failed to thank Marie-Hélène. And always on behalf of both herself and her son, whom Marie-Hélène must have met three times in all.

He, too, wasn't home very much, having to split his time between two jobs, one as unstable as the other according to what the pastor had told Marie-Hélène during one of their long discussions when she recounted the neighborhood's history as if passing on a torch. Ma Robinson had told her about Emmett but also about his lifelong friends Stokely and Autherine, alias Stoke and Authie. One Saturday afternoon Marie-Hélène had run into Emmett when Dan had taken her to Whole Foods, against her will, because it was an upper middle-class supermarket with many shelves of organic goods that cost an arm and a leg. In addition to not having any money, she also balked at 'fueling the new health fad to get their hands on our pocketbooks'. She was in a good mood that day and had gone along with her boyfriend, even if she moaned about it just to make the point, but also wanted to avoid having the vegan Rasta bohemian impose bad habits on her.

That's where she ran into Emmett, squeezed into his security guard's baize uniform that made his frame even more impressive. Although only the second time they'd ever seen each other, Emmett recognized her and welcomed her with a big smile. He opened the door, moving aside with an exaggerated bow as if for an important figure, before greeting her: 'How are you doing today, Miss Marie-Hélène? Abigail can't stop talking about you. Thank you again, for her, for everything'. The conversation hadn't gone any further than a mere exchange of pleasantries. Marie-Hélène remembered it with a special feeling because Emmett's look was as gentle as his daughter's.

A week after this encounter, Granny Mary Louise passed on, her death caused by a sudden pulmonary embolism. It was a magnificent funeral, celebrated by the Ma Robinson of the olden days who managed to find inspiring words to talk about her childhood friend, making the gathering laugh and cry, and commend her soul to the Lord, waiting for the Second Coming of Christ as described by John the Apostle in the Book of Revelation. All, or almost all of Franklin Heights was crowded into the small church. Dressed to the nines, without ever saying a word to each other, Stoke and Authie flanked Emmett and the three girls.

Marie-Hélène remembered it all too well. It was the

third time she'd seen Emmett, and only about three months before his tragic death. During the ceremony Granny Mary Louise's son seemed absent, but not from the sudden shock that we feel at the sudden death of someone close. He seemed impervious to Ma Robinson's dazzling sermon, to the people weeping around him. Even when Marie-Hélène approached him and, lacking any words of solace to comfort him, had promised him she would continue tutoring Abigail, whose tears seemed never to run dry, just like those of her younger sisters who were undoubtedly crying because of all the people sobbing around them. According to Franklin's residents who had run into him, for the last three months of his life Emmett would keep that faraway look in his eyes and even in his gestures his mind seemed to be elsewhere.

Even though Emmett's mother was now gone, Marie-Hélène wouldn't see him at the house again, where Ma Robinson and other sisters from the church were taking turns to help the girls in their grieving and give them the urgently needed daily logistical support. They needed to compensate for the absence of their father who continued to drift, as the pastor put it, although she made sure he would come home to sleep at night so the girls wouldn't be alone in the house. Marie-Hélène made it her business to come by two or three times a week. On days that she was unable to be there she would exchange text messages or share stories with Abigail on Instagram. And yet her schedule was quite heavy: an undergraduate French course at the university, research for her thesis—thanks to a generous though still inadequate grant, she had decided that after her master's she would pursue a doctorate on the Haitian writer Marie-Vieux-Chauvet. And there was Dan who complained of not seeing her enough although they rarely spent a weekend without each other unless she was going home to see her family. Obviously, her parents and siblings held it against her since they, too, wanted to see her more often.

The three months following the death of Emmett's mother gave Ma Robinson the chance to gain greater respect for the young Haitian-American. Had God in His infinite mercy judged it wise to bestow a child upon her, she would have loved her to have had Marie-Hélène's generosity, her strength of character, her enthusiasm for work, her faith in life and in the Lord. But the time had passed, she was no longer of an age to be either grandmother or mother to Marie-Hélène. And yet, did the Almighty not allow Sarah to give birth at the age of ninety? Nonsense. She had never put up with a man's whims. And she wasn't going to start now. In the meantime, she was enchanted by Marie-Hélène who was brimming with ideas, one of which was the creation of a website, something Ma Robinson would never have thought of. To the extent that her studies allowed it, she was also involved with the support network that, sadly, wouldn't stop growing. The pastor would have preferred the reverse, even if that activity benefitted from her ministry's impact. Lately, for the first time, she had seen a new population come for assistance who were not from Franklin Heights, like the Hispanics from South Side for example. The newcomers, mostly women, single mothers primarily, were recognizable by the embarrassment they showed when they came in and when they left, bags in hand, as if the entire world was watching them or would know where they'd done their shopping.

Emmett had never gone there, not even when his

mother was alive. A combination of pride and shame prevented him. Still, he had known Ma Robinson since he was born, she was a sort of alternate mother for him. Now in his forties, it was hard for him having to resort to welfare to feed his family. Yet he wasn't a slacker, he pulled his weight trying to improve their everyday lives. But for him, as for millions of others, it was the unadulterated and disturbing reality. The salary of the first two weeks of the month went to pay the rent; then the next two weeks' paycheck barely sufficed to cover the monthly bills and the groceries for at most two more weeks. Not counting unexpected expenses. It was really hard to survive month to month. The loss of his mother had thrown him into a depression that made him even less inclined to accept the situation. Ma Robinson had to make the most of his absence to bring the girls food prepared by the sisters at the church, stock the fridge a little, just to handle that pride that was eating him up inside.

He was also carrying around the shame of his failure to realize his dream to become a professional football player that would have elevated him to the status of a role model for millions of kids in the country. Especially for those coming from the kind of neighborhood to which he was forced to return, tail between his legs, to live in the same old dump where he was born and had grown up. And that wasn't all. After leaving the house to set up a home with one of Authie's friends, enough time to have fathered the third daughter, he had come back a second time and, worse, had been forced to rely on his mother's inadequate pension. He'd failed all the way, although he had shown the youngest ones another path different from the street, of dealing drugs, and the violence that was destroying Franklin Heights and so many neighborhoods like it across the country. Even though no-body spoke about it anymore, and people had long since turned the page, he was still dragging that sense of failure around like a ball and chain. Subscribing to a life of disap-pointments, everyone had grown used to chasing one pipe dream after another to hang onto until the end of life. That's what they call the American dream.

Shortly after the death of her old friend, Ma Robin-son insisted on meeting with Emmett on the pretext of dis-cussing the girls with him, since she was sure that he loved them beyond measure. Mary Louise's son had listened to her with an absent gaze, even when she brought up his mother's memory, whose fighter's temperament she saw again in Abi-gail. She didn't let go, that little one, thanks in part to young Marie-Hélène's dedication. But for her to be able to continue to hang on and be an example for her younger sisters, she needed to have a model herself, the model of a more alive father—the term Ma Robinson had used. That's what edu-cation was, setting an example. Not just uttering words that may say the opposite of what is deep inside us. Setting an example isn't delusional. It would also be a way to honor the memory of Mary Louise.

'You are right, Pastor,' Emmett had admitted. 'You are absolutely right. As usual, your words are golden. Oh, yes. As usual. But what do you want? When bad luck follows you...'

He had let a long silence go by that, knowing him, Ma Robinson chose to respect. He had always been a boy of few words. Maybe in a rare flight of trust he had ended up ad-mitting that he shouldn't have come back if all he had done was offer the neighborhood this pathetic spectacle. Not only to those who had seen him leave, but also to the young who had undoubtedly heard the mention of his name.

'You shouldn't retrace your steps when you have failed to attach your dreams to the peak of your ambitions at the time of your departure.'

The sentence sounded like a universal truth, a kind of absolute theorem whose evidence left no room for discussion. For a moment Emmett kept his mouth half open as if he wanted to keep talking. But he had added nothing more. It was then that the pastor understood that he had never really come back. Or, rather, that he had come back shattered. Like the migrant between two foreign policemen forced to return to the point of departure, a skimpy bundle over his shoulder with his tattered dreams inside. Those were the exact words he had spoken to the pastor that day, which she reported back to her little group: Marie-Hélène, Dan, Stoke, and Authie, not long before Emmett's funeral and the big march they were getting ready to organize.

The little group was all the more resolved to make an impression since nasty rumors broadcast by the continuous news on television were now circulating on the internet. According to these, in addition to suffering from who knows what serious condition, at the time of the arrest Emmett was supposedly under the influence of an illegal substance that had made him aggressive toward the police officer. Presumably, it was this combination of illness and drugs that had caused his death. Not the officer who had merely defended himself by applying techniques he'd been taught at the police academy. Those who were wildly carrying on about murder, assassination, voluntary homicide, systematic police violence against one section of the population, were endangering the unity of one of the greatest—if not the greatest—democracies in the world. 'I can't endorse these words', stated one politician whose opinion came through one of the many tweets of the moment.

Listening to these arguments, Dan, who had never met Emmett other than that one time in front of the supermarket, couldn't hold back an emphatic 'sons of bitches' before apologizing to the pastor under Marie-Hélène's blistering glare. Ma Robinson told him to calm down. Obviously, she said, it was the line of defense by the police officer's lawyer, by testing the waters of public opinion in a likely attempt to influence media-addicted members of a potential jury. False information repeated ad nauseam winds up being taken for truth. Hence the importance of keeping a cool head to better organize a counterattack. In the meantime, they had to focus on the essentials, namely the funeral—which she was taking care of—the march, and a few answers to be circulated on the internet: Emmett did not suffer from any serious condition that would have led to his death. No, he did not use drugs. And even if he had, would that make him into a person without any rights? Did he deserve to have his life cut down under such circumstances?

PREPARATIONS

AFTER FIRST CONSULTING Emmett's oldest daughter, Ma Robinson set the funeral for the following Sunday, hoping to gather the largest possible number of people for the march that would take place immediately afterward. 'We have one week to get it all organized', she said to her staff, which included the request from the appropriate authorities for a permit for the rally. That way nobody could accuse them of anything, not the police nor the White supremacists, even if the latter always criticized whatever they did. Recently, encouraged by the irresponsible tweets of the President, they were feeling more empowered. As for the authorities, the city council in particular would look really bad if it were to prevent a lawful, peaceful march from taking place. That might encourage uncontrolled, less peaceful demonstrations, which were already beginning to happen around the country, and expose themselves to criticism from all sides.

Since the previous meeting with the pastor and the others, Dan couldn't hide his elation. He was living in a state of permanent excitement that would have given anyone else a heart attack. He barely slept. But when needed he had a strong heart and a cool head. His mind was simmering with ideas on how to prevent the demonstration, planned for right after the service, from turning into a funeral procession, chanting slogans echoing from a voice beyond the grave and arms wearily waving signs without much conviction. He insisted it be spirited, a meeting of brotherhood and solidarity as Ma Robinson had summed it up, moving to thunderous music that would generate passion and hope. Like a life serum injected into a society that is about to give up the ghost.

That said, choosing music they could unanimously agree on was far from a simple matter. Between Ma Robinson, only interested in gospel music, and Emmett's two childhood friends who were followers of eighties' R&B, everyone had their own ideas about the kind of music that would set the appropriate mood for the march. In Marie-Hélène's opinion, rap was just for the young and considering the message they wanted to convey, could seem too aggressive and might risk alienating the older demonstrators. It wasn't the vibe, for example, of a Ma Robinson who didn't take kindly to dirty words, as she said, that so often comprised the lyrics. A vocabulary that also shocked the well brought-up Marie-Hélène who had been raised with a respect for propriety, all the more in a country that was not originally hers.

Never mind! Dan knew music that everyone would

be in sync with. For him the most unifying was Bob's. The thought was very exciting for Marie-Hélène who assumed he meant Bob Dylan. She was in love with him and his "Just Like a Woman", which she discovered when he received the Nobel Prize. As a student of comparative literature she swore by anything Dylan: 'His texts are simply sublime. True poetry set to music.' And, trying to convince her friend, she launched into a frenzy both inspired and abstruse of which only academic literary critics have the secret. Dan, the historian used to dealing with tangible facts, restrained himself from bursting out in laughter and hurting her feelings—she could be so touchy at times. Nevertheless he couldn't help objecting:

'We're not in the sixties anymore, honey. True, the words are fine but they lack life. Listening to these songs and seeing Dylan's face, it feels like your mother's funeral. And that's precisely what I want to avoid. I'm talking about the one and only Bob, Mr. Marley.'

'That drug addict with the bird's nest on his head?'

'It's a lot more lively don't you think? Besides getting people dancing, it's music with a fitting message.'

Dan imagined portable speakers, volume pushed to the max as the demonstration would come alive, to the beat of "Get Up, Stand Up", "Redemption Song", and "Buffalo Soldier". Titles to the tunes of fiery slogans whose words he knew by heart. Taking off his cap to let his dark brown dreads that contrasted with his almost cottony complexion, fly from side to side around his shoulders, he began shaking his head from right to left, jumping from one foot to the other, his throaty voice repeating the lyrics of "War", a genuine declaration of war on every form of racial and social discrimination that the Jamaican singer wanted to eradicate from the face of the earth:

> *Until the philosophy which holds one race superior*
> *And another inferior*
> *Is finally and permanently*
> *Discredited and abandoned*
> *Everywhere is war*
> *Me say war*

> *That until there no longer*
> *First class and second class citizens of any nation*
> *Until the color of a man's skin*
> *Is of no more significance than the color of his eyes*
> *Me say war*

Like Bob Marley, he, too, didn't want a philosophy that advocated the superiority of one race over another, of a society with first and second class citizens where skin color was more important than the color of one's eyes. Before he could go any further, Marie-Hélène stopped him short and said, her gaze fixed on his: 'You won't play "I Shot the Sheriff", right?' Faced with his hesitation, she repeated: 'Right?' Despite himself Dan had to give in.

The music question resolved, they had to think about slogans and the global message the organizers of the march intended to deliver. 'Brotherhood and solidarity, that's fine, but justice, too,' a restless Authie persisted. That was the first reason they were taking to the streets on Sunday: 'Justice for Emmett and his daughters'. Ma Robinson had insisted that

Stokely and Authie, who hadn't spoken to each other in ages, would be part of the organizing since the event had brought them back together again. Not only did she want to mend the bonds between the two remaining musketeers in honor of their deceased friend, it was also a way of making sure that the residents of Franklin Heights wouldn't feel deprived of their battle by people coming from the outside, no matter how caring they surely were.

All too happy to be part of the tribute to his childhood friend, Stokely had gone through a lot of trouble to interest the neighborhood youth, too. For these young people, whose relationship to time lay in the here and now, the deadline was essential. He also insisted on the idea of a short-term goal, march for the incarceration, then the trial of Emmett's murderer and his accomplices. His involvement seemed to be bearing fruit, in view of the unusual ferment that pervaded Franklin. Although early in the spring, some of the young were wearing black T-shirts they themselves had sprayed with white letters: 'Justice for Emmett'. The same slogan they repeated after greeting each other with a ritual of their own: high-fives, a quick hug, and holding the left fist to one's forehead.

'Justice for Emmett, bro.'

'Justice for Emmett, sis.'

Even more importantly, in three days the fund that Stokely had suggested they create had collected more than a hundred-and-fifty-thousand dollars, including donations from well-known artists and athletes. A player from the Green Bay Packers had contributed twenty-five thousand dollars in the name of his family. He must have heard that Emmett was a former university football star. And it didn't stop coming. 'Real manna from heaven,' Ma Robinson re-joiced. 'Blessed be the Almighty!' Stoke was so proud when he was told that he showed off a few dance steps under the delighted look of Marie-Hélène and Dan and some friendly teasing from Authie, a sign that the two had been reconciled for good: 'Stop puffing up like a turkey, or you'll explode'.

However, this achievement need not put the prepara-tions on the backburner. For a completely successful demon-stration, for which the authorities had given them the green light, they still needed to do some hard work on at least two fronts: slogans and sign-making on the one hand; stories to be posted to the web on the other. The preceding days Stoke-ly, Authie, Marie-Hélène, and Dan were in the backroom of the church for a regular brainstorming session. They quickly agreed on the basics: to condemn the police violence, mes-sages needed to be short and well-chosen. Direct and easy to read, Marie-Hélène emphasized. If only with the goal, among others, to rally to the cause any moderates among the enforcers of the law. It was her mantra. The objective was first and foremost to ensure that the greatest number of participants would feel concerned. As if a friend, a cousin, a brother, or even oneself were in Emmett's place.

The brainstorming sessions gave rise to slogans that grew increasingly demanding. 'I am a man,' which Stokely proposed, was refuted by Authie who asked him if women didn't count. 'Just look around you, man. Who raises your kids, right here in Franklin, when you go running after the mirage of the American dream or the ass of your mistress?' Stokely tried to justify himself arguing that Emmett was a man, not a woman. 'So? That doesn't make him any less of a human being,' Authie retorted, proposing 'I am a human being', which the other two agreed with. 'Three to one,' Authie was very pleased with herself. Not to be outdone, Stoke offered 'Let my people breathe,' which the demonstrators could chant to the tune of "Let My People Go", Ma Robinson would like that. 'Brother, I'm Dying', was Marie-Hélène's idea, playing on the title of a memoir by the Haitian writer Edwidge Danticat. Next came 'Dead for ten bucks', 'I had a dream', 'Hands up! Don't shoot', and more.

To Dan, who came out with a whole panoply of much tougher ones, these were sentimental slogans: 'Fed up', 'White silence is violence', 'We're already dead, might as well die for a good cause', 'No justice, no peace', 'The fire next time', a James Baldwin title, 'Burn, Baby, Burn', 'By any means necessary', a slogan incorrectly attributed to Malcolm X, Dan stated, as it had actually originated with the Martinican Frantz Fanon.

During his long hours of insomnia he had plenty of time to drop ideas that came haphazardly to his mind onto his cell phone. He wanted to go farther. In his eyes, the police were nothing more than the guard dogs of a brutal capitalism that in the long run should be gotten rid of in order to end up with a more just and more rational society. 'Occupy Wall Street is of no use, but burning it as a symbol of the system, yes. And the sooner the better.' If it were up to him he would have established a people's tribunal to judge the perpetrators of these crimes and implement the sentences handed down. In the name of the people reduce the numbers of all those who would stand in the way, as the French did during their Revolution. The tribunal's motto: 'An eye for an eye and a tooth for a tooth. The good old law of retaliation.' Or better yet, he got carried away: 'He who lives by the sword will perish by the sword, that attribute of justice speaks to everyone.' Marie-Hélène found him so impassioned—too much for her taste—that she called him Ogou Feray with kosher sauce.

'Ogou Feray, who's that?' he asked

'The Vodou spirit of war,' she replied in a neutral tone.

'That's brilliant, it suits me.'

The next morning he came to the meeting with a watercolor of a warrior dressed all in red on a galloping white horse, waving a flag with the vèvè of Ogou on it and crowned by a Star of David. The eyes of the figure were shooting angry bolts of lightning. He had drawn it himself after doing research on the internet to identify the symbolic attributes of the *lwa*. Ever since he was a kid, drawing had always been an outlet for him, an activity that calmed him when he was really mad at someone or something. He arrived all smiles, expecting Marie-Hélène to be pleased, but ironically the watercolor shocked her, as her religion didn't mix well with Vodou, which she saw as a vulgar superstition.

The squabble behind them, the two lovers threw themselves body and soul into the preparations for the demonstration. Dan suggested to Marie-Hélène that one of the stories to be posted on the web should be the poem 'Sales Nègres' —"Filthy Negroes"—by the Haitian writer Jacques Roumain, from the collection *Bois d'Ebène* that she had given him for his birthday. His suggestion didn't come out of the blue. Marie-Hélène herself had reported an event, comical to put it mildly, that had occurred at her previous university in Chicago where ninety percent of the professors and more than two-thirds of the students were white. The administration had initiated a workshop on the best way to deal with the 'Black question' at the university. After all, why not? The absurdity came when it suggested opening the workshop with a group meditation that would help them find the courage and the serenity to approach such a thorny subject.

'The worst of it was,' Marie-Hélène fumed, 'that everybody there went along with the game.'

They split the poem into several stanzas, which they planned to post on the church's website and on social media, one at a time until the day of the funeral and the demonstration. In this country where the term "nigger" when uttered by a White person was taboo, downright offensive—even when quoting a Black—he would have to say 'the N word' if he didn't want to be burned at the stake, and to feign emotional turmoil if he happened to do so in the presence of someone White. So they had to admit that letting Dan read the poem would be a provocation. 'And therefore counter-productive,' Marie-Hélène concluded, who had to temper the fervor of her partner once again, as he was determined to throw their hypocrisy in the face of these people.

> *Well, it's like this:*
> *we*
> *negroes*
> *niggers*
> *filthy negroes*
> *we won't take anymore*
> *that's right*
> *we're through*

They then agreed that Marie-Hélène and her Ivoirian housemate would read it together. Dan, on the other hand, would have the satisfaction of a brief appearance in the posting to read the line 'filthy Jews'. Playfully, Marie-Hélène suggested that he also say 'filthy proletarians'. 'With your bourgeois East Side city face you'll be very convincing in that role,' she let slip, deadpan. They gave the line 'filthy Arabs' to the Maghrebi-French girl whom they had a hard time persuading; she claimed she was Berber. Calling her an Arab, the name of the invaders of the land of her ancestors, was simplistic and discriminating, though in the end she agreed to do it when asked by the Ivoirian, on whom she had a barely concealed crush.

> ... it will be too late I tell you
> for even the tom-toms will have learned the language
> of the Internationale
> for we will have chosen our day
> day of the filthy negroes
> filthy Indians
> filthy Hindus
> filthy Indo-Chinese
> filthy Arabs
> filthy Malays
> filthy Jews
> filthy proletarians

On the days prior to the event, the followers of their various networks saw the four university students do a poetry slam of Jacques Roumain's poem:

And here we are arisen
All the wretched of the earth
all the upholders of justice
marching to attack your barracks
your banks
like a forest of funeral torches
to be done
once
   and
      for
         all
with this world
of negroes
niggers
filthy negroes

Since each of them had to manage their own network, Dan dismissed his parents from the outset as they had voted for the puppet with the toupee without ever showing the slightest sign of regret. He told himself that it was useless to waste his energy on trying to convince them. In any event, he needed people who were connected with others who in turn had fairly extensive networks, and so on. In addition to their political ideas that horrified him, his parents were well over fifty and not hip enough. Hence his decision to focus his efforts on friends and acquaintances of his own generation.

His decision was well made, he would start with those closest to him, friends first, then acquaintances whom he saw regularly, before widening the circle as things progressed. This way and without too much trouble he could rally his former undergraduate classmates from Marquette University, mostly good Catholics full of fine beliefs. When he became a graduate student he chose the state university, a matter of being true to himself, to the great chagrin of his parents who wondered what in the hell he was doing at what they characterized as an unemployment factory. From there he would go on to his classmates at Golda Meir High School, the majority of whom had already entered the working world, some had even begun to make a name for themselves in Milwaukee's fine society. Fortunately, he had had the good sense to stay in virtual contact with them. Some of them had close to five thousand social media 'friends'. From what he could tell, they hadn't forgotten him. They never missed an opportunity to 'like' his posts or comments. Oh, he wasn't fooled by those friendships, but if he managed to convert just half of them to the cause if only for three or four hours, the time of the demonstration, that would be something anyway.

As the hours went by, Dan had the good feeling of following in the footsteps of his grandparents, especially his maternal grandfather. Fate had driven them far from their roots, taken them to Milwaukee, without their forgetting or losing interest in others, their human sisters and brothers. It was from this inherited memory that his interest in contemporary history was born, whose living witnesses could still report on their own version of the events before these were transformed into a national work of fiction that all too often tended to exclude the other.

He would do anything to have the march entered in the annals of Milwaukee. It would make him worthy of his grandparents. Worthy of Marie-Hélène as well who, in a year-and-a-half, had occupied a huge place in his life. He kept postponing the moment to talk about her to his parents, even though his mother was dying to know where he spent most of his weekends. One day, tired of not running into him for a whole week—she left for work early in the morning and he came home late at night—she told him defiantly: 'You know, if you want you can move out to wherever it is you're sleeping.' But Dan didn't fall in the trap. He, and he alone, would choose the moment to talk to them about it.

Distance being in her favor, Marie-Hélène's position was easier. If need be, all she would have to do is to tell her parents she wasn't coming to Chicago on weekends because she had work to do or she had to help the pastor. And that would be the end of it. Only three weeks before, they had planned a weekend away to celebrate the beginning of spring in Madison, and she had canceled at the last minute after a phone call from her family. Her younger siblings had complained they hadn't seen her in a long time, that they needed her to help them with their high school problems. 'Surely a ploy by my parents to get me to visit,' Marie-Hélène was sorry to say, but she'd gone anyway leaving him alone and still longing for a romantic weekend. Organizing the march was beginning to present itself as a baptism of fire for them as a couple, meant to bind them together for the years to come. At least, that was Dan's secret wish, who already saw them making pilgrimages to Haiti with their children and grandchildren.

OF GENDER AND COLOR

THE DAY AFTER EMMETT'S death, Police Officer Gordon had taken refuge in his well-kept home overlooking scenic Lake Michigan. It was located in Cudahy, south-east of the city. Its lawn mowed down to the millimeter, the house was literally two steps from Sheridan Park where he jogged throughout the year to maintain a physical condition of which he was very proud. In the spring and summer he felt it was his duty to bring his family there, often without driving, contrary to most of his neighbors. It was just a short walk that ended when they had to cross South Lake Drive—a thrill for the girls because of the heavy traffic in both directions—which backed onto the park. The only disadvantage of this white middle-class suburb where he'd decided to plant his family was the proximity to General Mitchell International Airport and the incessant noise of planes taking off and landing. Over time he had made his peace with this. Despite the word 'international' the city had attached to the name to show off, it was the Chicago airport that got almost all of the long-distance flights and most of the regional air traffic. 'And,' he liked to say, 'that's life, every rose has its thorns.'

Since the previous evening, the house had been surrounded by a pack of journalists anxious to get a word from him or a member of his family. A fake platinum blonde from a very popular television station—Gordon had recognized her—was holding a sign above her head on which was written in black marker '$10,000 for the exclusive rights'. An amount that would surely help him pay part of his mortgage. For now, not one of them had managed to get his or his wife's cell phone number. Just a matter of time, he thought resignedly. These vultures always get what they want. Fortunately, he'd just disconnected the family's landline, which would have been easier to trace even if it was unlisted. They all wanted to throw him to the wolves, showing their viewers the monster responsible for Emmett's death, organizing debates, sometimes with just anyone, sometimes with so-called experts, such as university professors, sociologists, shrinks, all too ready to shout out in order to have their precious opinions heard. As if it were the first time this was happening in the country, that a Black man perishes while being arrested by the police.

At the police academy they were taught to draw and fire their weapon first and then ask questions, shoot first then talk, if in the meantime the other hadn't been sent to meet his maker. What's more, it wasn't unusual that the officer himself was Black. And there wasn't a single damned journalist among them who wouldn't wave their mic in his face and, acting like the attorney general, demand that he account for himself even though they had already unanimously convicted him, voted on by a people's court whose members stayed well-hidden behind the anonymity of their social networks. No really! They could shoot each other with impunity. But he didn't have the right to do his job in peace without having a bunch of hyenas jump on him, a job for which he was paid by public funds; the job of law enforcement that, incidentally, he had neither written nor voted on.

What those hypocrites didn't say either was that White folks, too, made their share of blunders. To a lesser extent he was ready to admit, but that was because on the whole they broke the law less often, period. 'There's no use making a mountain out of a molehill.' In any case, when that happened no one said a word; at least not that much. It didn't create all this uproar. The officer wasn't harassed, hounded, reviled, and his reputation dragged through the mud as his had been for the past two days now. Specifically, what was he being criticized for by these self-righteous zealots who dreamed only of toppling statues of great men like President Thomas Jefferson or General Robert E. Lee just to appease their guilty, White-privileged conscience? He hadn't invented these neutralization techniques. He had learned them at the academy. They were practiced all over the country to control an intractable suspect during his arrest, as his colleagues in New York had done some years before in the case of that other man, Garnier or something like that. Pinning the individual face down on the sidewalk to put handcuffs on, one knee on his back and the other on his side to keep him down on the ground and render him immobile. Was it his fault that the subject ran out of air because he was under the influence of drugs and suffered from some respiratory disease? Conceivably he was only pretending so they would take the cuffs off. He would really like to see what all those accusing him would do in his place. 'How the hell do we handle a guy who is thrashing about, who weighs a ton, like most of those people with their unhealthy lifestyle spending their time stuffing themselves with fried chicken and sweet potatoes?' Some of them, who were employed en masse by the police to calm down the community after the riots following the Rodney King affair, well, they couldn't even walk three hundred yards without running out of breath.

Besides, he wasn't the only one there, what about his three colleagues, two of whom had trained with him. One of them was "of color", even if you couldn't tell at first. It took a keen eye like his to notice it. He, however, was different from the others, he didn't spend his time complaining about his lot, playing the victim all the time, on TV, the web, everywhere, it was always about them. Even when it came to being hired for certain jobs that were guaranteed, their quota comfortably waiting for them. Same thing with women; equality they say. Even then, they were incapable of holding a job. And what if just for once they'd be responsible for their own destiny rather than sit on their fat asses waiting for their welfare check or for the state to take care of their bills? 'We're not in some damn communist country.' What did those freeloaders think? That he was born with a silver spoon in his mouth? That he wasn't busting his butt like everyone else to pay the bills for the house, the car, to take care of his family? And in his free time he often took on private jobs to make ends meet. That's what he had to do with a stay-at-home wife—to his honor—and two daughters who needed all sorts of trendy things.

And then, at the moment of the arrest, there was the Asian, too. He quite liked him. He was from Cambodia originally, like his wife. A really hard worker who didn't shy away from accumulating additional hours without complaint. And not just to make his life a little easier either. The guy was driven by the same sense of duty as he himself was. Officer Gordon never had any problem with guys like that, in contrast to those others who for no apparent reason would talk to you about the cottonfields and how that era was gone, how everyone supposedly had the same rights now. They'd arrived on the same boat, at the same time as us. Even though, had he wanted to, he could have answered that his ancestors had traveled on the upper deck while theirs were crammed in the hold like fucking sardines, soaking in their excrement, their vomit, and their awful howling. But out of Christian charity he'd never said that to them, nor that he'd ever heard any TV documentary mentioning people like them being among the passengers of the *Mayflower*. Yet, they insisted, the only word out of their mouth was equality instead of rolling up their sleeves and hustling like the rest of them. But no, they had their rights and so on and so forth, while if anyone took precedence it would only be the native population who, as the true owners of America, could have laid claim to it. But they had been overpowered, wiped out, robbed of their lands, and in exchange were left with the Gospel and other such bullshit. All of it to justify their gross laziness.

In that they were a match for the women of this country, whether White or Black. Always mad, always demand-

ing things. The kind that tells you: 'Women have been sub-
jected to White patriarchy for centuries, now it's our turn.'
It's nature that created color and gender, right? He hadn't
clamored to come into the world as a man. No one had
asked his opinion, he just accepted it. Those women would
like to have castrated men if they had not gone about it a
different way. One reason he'd set up house with a woman
from Cambodia. At least she remembered that this country had welcomed her people and she didn't approach you
with ludicrous demands, making you ask permission for everything all the time, even after they were already together:
French kissing, a little breast groping, the position and dura-
tion of intercourse. And if they had given their written consent, they still reserved the right to draw the fatal weapon at
any time, claiming that they were under duress when they
signed, because 'you're a predator, a narcissistic pervert, a
passive-aggressive, a manipulator' who forced them not to
like their periods anymore, refused them a little cuddle at
moments when they were so in need of some tenderness.

That's what Officer Gordon was thinking about as he was
shut away in his house. Although they didn't dare camp on
his lawn as yet, he felt his home literally assaulted by a pack
of reporters, drawn by the scent of his blood in their imagi-
nation already coagulating in his veins after the lethal injec-
tion. A violation of private property that would have allowed
him to shoot on sight, as the law to defend your property
permits. He was in such a rage that he didn't give a damn
about making his case worse. He had to guard his family's
privacy. It was because of the press that Dylan, their dog,
was confined to the back yard, forced to run and do his busi-

ness there, concealed from cameras and microphones by the hedges and the oak tree. He knew that he would have to face them sooner or later, they had to go shopping, after all. Fortunately, both their cars were parked in the garage that he had built with his own hands, and not outside along the sidewalk like those of his neighbors. When the time came they would be inside the car, doors locked and windows up, and all he had to do was open the electric garage door and speed straight ahead. He knew how to shake them off. He would shop for groceries outside town where the vultures weren't likely to be waiting for him.

He grabbed the TV remote control, off since the night before to spare his family the torrent of hate from journalists and so-called witnesses. Black and and guilty for just being there by chance. Or some White individual spouting politically correct stuff morning noon and night on television, the internet, at church, at work, because in this country everyone mistrusted everyone else and wanted to have a clear conscience at low cost. He had confiscated his daughters' Ipad and cell phone for the same reason. Their mother hadn't taken them to school that morning so they wouldn't be harassed by the jackals when they left or when school let out. Worse, so they wouldn't be attacked inside the school itself. He could just imagine the other kids, influenced by their social networks, the TV, or their own parents, treating his girls like children of a murderer, and racist, and all the mean things children can say to each other. As their father it was his duty to protect them, the flesh of his flesh. His family was the rock to which he clung at moments of great upheaval. As long as they held on he could, too. Still, the night before he'd felt his wife tense up when he drew near her in bed. He wanted a bit of comforting, but she pretended to be asleep. Her stiffening had betrayed her as if she were trying to protect herself from a monster. As long as she didn't lose her nerve. Not her, not now. If that happened, everything would fall apart for him.

Taking advantage of his girls' playing in the older one's room, he turned on the TV and came across the announcement on the news that he had been suspended from duty. His superiors had suspended him. From one day to the next, accelerating the process to cover their backs. Those pencil pushers had acted like all other managers these days, scared shitless at the slightest sign of a problem. They didn't even have the courage to call him in and tell him face to his face; or at the very least to call and tell him by phone. 'Officer Gordon, we regret to inform you that...' He would have taken the shock like a man, but above all he would have appreciated being told before the vultures circling his house found out. If the protests continued to spread throughout the country, he expected that his superiors would take it a step further at any moment. That they would terminate him, pure and simple. If that's how it was, he wouldn't do them any favors either. In that case, they just didn't know him. He was going to contact his lawyer.

Officer Gordon had it right. Barely three days had gone by when the news of his discharge came down. Bowing to popular opinion, the cowards who were in charge of his department had it in for him. As he would later find out, they had committed a thinly veiled blackmail of the union representative to get him to dissociate himself from the case, 'it's about the image of the profession', and all that. He had lost the job of a lifetime, in addition to becoming a pariah whose mug was plastered on every screen in the world. To make matters worse, his wife decided that same day to find shelter with her daughters at her family's house. You'd think that she was conspiring with his superiors to destroy him. He was neither inclined nor had the courage to ask her to stay. She could have, should have, understood that all by herself. Understood that in the eye of the storm he needed them. He wasn't the kind of man to implore anyone. Except God.

Even without their screens and despite their tender ages of five and seven, the girls understood that there was something serious going on. Their mother came to pick them up from school early the day before and they left in a big rush. From that moment on both girls wouldn't stop asking why. Why didn't they go back to school that morning? Why were all those people and vans with cameras parked in front of the house? They were forced to keep the curtains closed even during the day. Were they going to be on television? 'No, quite the opposite, my darlings.' And if by some unfortunate accident they should come face to face with these bad people, they were not to answer any questions but call their parents right away. They had to find the right words to explain that it had something to do with Papa's work without telling them why. When the older one knew they were leaving for their maternal grandparents' house, she wanted to know why their father wasn't coming with them. As long as they were going away why not all together?

As much as they didn't want to admit it, their mother had given him no choice. She had reserved the plane tickets without having the decency to discuss it with him first, as would happen with a tightknit couple who respect one another. Once the tumult died down, he would pick up the car from the parking lot at the Chicago airport instead of Milwaukee's, she told him, otherwise they would run the risk of being spotted by the scandalmongers ready to alert media outlets there. True to her ways, his wife had developed the plan down to its smallest detail before telling him. She had confronted him with a fait accompli, like the wimps who sacked him. She'd done it her way, without raising her voice. Since she was a homemaker, she didn't need to notify an employer and negotiate an extended leave of absence. She told him—the irrefutable argument —that it would be better for the girls to live with their grandparents for a while, without indicating either the length of the stay or a prospective reunion. She would go with them, of course. All he remembered was that she preferred him not to. She didn't want her children to be stalked like criminals. She'd said 'her' children, as if they weren't his as well. The end result was that she was taking them to California, the other end of the country where nobody knew them. 'Well anyway, not as well as they know you,' she added leaving him unable to grasp the exact meaning of the insinuation. He had to take the heavy suitcases to the trunk of the car himself, like a condemned man forced to dig his own grave. Then they left, the vehicle chased down the street for several yards by a pack of scavengers.

Officer Gordon was alone in their large house, empty of the rowdiness of the girls, the hushed smile of his wife, the smell of her cooking, which he had learned to love and, in many ways, preferred to any other. It was a lot healthier than what he was used to before he'd met her. How was he going to spend these days, these weeks, without his Three Graces? Holed up in dark rooms with a horde of predators baying for his blood. Without being able to enjoy the beautiful spring-time sun of this time of the year when Milwaukee was so dazzling in its greenery, exhaling a multitude of fragrances from flowers and trees, especially at nightfall, and the diverse and wide-ranging bird calls at dawn. As if all of nature was reborn. He could almost feel the nauseating breath of these hyenas on his neck, their filthy fangs eager to tear his calves to shreds.

One thing was sure, he wouldn't starve. Proof that she had prepared her plan without mentioning it to him, before leaving his wife had filled the fridge and the freezer with a ton of food that she'd been cooking for three days. His favorite dishes. He was so embroiled in his thoughts that he hadn't even noticed. There was enough for the length of a siege; the dishes were portioned out in aluminum foil containers, labeled meticulously as was characteristic of her; all he had to do was reheat them. It was a last kind gesture, a sign, if he needed it, that she still loved him. He must not go to pieces.

The ringing of the phone brought him out of his ruminations: a colleague warned him that they were coming to pick him up. The investigating judge had decided to charge him with involuntary homicide and had ordered his pre-trial detention. One of his superiors had even told the press that it was better this way, in prison he would be protected; outside he might risk getting lynched by an irate populace. Officer Gordon turned the TV on again: the information was already aired as 'breaking news', his face appearing large on the screen. The colleagues who had been with him during the event would also be incarcerated as accessories to murder. If he wanted, he could be let out on a one-million-dollar bail.

THE CHOICE OF THE ETERNAL

On the day of Emmett's funeral a tropical storm struck Milwaukee unlike anything anyone had ever seen before. It poured for almost the entire morning even though the weather had been downright summery just a few days before with the mercury approaching eighty degrees at noon. Men were going around in T-shirts, flipflops, and Bermudas, while the women were wearing tight shorts displaying their pierced navels. Just for fun, some boys had opened a fire hydrant the way they saw it on television every summer, generating a powerful geyser that almost sent one of them to the Emergency Room. Still, that didn't discourage them from their recklessness, as they began to redirect streams of water like a shower, spraying cars that happened to drive by.

The storm started with a bang as dawn was disappearing, propelling hailstones the size of large agate marbles against the windows, waking Ma Robinson, conditioned by her past life as warden into being a light sleeper. The powerful downpour continued uninterrupted, as had never been recorded in Milwaukee's meteorological records, according to the oldest inhabitants. Joining the pastor at the church very early to help with the final preparations, Dan and Marie-Hélène were afraid that these unusually prolonged showers would keep people from going out. Besides, the temperature had dropped during the night, reverting to what was more normal for the time of year. And the forecast for the rest of the day wasn't exactly reassuring. Marie-Hélène and Dan, keeping their eyes riveted on their smartphone, were hoping to find a last-minute announcement that would refute the earlier ones and put their hearts at ease.

While they were each about to mention a new Flood—not as a metaphor—the pastor was busy putting the finishing touches on her sermon as if everything around her was at its best in this best of all possible worlds. In her seventy-five years she had seen so much, had experienced so many miracles, and she knew the Creator had a plan for everything and every person. If it was His will, it would rain all day long and Milwaukeeans would stay in their living room watching reruns of the Jerry Springer Show or some other stupid broadcast, drinking soda and stuffing themselves with unhealthy takeout food, if they could afford it. Unless it was bright and sunny, in which case they'd opt for a blaringly loud barbecue on the shores of Lake Michigan. But if He in His heaven decided otherwise, these same people wouldn't hesitate to brave the elements: storm, flood, late snow, anything to come out and bid a final farewell to Emmett. The Lord of Hosts would judge for Himself whether He would bring them another victory in the never-ending battle that was life for every human being. As for her, she'd fought the good fight, finished the race as Paul the Apostle said. In a word, she had done her share and her soul was at peace. She was leaving the rest in the hands of the Almighty. To each his job.

While Marie-Hélène and Dan were bustling about, Ma Robinson told herself she had bigger fish to fry, things to think about that were far more crucial than a mere whim of nature. For instance, should Abigail speak from the pulpit to shout out to the world all the love she had for her late father? It was a very fashionable thing to do. And the social media would rush to make her into an international icon whose words would be dissected in sterile debates in the so-called developed nations, quoted by heads of state worried about their status in the polls, time to find another piece of more glamorous news, more in tune with the times. In Stokely's opinion, it would not only stir people but would also encourage them to loosen their purse strings for the online fundraiser. Who knew, the funeral might be aired on television or on YouTube. Bill, Mark, Jeff, or Oprah might be touched by it and be willing to let go of a small part of their surplus of billions, 'just a drop in the ocean for them, Ma.' Some elite university would benefit from it as well, getting publicity at little cost when they would announce that they had created a scholarship for the girls once they had graduated from high school. That way their future would be guaranteed.

'It's the only thing that works, Ma. We're living in a

hell of a showtime society,' Stokely, the former convict said.

'No bad words in my church, Stoke. No bad words,' the former prison warden reprimanded him.

Media coverage of the funeral, too, would contribute to pressuring the judicial system, forcing the incarceration of the killer, if only so he wouldn't be seen walking around freely while awaiting trial, which would happen God only knows when, while his colleagues across the country continued to commit other crimes of the same magnitude. It wouldn't be surprising if they'd release him on bail that very day. With a system like this, it was logical that there were so many poor people rotting in jail. At least, that would be something, Ma Robinson told herself. That son of Satan would be hit where it hurts.

So, should Emmett's oldest daughter be asked to the pulpit? In her soul the pastor had already made her decision. She was convinced that it wasn't the role of a thirteen-year old girl to have to act like a trained seal on the podium while reading a speech in a quavering voice that an adult had prepared for her. They had to let her grieve at her own pace when the time came, with her own words, instead of stirring the still hot ashes of her father's remains. It might well upset her even more. That's what Ma Robinson was thinking. Maybe it was old-fashioned but at her age one didn't change anymore. Yet, somewhere inside her the pastor still felt a hesitancy. Since time was running out she ended up by making a Solomon's judgment.

She would have her read a passage from the *Epistle to the Thessalonians* before the sermon, which says that 'and the dead who are in Christ shall rise first'. Abigail's father had been raised in faith by his saintly mother and deserved paradise, even if it wasn't her role as a mere mortal to interfere with the plans of the Eternal One. Emmett's ex-fiancée, who seemed to be a woman of great compassion, would precede the girl in the order of service. Nancy had contacted Marie-Hélène via a private message on FaceBook, had explained who she was and insisted on having a chat with the pastor. It was a very warm conversation. She told her about Emmett's university years, about which no one in Franklin knew much, about their encounter that had been both beautiful and turbulent, the feeling that he hadn't been up to the expectations placed in him, information that Ma Robinson was welcome to use for her homily if she thought it would be appropriate. With deep emotion the two women remembered the mother of the deceased who had died three months earlier. When Nancy heard that news she was deeply distraught. She had happy memories of her only visit to Milwaukee and of the woman who almost became her mother-in-law. That Nancy really was a woman with a heart, which is why the pastor decided to entrust the first reading to her.

Authie would close this part of the ceremony and so Abigail would be well flanked. Ma Robinson absolutely refused to feed her to the tabloid media that, plainly or incognito, would certainly be present at the funeral. She had to protect her from this unscrupulous breed. Everybody was constantly taking pictures with their smartphones these days, filming anything and everything, willingly displaying the most intimate images or re-selling them to the media, posting photos and videos on the web of a corpse in his coffin without the permission of his loved ones, without any respect for the dead. It was the message she conveyed to the others before making her final decision; the message she asked Stokely to give to the neighborhood's youth: unify around Abigail and her sisters. Prevent the vultures from jumping on them and tearing them into small, bloodstained pieces to be flung at a following addicted to on-screen voyeurism.

Around nine-thirty the rain suddenly stopped. The sun chased away the low dark clouds to make way for a gigantic rainbow that majestically unfurled its colors above Lake Michigan, mocking the weather predictions that Dan and Marie-Hélène kept checking as if humanity's fate depended on it. Their eyes opened wide in amazement when they saw the sun, whose sudden return even the Weather Channel had failed to predict. From the corner of her eye, the pastor saw how they threw themselves into each other's arms in a rapturous—'Yes! Yes! Yes!—in such an explosion of delight that one would have thought they were diving into some forbidden games. 'Just let it last,' Marie-Hélène prayed with folded hands, in a mixture of mad delight and mistrust. 'Jesus, let it last.' Ma Robinson, on the other hand, knew that the God of Abraham, Isaac, and Jacob wasn't given to miracles. The old lady smiled and went back to her sermon.

In the meantime, Emmett's former fiancée, the coach who had trained him during his college years, his wife and their youngest daughter, who was now a beautiful woman in her thirties, were finishing their breakfast at the Hyatt Place in downtown Milwaukee. They'd arrived the night before to avoid getting up at dawn to catch a plane, rushing to be on time for the funeral, and to participate in part of the march before taking their flight back. It was a lot for just one day. But it was not the only reason for their decision. That evening the Bucks, the city's NBA basketball team, which had been doing extremely well, were playing the Chicago Bulls. Led by a fiery Antetokounmpo, the Bucks should be able to walk all over the Bulls that, without a real star on their team, was no more than a shadow of its former self. Even if in his eyes basketball would never be the same as football, Coach Larry would never want to miss this regional confrontation. He had purposely reserved a hotel not far from the Fiserv Forum, the stadium where the Bucks played.

Nancy had taken care of the rest. As they landed in Milwaukee her heart filled with a bittersweet memory. Although she'd paid for her ticket she apologized to Coach Larry and his family who would be going to the game without her and fled to her hotel room with a dinner tray that she barely touched and a bottle of chardonnay that she emptied to the last drop. The memories had come flooding back in such powerful waves that her spirit wouldn't have been able to bear the lights and noise—the sensory overload—of being at a basketball game. On the morning of the funeral the four of them met up again in the hotel's restaurant. After breakfast, they went to the front desk to ask whether they could borrow an umbrella, decided to face the terrible weather since they wouldn't want it said they'd made the long trip in vain—when the rain stopped unexpectedly, giving way to a clear and bright sunny sky. From the bay window on the fifth and highest floor they caught a glimpse of the rainbow's end, displaying its splendor above the lake. They were thrilled. Nancy went down to the lobby to order an Uber, expected within five minutes, time enough to brush their teeth and for the ladies to apply a little make-up before coming down.

A little farther north, in Franklin Heights where they had always lived two blocks apart, Authie and Stokely, surprised by the storm, had abandoned their plan to get to the church an hour early to help Ma Robinson with the final preparations. Heartsick, they had to wait for the rain to end so they wouldn't ruin their elegant clothes and arrive at the ceremony soaked to the skin. Stokely had taken out the dark suit he wore on special occasions that was a bit tight around the waist, making him appear heftier than he really was. His rebellious love handles refused to melt away in spite of his twice-a-week participation in warm-ups for football matches with the kids that he coached and looked after. He was only a step away from turning fifty, a time of life when one feels one's age. His gait, which his sidekicks used to refer to as loping because of the way his feet barely touched the ground when he walked, was less feline and heavier now.

Authie wasn't much better off. But she could claim that she'd always had her curves. 'It's to fight off the Milwaukee winters, it keeps me warm,' she used to say in defense when she was a teenager faced with the sarcasm of the other two musketeers. It didn't prevent her from getting really dressed up as well, in a bright blue dress that she had a hard time squeezing her more than ample body into. Luckily, the looser off-white jacket that she wore on top served to hide her flaws, except for her imposing behind, which she knew that bastard of a Stoke would make fun of after the ceremony was over. He was the type to let her go first, not out of gallantry but to admire the view, as he said.

The rain gone, and after their three-decades long rupture, the two friends left their house at more or less the same time, running into one another without having planned it that way. Acknowledging the coincidence, they half-smiled at each other and decided to go the rest of the way together. 'You'll quit picking on me,' Authie said, remembering the gibes of their long-gone childhood. Perched on heels a good three inches high that caused her to move along very gingerly, the 'sister' accepted the arm her friend offered to keep her from stumbling and splashing in a puddle, and ending up flat on her back. Besides hurting herself, she would have ruined her clothes and gone through all that trouble for nothing, she said as a thank-you to Stoke. And so they went, steadier on their feet, supporting each other. Anyone who saw them without knowing who they were, would have taken them for an old couple moving along laboriously on the path of life.

THE MA ROBINSON SHOW

Fifteen minutes before the ceremony began, the church was packed and from the ranks rose a muffled din, much like a prayer comprised of a thousand whisperings. Although the majority of those gathered were Franklin Heights residents, the pastor's discerning eye immediately spotted unfamiliar faces among the crowd whose number kept growing as the minutes rolled by and the atmosphere in the church warmed up. There were Whites, Latinos, and Pakistanis, undoubtedly members or friends of the family who owned the grocery store, whose nephew's 911 call had cost Emmett his life. As well as sending a wreath they had insisted on sharing the funeral costs. Nevertheless, when the nephew expressed his wish to attend, Ma Robinson had firmly advised him against it:

'Better not,' she'd whispered. 'For the sake of the so-lemnity of the service, and your safety, better not.'

She'd stipulated it twice to be sure she'd been heard without having to raise her voice. On the contrary, she spoke in a sweet melodious tone unusual for her. Those who knew her recognized that it was precisely at those moments that she should be obeyed at the peril of watching her turn into a tornado—her warden's spirit taking over from the compas-sionate woman of the Church—and running into waves of rare, impassioned rebukes.

Nancy, Coach Larry and his family were seated in the first row on the left, not far from the gleaming beige coffin with gilded handles and encircled by wreaths of fresh flow-ers, sent from all over, even from the city's democratic may-or, eager to take care of his electorate. (The emotions in the community, in the country, and in the world, were such that it would have been a political error to proceed otherwise.) Right next to them sat two of Emmett's teachers from the Benjamin Franklin School. They hadn't mentioned to any-one that they would attend the funeral. At first they thought they could do so without being noticed, telling themselves that nobody—if there even was a former student still living in the neighborhood—would recognize them in these two little old ladies, one Black, one White, stepping out of a taxi well before the service was to start so they would be sure to be on time as they walked arm in arm into the church's courtyard. They were convinced they'd pass by unnoticed even by those rascals Autherine, alias Bodyguard, and Stokely-Gorilla, unless like Emmett the latter had also come to an untimely end.

They hadn't counted on Authie's gift for remembering

faces, adept at identifying someone after thirty years even if she'd only seen them once. She asked Stoke to go over to them and went to alert the pastor who had them placed to the left of Abigail and her sisters, Emmett's only blood relations present at the funeral. His mother had come from the South more than half a century ago by herself, without any close relative, while his father had vanished into thin air without leaving a trace. As so often happens in migration stories like theirs, contact with those family members who had stayed behind had fizzled out over time. It would take an ingenious person to track down a cousin or an old aunt from Louisiana to come and bow over his remains at the moment of interment.

Sitting to the right of the girls, 'Auntie' Authie was both prim in her attempt to appear composed while her face was devastated with suppressed suffering. For a while she had been friends with the mother of the youngest daughter until she, too, disappeared. Who knew, she wondered, where that one was hiding at a time when her daughter would be so much in need of her. No doubt she was chasing fantasies of love in the wake of some Prince Charming who would soon walk out on her for a younger and prettier version, exactly as she had done to poor Emmett. Once the two teachers were seated, Authie decided it was wiser to sit down as well, since her high heels wouldn't let her stand for very long. Nearby were Dan, Marie-Hélène, and their housemates who had been kindly requested to help seat the last arrivals in a space that, including the balcony and the ground floor, was filling up with an enormous number of people, beyond what was reasonable or regulatory.

So much so that they had to put fifty folding chairs in the church courtyard. Very soon, even those were no longer enough. Hundreds of people stood outside, crammed together, overflowing from the courtyard onto the sidewalk. Fortunately, the evening before, Stokely had suggested to Ma Robinson that they bring two huge loudspeakers, which an electrician friend had offered to let them use.

'What do you want us to do with them, Stoke?'

'You never know, Ma.'

'Why break your back with those heavy things if they serve no purpose?'

'Perhaps, Ma, the faithful will multiply like the loaves and fishes of the Nazarene.'

'Stop your blasphemy, you old rascal.'

'Better be ready for any eventuality, Ma. No big deal if they're not used.'

'Fine, if that's what you and your friend would like. But I warn you, I don't want them in my way during the service.'

'No worries, Ma. We'll take care of everything.'

Stokely's friend came that afternoon with the speakers stacked in the back of a pick-up that four burly men helped to unload. In no time he'd unwound the cables, slipped them under the carpet along the wall—he insisted on doing things according to the rule book—before connecting the speakers to the church's audio system. Mercifully, they had the good sense of putting them inside for the night, or else the early morning storm would have rendered them useless. When the rain stopped, the same guys from the night before appeared out of nowhere, closely followed by Stokely, and set up the loudspeakers in the courtyard on either side of the front entrance, facing the street. Now, the hundreds for whom there was no place inside could follow the religious service and the sermon in which Ma Robinson would outdo herself.

In the meantime the choir, whose members were draped in mauve satin robes with a white V-neck collar and full sleeves, offered its very best with an interpretation of "Amazing Grace" as a high point, which overwhelmed the congregation, both those who believed in heaven and those who did not. Then Abigail read a passage from the Gospel where it speaks of the resurrection of the dead in Jesus. '*For since by man came death, by Man also came the resurrection of the dead,*' she read in a slightly tremulous voice. It was done exactly as the pastor had orchestrated it, with complete restraint, but no less moving to the assembly, especially to Emmett's two former teachers; and to Nancy, who caught herself thinking that Abigail could have been her daughter, the oldest of the three children she had dreamed of having with the love of her life.

The recitation of the 'Elegy for Emmett Till', a poem by the Cuban Nicolás Guillén, suggested by a Hispanicist colleague of Marie-Hélène, formed the highlight of the readings. 'The adolescent of whom the poem speaks also came from Chicago,' he had explained to her. Spending the 1955 summer vacation at his uncle's in Mississippi, he was kidnapped by armed white men, tortured and assassinated. His mutilated corpse was found in a river three days later. He was fourteen years old. His killers were acquitted by an all-white jury with the support of the sheriff. Marie-Hélène had to do everything she could to convince the pastor who flinched at combining the reading of pagan texts with the sacred word. She was aware that it was a current trend that led people to slam exultantly in the pulpit. As if it were normal to mix apples and oranges and change the sacred space into a new ecumenical patchwork. But, she was told, it made sense here. In addition to the reference to Emmett, she surely owed this much to his young daughter.

> *In North America*
> *the mariners' rose*
> *has its southern petal stained with blood.*

The poem spoke of:

> *a black man always burning/*
> *the obedient Black,/*
> *his torn bowels wrapped in smoke/*
> *his guts choked with fumes/*
> *his abused sex...*

He described the protagonist as 'this adolescent angel/ on whose shoulders/had not yet healed the scars/of where there once were wings.' He was 'a boy with [...] his picture of Lincoln/a U.S. flag... /black. /Black, murdered, alone: this boy who tossed a rose of love/at a passing girl/who was white.'[1] At these words Nancy couldn't help but wipe away a furtive tear from the corner of her eye. The coach's wife saw it and quietly slipped her hand into Nancy's while keeping her eyes fixed on Marie-Hélène's colleague as he read both the Spanish and the English text. After the readings the choir performed two more Gospel songs, one of them

---

1 Translated from Spanish by Robert Márquez and David Arthur McMurray

"I Just Wanna Live", in which a young soloist who, a teenager, could have been Emmett Till's age, fervently implored God to remain by his side and protect him since, in spite of all his efforts, he was unable to find a place where he could feel safe.

Then came the Ma Robinson show. For the funeral of Emmett's mom three months earlier, her lifelong friend the pastor had already surpassed herself with a sermon that had more than enthralled the congregation. Even the youngest ones were talking about it. Until this springtime Sunday. According to the elders of the church, her brothers and sisters in Christ, no sermon like this had been heard since the Reverend Martin Luther King, Jr.'s famous "I Have a Dream" speech. There is no doubt that she had in mind the crying injustice of Emmett's homicide. There is no doubt that she was improvising on the spot, inspired by the presence of television, of the hundreds of men and women who had come running from the four corners of the land to the crumbling neighborhood of Franklin Heights, ravaged by society's thousand ills, to bid a last farewell to one of Milwaukee's sons. Some might say that the comparison was exaggerated, for Dr. King's sermon remained a part of history, better yet had made history. But that Sunday even nonbelievers had to admit that the pastor was on intimate terms with the divine.

Ma Robinson spoke passionately, at great length, stopping every now and then to wait for the congregation's approval, which never failed to come back with 'Amen!', 'Yes, Lord', and 'Hallelujah'. She combined anecdotes with Biblical quotations, unspooled verses as if she were unwinding a skein of yarn, abandoned the sermon she'd prepared to the last comma to venture into a connection between a parable of Christ and the recent news. Every now and then she wiped her forehead with an immaculate handkerchief before starting up again more fired up than before. She seemed thirty years younger. The gathering was hanging on her every word, her facial expressions, her gestures, her silences, too, as is she were running out of inspiration or wishing that the participants would immerse themselves in a barely uttered phrase, like wine lasting long on the palate. Serious for the most part, the congregation occasionally burst out laughing, the former warden knew how to mesmerize her people. This Sunday morning's sermon was the testament she bequeathed to them as well as to the visitors, at a time when it was fitting to bring together a more and more divided country. For, she said, 'if a kingdom is divided against itself, that kingdom cannot survive; and if a house is divided against itself, that house cannot stand.'

'I remember,' the pastor recalled, 'the sign that a young white woman was waving around furiously during the march that was organized to condemn the acquittal of the police officer responsible for the death of Eric Garner, the first one before our lamented Emmett who spoke the words we are repeating today: "I can't breathe." In December 2014. The sign read: "It's not enough not to be racist. We must be antiracist." The same words she was shouting as she marched, her face distorted in anger. It still brings tears to my eyes. Seeing that determined young White girl walking on in the middle of the crowd made me think that not everything was lost. There is hope. More than fifty years ago, at the time of the marches of 1963 and 1965, she might have locked herself inside her house to watch those go by whom her parents or the society had taught her to see as a pack of fanatical savages.'

'Of course,' Ma Robinson went on, directly addressing the non-Blacks in the audience, 'some members of your respective families, your loved ones, will tell you that it's not your battle. You are not responsible for the actions of your great-grandparents. You did not enslave anyone. Some of you weren't even born when segregation, which treated part of this country's population like third-class citizens, officially ended. You have never been a member of any hate group, the great sacrilege of the cross of Jesus Christ. You haven't fired on any unarmed Black adolescent or taken anyone's life, in any way at all. You are not responsible for anything at all. You are White as the driven snow. Innocent as a newborn lamb. That's true. At least on this point. As for other sins...' She paused before letting out a mischievous chuckle swiftly stifled in a prolonged sigh. It made the congregation laugh. 'Know that God sees everything, hears everything. It is up to each of you to settle your accounts with Him.' And she went on.

'Of course, pariahs will be quick to accuse you of wanting to buy yourself a clear conscience at a bargain price. They will tell you unequivocally: "You are here because you feel guilty. Your whole life long you have closed your eyes and turned a deaf ear. Where were you when they killed Michael Brown? Where were you when they burst into Breonna Taylor's apartment in the middle of the night and riddled her with bullets in front of her partner? Where were you when they executed Ahmaud Arbery in cold blood?" I could give you a list as long as my arm and continue until the second coming of Christ. You will hear harsh words that will raise doubts about your good faith, perhaps you have already heard them. I can well imagine what you felt, what you will feel at moments like that. It hurts, it hurts a lot to know that people doubt our sincerity.'

'It's true, we shouldn't look the other way,' the pastor acknowledged. 'We live in a country where from the very start those like me have been on the side of the dominated. From the hold of the slave ship until today, via the cotton fields and the bitter time of segregation.' She seemed to hesitate for an instant, then continued. 'You are among the privileged by force of circumstance. Please don't take the word "privileged" wrong. Among those who will be coming with us shortly to beat the pavement where the police officer crushed Emmett's face without giving him a chance to breathe, I know that many of you have a hard time making ends meet. I know that, oh yes, I do. I know that you wonder anxiously whether you'll be able to register your sons and daughters in some community college, at least. Whether they won't have to go into lifelong debt to be able to make it when the children of so many others have plenty of choice. But in this land of ours, from the strict point of view of the racial barrier that will shortly take us out into the street, we are not in the same boat. We must not turn our head away. Oh no, Lord. Amen?'

'Amen!' the congregation replied.

'It's precisely because of this that I want to thank you from the bottom of my heart. Thank you for them, thank you for us, human beings. You do not owe us anything, oh no, Lord, you do not owe us anything. You could have turned your eyes away, like millions of others, and gone your way. But you understood, better yet, you felt from deep inside yourselves that we need solidarity to make this stop and you have reached out to us. You felt that you wouldn't be fine if your neighbors aren't fine. That you wouldn't be safe if your brothers and sisters aren't safe. If they're hunted down day and night, humiliated, beaten, executed like wild animals on a street corner. By doing so, you admit that there is only one single unique community. It is the human community. That's what I used to tell the girls in prison when they would fight over a false identity invented by the rulers of this world, while they were behind bars in their shabby cells. Victims of the same rejection by a society that had forgotten about them as the dregs of humanity. You reacted like human beings. And that is to your credit. In the name of this great human community, the only one that I accept and recognize, I say thank you. Who you are, where you come from matters very little. Thank you.

Very often, it is true, people prefer seeing the glass as half empty. They are the ones who say: "Where were you before? You are buying the Bread of the Spirit on the cheap," and awful things like that. They forget to see the glass as half full. A few years ago, you sister, you brother,' the pastor said as she pointed her finger at the gathering, 'you would have stayed home, nice and warm, to avoid trouble. Or because it didn't concern you. Today you are here, with us. Among us. That is all that counts. Nothing else does. Those who blame without knowing, well, they are wrong. Those who accuse you of being part of the problem, well, they are wrong.' A brief pause, then she added: 'Stupid, as they say today, as if we hadn't been young as well.' The room chuckled, covering their mouth with their hand. 'Emmett spoke that way, too, to make people forget he was well into his forties.' This time the congregation indulged in a hearty laugh. 'To those sceptics

I say: you should be part of the solution. If you are thirsty and someone gives you half a glass of water you don't say: "What a skinflint! The glass isn't full." You drink, you get a bit of energy to keep going, to keep fighting to get more. "I was hungry," she said quoting Christ, "For I was hungry and you gave me food, I was thirsty and you gave me drink, I was a stranger and you welcomed me."

'Beloved sisters and brothers, in the fight that we have been waging for so long, how sweet it is to find men and women by our side to help us win the battle. Shortly, when we march in honor of our lamented Emmett, there will be people from all walks of life. Be careful, I beg you, not to lapse into provocation, gratuitous, or worse, counterproductive. Be careful not to heckle our white sisters and brothers with words like: "Thank you for coming but you are all racist and privileged." As if the men and women by our side should in turn be made to feel uncomfortable at all costs, so they will sense in their own flesh what we feel all too frequently in this society. I've heard that already. I know where it comes from.

With every new humiliation, every brutal loss of a father, a brother, a sister, you have the heartbreaking impression of a story eternally repeating itself. The impression that it will never stop, as the former teacher of the unfortunate Emmett confessed to me just before the sermon. With her colleague, she was already with us in the eighties; and today, they have both picked up their old activist cane to climb with us up the mountain at the foot of which we now stand. The distressing impression endures that there really isn't any progress. Since the dark days of segregation. Since the ghastly Black Wall Street massacre in Tulsa. Since the assassination of Emmett Till. Since the attack on Rodney King and the riots that ensued. I know the origin of your speech of distrust, even of hatred at times. It has its roots in the old law of an eye for an eye that the Messiah taught us to get rid of as of a worn-out garment and replace it with love for our fellow human.

I understand the origin of your views but please allow me not to share them. One does not heal evil with evil. If you cannot put your resentments aside, at least be pragmatic. This type of discourse is not the most useful when facing an audience that is already yours. Surely, we aren't minors, we can fight on our own to defend our rights. But if there are men and women of good faith ready to support us in this battle why refuse the extended hand? If there are women and men ready to help us carry the burden, why tell them not to?

Beloved brothers and sisters, be proud of who you are, but don't make the mistake of retreating. And don't let others force you to retreat either. Not even in this beautiful term of African-American that, I have to admit, I sometimes find problematic. Besides, why "African"? Do the others call themselves "European-Americans"? I will tell you this: you should distrust what might be just as insidious and stigmatizing. Oh, we are proud of our African heritage. Not necessarily so. The truth is that behind this term some still think of the good old Negro they no longer dare to mention. Or of the gentler, segregation era "people of color" that still comes out of their mouth sometimes. As if they themselves were colorless or were the color of light. There is worse. By defining oneself that way, we bring grist to the mill of those who want to keep us away from the world's forward momentum. From the world's beauty. From the light that is to shine beneath the footsteps of every human being. Afterwards they'll be glad to say: "See, they give themselves that name. To stand apart. To separate themselves from the group that, one way or another, we've been trying to hold together for centuries now. All we are doing is respecting their way of referring to themselves. We can't go against their will." But they, who are they? When they speak of themselves, in their books, their media? Who are they? Men, women, children. Human beings. Nothing else. "I too am America" said that good brother Langston Hughes.

For the rest, whoever we may be, here today to pay final homage to our brother Emmett who died under the abhorrent circumstances that you all know, here we are all of us: Black, White, Latino, Asian—all of us are here; let the naysayers talk. Let the sowers of hate talk. Let them talk and let us march. Let them be, brothers and sisters beloved by the Lord, and let us move onward. Let us build bridges, solid bridges between us, there where malevolent spirits and kill-joys seek to divide us. We are standing on the side of what's right, the human side. We are "neither Jew nor Greek", as Paul the Apostle wrote in the Epistle to the Galatians, "neither bond nor free, neither male nor female". And I would add, neither Black nor White. Neither Latino nor Asian. For "[we are] all one in Christ Jesus."

In this struggle that is as old as humanity, we shall surely suffer defeat, as we already have. Perhaps we shall suffer still heavier ones. Perhaps we shall even have to drink the chalice down to the dregs. To the point where we may sometimes let ourselves grow discouraged. Have our morale flattened like an old tire that's been fixed a thousand times over, where there's no room for even a single patch anymore. To think that we have gone three steps back after taking two steps forward. But we know how to rise up again, I am convinced of that. With the help of the Almighty. We know how to dig deep within ourselves for the strength we need to keep moving ahead. For we are on the right side of history. Which will end up victorious, whether we like it or not. Which will end up victorious, I tell you the truth. In fifty years. In a hundred years. In a thousand years. It doesn't matter. The day will come and it will be victorious. Oh yes, Lord.'

And in a voice that seemed almost totally worn out, the pastor launched into "We Shall Overcome", which the choir and the congregation joined, swaying hand in hand, eyes closed, tears streaming down the cheeks of some who didn't try to wipe them off.

GOD'S POINT OF VIEW

AT THE STROKE OF noon the final gospel song was heard and the faithful, still overcome by the sermon, had almost all left the church. The coffin was hoisted on the shoulders of six strapping men, Stokely being one of them, was set down, pushed, then expertly guided into the hearse, as the family of the deceased immediately got into the car and headed for Union Cemetery for a hasty burial. A final blessing by the pastor, a rose on the casket, a fistful of earth poured out with a heavy hand at the moment the casket was lowered by those who had been asked to do so, and it was over. The reason for all the rush was that they needed to catch up with the march, shortly beginning under the interim leadership of Marie-Hélène.

While her partner was already busy enlivening the atmosphere with Bob Marley's music, produced by a mobile speaker in Rasta colors slung over one shoulder, Marie-Hélène was distributing posters that had been prepared the night before. Not that many, actually, since slogans had been shared on social media so that a fair number of people came with the ones they had made at home. The demonstrators were reminded of some final guidelines: 'No controversial comments, not every policeman is a killer, no provocations, this is a peaceful rally, stay within the safety zone...', and the procession took off through the streets of Franklin Heights under a sunny sky cleared of the last visible traces of the early morning deluge, other than some lingering drops that clung to leaves in full bloom. Propped up on the bed of the pick-up truck that belonged to Stokely's friends, a gigantic head-and-shoulders portrait of Emmett contributed by a local artist led the march, its brushstrokes in their dazzling bright colors reminiscent of some of Basquiat's paintings. The son of the late Mary Louise was depicted in his usual good nature, his gentle look, and with the hint of a smile on his lips.

Dan had put in his two cents' worth to plan the itinerary, dreaming of lighting a spark in this Midwestern city asleep on its nauseating laurels where the question of race was concerned. He had been forced to argue hard, first with Marie-Hélène who was split between her activist's enthusiasm and her immigrant's syndrome inclined to keep a low profile in a country of which she was, nevertheless, a citizen; then with Ma Robinson who was afraid to make any waves that might do disservice to the cause. To tell the truth, the former prison warden was a veritable control freak, she loved being in command of everything from beginning to end in the decision-making chain. Her motto: 'You are never better served than by yourself.' The idea that some unidentified elements would steal 'her' demonstration and come and mess it up was intolerable to her. Still, Dan had some ironclad arguments, borrowed among others from Dr. King's "I Have a Dream" speech, which he had at his fingertips and knew how to handle judiciously, thereby managing to convince the old pastor.

'Go ahead with your roundabout itinerary, young man. However, tell your Rasta friends, no matter what their color, not to even try smoking their weed at my demo if they don't want me to kick their ass', she concluded—half-warden, half-pastor.

Barely half an hour after the procession began, a determined Ma Robinson moved to the head of the march flanked by the three orphans, Authie and Stokely, as well as Nancy, Coach Larry and his family who, as the pastor said, having come such a long distance deserved to take part in the burial. The two teachers had also gone to the cemetery before they went home to rest, encouraged by Ma Robinson. Her persistent thoughtfulness might give the impression that she was much younger although, give or take a few years, the three of them were of the same generation. She couldn't stop thanking them for having come to pay tribute to their former pupil.

'It's not in the natural order of things. We would have preferred it to be the other way around,' old Mahalia said.

'Or under happier circumstances,' her colleague added before the two of them slipped away slowly and cautiously, helped into two separate taxis by Stoke and Authie.

Arriving at the march, Authie had exchanged her high heels for the more comfortable sneakers she had in her backpack. Despite her weight, she moved along at a good pace, laughing heartily with her old buddy Stoke, whom she instructed for the umpteenth time to say a prayer of thanks to the soul of their departed friend who had allowed them to reestablish their friendship. 'Otherwise you would have had to wait until you, too, were six feet under. Yes, really, I would have come to make sure I was finally rid of you. It's not as if you had any other family besides me,' she teased gruffly. Laughter was her way of warding off the grief at the moment they buried the one she regarded as a part of herself. A grief that had been torturing her body ever since she'd watched the scene live on television, as had so many millions across the world.

Next to them marched a well-known player of the Green Bay Packers—undoubtedly the one who had donated the twenty-five thousand dollars to the fund, which he had the grace not to disclose. He had contacted the organizers that very morning via Twitter to let them know he would participate. The news made Marie-Hélène and Dan jump for joy, 'Wow! Brilliant! That will make a lot more people come,' while it left Ma Robinson unmoved although she wasn't averse to the athlete's presence:

'Fine, he's assuming his responsibilities,' she commented soberly.

The Packers star reported in an interview on CBS Sports that it had come as a revelation to him that morning when he woke up. There was no game or training session scheduled for that day. It seemed obvious to him that his place should be in the street with the others that Sunday.

Was he contractually permitted to be there? There were so many restrictions in that damned contract that he no longer knew what he was and wasn't allowed to do as an individual. Maybe he should even have to ask his employer's authorization to take a piss. He was well paid, he wasn't complaining. He could have called his agent to make sure but at the time that hadn't occurred to him. In the end, he didn't care. 'There are moments in a man's life,' he explained to a journalist who had come to interview him during the march, 'when you have to be consistent with yourself, when that consistency comes before all else: your image, your employer, the money...' In any event, at age thirty he had enough money to give his family and his descendants a comfortable life until the end of their days, he figured, as he matched his stride to those around him.

Certainly, he had Colin Kaepernick in mind, a football player like himself, whom he had faced on two or three occasions. A Milwaukee native, the mixed-race quarterback had paid a heavy price for taking a knee as the national anthem was played to condemn police brutality against Blacks and minorities in the United States. He was dismissed from his team and blacklisted by all the other NFL teams.

'Sports and politics don't mix,' the spokesman of the San Francisco team, Kaepernick's employer, said.

'And what about the raised fists in their black gloves of Tommie Smith and John Carlos at the 1968 Olympic Games in Mexico?' a journalist asked.

'They were wrong.'

It was the message that Kaepernick's employer insisted on, no doubt for fear that the show would be boycotted by the majority of white spectators and television viewers.

Here, more than anywhere else, customer is king. And furthermore the show must go on, no matter what. In addition to losing his job, the Milwaukee player was called a 'son of a bitch' in his usual refined vocabulary by the occupant of the White House who was then a presidential candidate. Other hate messages had flooded the internet, accusing him of biting the hand that feeds him.

None of it prevented the Packers star from deciding that morning to participate in the demonstration. After receiving the enthusiastic response from the organizers, he phoned a white teammate who lived a few houses down in the same gated community as he did and who was expecting him for a family brunch. When the quarterback told him why he wanted to cancel, his friend thought for a moment, then said: 'Don't move. Give me five minutes, I'll call you back.' Fifteen minutes later he rang the doorbell with his wife and children dressed for the march: 'Shall we go?' That's how, next to a former prison warden used to subduing strong heads and now fishing for souls, the two players and their family found themselves in the front of the group that left Franklin Heights, a Milwaukee neighborhood they had vaguely heard about in local news.

Police barricades were ostentatiously placed at strategic spots along the route, at best in order to prevent things from getting out of control or, if necessary, quickly quelling them. The municipality had requisitioned all available Black officers, called back those who were on vacation in order to appease indignant citizens, without being accused by the Republican opposition of backing one part of the population to the detriment of others by, in addition, making concessions to rioters and hoodlums. The image of Milwaukee, close to being number one where discrimination was concerned, depended on it—'the most segregated and racist place I have ever known in my life,' the white president of the Bucks, the city's basketball team, had declaimed.

The route had been planned and negotiated inch by inch with the mayor and the police commissioner. Leaving Franklin Heights, it was supposed to go down Keefe Avenue to 20th Street, along Union Cemetery, then turn left at Fond Du Lac Avenue before heading for City Hall, a handsome Neo-Renaissance building constructed at the end of the nineteenth century on the other side of Kilbourn Bridge, which runs across the Milwaukee River. 'Very symbolic,' Dan was ecstatic, thinking of the Edmund Pettus Bridge, which had become a place of pilgrimage after that Sunday in March 1965, which had witnessed the Selma police together with members of the Ku Klux Klan violently crack down on the march of Dr. Martin Luther King, Jr. Time and again his enthusiasm and his knowledge of the history of the civil rights movement delighted Ma Robinson.

Truth be told, that hadn't entered the mind of the old woman for a single moment. When the young Rasta discussed the route with her that she found seriously appealing, it was primarily because it would use main roads and avoid being cornered in case of a skirmish with the police or, worse, with extreme right militias, staunch defenders of the Aryan race and other supporters of the great replacement theory. In view of the turmoil that Emmett's murder had provoked and the media coverage of the march, the police should just stay calm for once. On the other hand, these reactionary fiends always sought the spotlight and the march was handing them an golden opportunity. Until now, thank

God, they hadn't shown up. 'May it last,' the pastor prayed inside herself as she moved ahead unfailingly. The events had unquestionably reinvigorated her. Upon her arrival she would give a brief address on the esplanade in front of City Hall, followed by Stokely—who was dragging his feet, terrified at the thought of having to speak in public—and Authie, who had been named substitute mom by Ma Robinson, since the mothers of the girls hadn't given any sign of life. The three of them would speak of Emmett's battle, his faith in humanity and the American dream before the rally would break up to the melody of "Free At Last"—the choir was present as well—so that the participants would leave in peace and joy.

Journalists were milling about everywhere, even standing on the roofs of vans; the Fourth of July Parade wouldn't attract this many in the city of Vel Phillips, first woman Secretary of State from Milwaukee, a civil rights activist and a jurist. They could be seen hanging out of the windows of tall apartment buildings, for which they must have paid a stiff price to the residents, trying to get the best possible angle for a photo or a video recording since the march was being aired live on television and social media. Some of them were weaving in and out of the crowd, microphone in hand, trying to find a 'good customer' willing to offer a catchphrase, a polemic if possible, which would be picked up in a continuous loop on TV and create a buzz on the networks. Nancy, who had somehow been identified as the ex-fiancée, was beckoned to bear witness on her experience of living with the victim as a mixed couple in a country where communities tended to rub shoulders without ever intermingling, an exercise the professor of African-American Studies refused to take part in.

Above Milwaukee a dazzling blue sky made room for a chaotic ballet of police and news channel helicopters, generating a cacophony when combined with the slogans and chants that had been either created in advance or made up on the spot; to the variety of diverse music that saw rap as well as Dan's reggae stealing its limelight; to the folk and country music of those nostalgic for the sixties; and to the frustrated look of someone searching in vain for a quiet place to collect their thoughts.

'It's a matter of honoring the memory of a human being, damn it,' the most cantankerous protested. 'We're not in a goddamn marching band.'

Roughly forty-five minutes after she joined the march, something happened that Ma Robinson wouldn't hesitate to characterize as a miracle, and that the copious presence of the press would lead one to anticipate. Indeed, as the procession advanced, small groups of demonstrators kept rushing into its midst, coming from every corner of the city, from the nearest metropolitan areas, and some even from Madison. Social media? Local radio and television stations that had announced the event the night before? Word of mouth? The Lord of Hosts, the pastor decided. He had taken His side in the case, He had weighed it on his Scale, He had found it to be greatly unjust. The small group of a few hundred people that had left Franklin Heights was in the throes of changing under its own eyes into an army of thousands, then tens of thousands of determined citizens who were sick and tired of the direction the country was taking, fed up with the incompetence, the cynicism, and the vulgarity of a President for whom some of them had voted, nevertheless, fed up with the Governor of the State who had supported him and done much worse, besides. Whites, Latinos, Blacks, Asians, women and men from the different communities that made up the United States, joined the demonstration along the way, like passengers getting on a bus in their neighborhood or running a few hundred yards to catch it at the nearest stop. This whole multitudinous throng pressed on in faith, as if the march inspired them to create a single humanity, with the same hope for a kinder tomorrow anchored in their heart.

THE DAY WILL COME

HALFWAY AT THE intersection of West North and Fond Du
Lac Avenues, Black Lives Matters activists started breaking
into the march. Their contingent consisted of mostly young
and experienced women who had joined the struggle seven
years earlier, shocked and then repulsed by the acquittal of
Trayvon Martin's murderer. 'The law has its own logic that
has nothing to do with morality or sentimentality,' the killer's allies rejoiced. That had only sickened them more, calling them into the streets in larger numbers, ready to do battle each time an equally racist incident of violence occurred,
breaking the already precarious balance of community relations in this unhappy country. The women took over the
demonstration in no time, controlling the procession from
the middle to the end, opening up their own black banners

with slogans in white letters, shouting 'Black Lives Matter' at the top of their lungs until it drowned out all other voices. That clearly was the result of know-how acquired in the field and of an action planned to its finest details.

Between their sizeable invasion—they had rounded up a maximum number of irate members from their own network —and the individuals who were steadily joining the march, after an hour-and-a-half the procession consisted of nearly fifty thousand participants, if not more. Later the police and the opposition would minimize the numbers—'a handful of protesters'—to remember only the escalation that followed, blaming it on the irresponsibility of an old communist hiding behind the vestments of a pastor—such irreverence!—and on professional activists, troublemakers whose place should have been in prison rather than in the street where they were preventing honest folks from enjoying a well-deserved day of rest and people who had to work hard on Sundays from focusing on their activities. Quite proud of their unexpected success, Marie-Hélène and Dan were waving their smartphone in front of Ma Robinson's eyes every three minutes as the numbers and images appeared, as the multitude, carried by an almost mystical impulse, was moving on toward City Hall under a lovely springtime sun that countered that morning's weather predictions once and for all.

At the rate the parade was advancing, City Hall would be in sight forty-five minutes later. They had reached Walnut Street when a rumor ran through the crowd, suddenly vigilant, heads up and ears on the alert, looking for a way out in case of a general stampede. Appearing from nowhere, three water cannons were set up two streets before the bridge at the intersection of Kilbourn and Vel R. Phillips Avenues. At the same time, police on horseback, quiet until then, rose up in front of the marchers, their long truncheons hitting the imposing flank of their animals whose muscles twitched intermittently as if pervaded by electric shocks, making them feel they needed to defend themselves in the face of what seemed like a hostile human mass. With an expressionless gaze beneath their helmets, the cops had their eyes fixed on the demonstrators without really seeing them. They seemed concerned only to prevent the crowd from reaching City Hall if there was even the slightest sign of trouble.

Her arms around the shoulders of the two youngest ones, Ma Robinson felt Emmett's daughters brace at the sight of the horses and the police. The littlest one started to cry. Paralyzed with fear, she could no longer move; her feet were stuck on the asphalt, refusing to obey her. The pastor leaned over and whispered in her ear: ' Don't be afraid, darling. Do you remember the story of Daniel in the lion's den? When God sent the angel. . .' She had no time to say anything else. A few young White men had spontaneously begun to encircle them, shielding them with their bodies to protect them from what they thought was an imminent attack. Their eyes flashing with anger, they looked as if they were in a trance, a trance fed by the slogan loudly and forcefully repeated: 'Black Lives Matter! Black Lives Matter!' Others, on the contrary, didn't say a word, their mouth covered with a cross of black tape, and their hands around their neck to mimic strangulation.

They were the generation of social media, Instagram, TikTok. At school they had barely skimmed the history of the struggle against slavery and segregation but they had become immersed in it through films like *Twelve Years a Slave*, *The Hate U Give*, and old TV series like *Roots*, rebroadcast on television or watched via streaming. They were dreaming of another world destined to be more just, where everyone would start out on an equal footing, would have the same chances, no matter what their ethnic or social origin or sexual orientation. Where there wouldn't be any simplistic amalgamation, definitively excluding any minority of which a single member had transgressed. Where one would be allowed a second chance. They were unselfishly putting all the fervor of their youth into the quest for this better world in which they wanted to believe. It warmed Ma Robinson's aged heart to see many among the demonstrators so determined despite their naivete, if not downright angelism.

What they couldn't see from this side of the bridge were the several thousand aggressive White militants concealed by trucks and the police who were hiding behind their shields and visor helmets. They had arrived at the front of City Hall only fifteen minutes earlier. Despite the tendency of these small groups to generate publicity, this operation had been planned in the greatest secrecy, with texts or in private circuits on social media, for fear that the information would be disclosed before they arrived. They seemed determined to stop the demonstrators from gaining access to the area around City Hall.

Some were openly carrying their firearms as permitted by Wisconsin state law, which was very effective since it allowed them to make an impact on the opposing camp. Others were flaunting jackets with a White fist, a skull, or a shortened Celtic cross, tattoos of crossed hammers on their iron-pumping biceps or their neck, all symbols of their membership in factions that advocated White supremacy. Still others, looking more placid than threatening, were sitting astride their Harley-Davidsons and giving the Nazi salute while taking selfies that they posted on their Twitter or Facebook accounts. There were very few women among them, other than some platinum blondes and two or three brunettes in studded jackets. A hulking guy whose muscles bulged under a black T-shirt, was haranguing them with a megaphone from the back, shouting the opening of slogans that the rest finished in a game of call and response that could have been inspired by Negro spirituals:

> 'Better shoot first...'
> '...and apologize later.'
> 'When the looting begins...'
> '...the shooting begins.'
> 'White lives...'
> ...matter.'
> 'Blue lives...'
> '...matter.'

As soon as they caught wind of the presence of groups like the Aryan Nation and others, the journalists rushed in their direction, having sniffed the potential of incitement that would boost ratings. The vans took off, creating an initial panic among the crowd that was swiftly reassured by the leaders: 'Stay calm! It's nothing. Stay calm!' As the press arrived on the other side of the bridge, pronouncements merged, pugnacious and hateful. The counter-demonstrators took full advantage of the platform on hand; like the

Proud Boys justifying their abject statements that they drew from the first amendment and its freedom of speech, so did the interviewers to clear themselves of any responsibility. Alerted via social media and by journalists, they responded similarly on the opposite side. They had to show that they could as well, that they weren't docile sheep being led to the slaughterhouse. Slaves at everyone's beck and call, endlessly exploited. Workers paid a few cents an hour to harvest cotton on the huge plantation of a white patriarch. That era was gone.

The more the minutes rolled by the more the hearts and minds heated up on either side of the Milwaukee River that, indifferent and impetuous, flowed on in its life, wide from the melted snow. Teeth clenched behind their visors, the police were preparing for a worst case scenario: a generalized brawl that would see the extremists on both sides clash, trading blow for blow. The tension only heightened, filling the air with screams, vituperations, rising to a palpable climax. Then suddenly it stopped again. A strange silence ensued. All at once, not a single slogan, not a single catchphrase was heard. You couldn't even hear the crowd breathe. Time was suspended. You couldn't hear the river roll in its unbridled course. Or the ducks, regular inhabitants of its banks, launch their noisy flight into the air and stifle into muteness the song of birds intoxicated with spring's presence. A silence of only a few seconds, but an absolute silence that seemed like an eternity to those who were listening, to the minds and later in the memory of the demonstrators. A little like the calm before a force-ten storm when the winds arrive, brutal, bending, breaking, tearing up roots, shattering everything in their way.

Ma Robinson reacted by telling Marie-Hélène and Dan to smuggle the girls out, away from the crowd. 'Right now,' she commanded as the two lovers hesitated, looking at each other in surprise as if to say that they hadn't made all those efforts only to be deprived of the finale. It would take the two of them. Her antennae on red alert, the former warden didn't leave them any choice but to obey. Some would call it a feeling or at any rate intuition brought on by the experience of a woman who in the sixties had marched for civil rights and all too frequently seen the gatherings degenerate into dozens of deaths, hundreds of wounded, massive imprisonment, and traumas that would often be transmitted inadvertently to their descendants. Left at her side were Stokely and Authie, to whom the pastor handed a megaphone asking them to thread their way through the demonstrators and tell them not to give in to any provocations.

'Our quest is a quest for justice. Our approach is an approach of peace and reconciliation. Of love, not hate.'

After marching for almost an hour, the two football players had abandoned the crowd, undoubtedly reminded of reality by their young children, who must have been hungry and mainly tired of it all. Nancy, Coach Larry and his family had slipped away a little earlier to go by the hotel to pick up their bags, catch a cab to the airport, and fly back to New York. So they did not witness the fateful continuation of the peaceful march in honor of Emmett, who had died suffocating under the knee of a police officer. They would find out about it when they landed, thanks first to Coach Larry's daughter's cellphone, and then to the television screens inside the airport.

When the deafening silence ended, voices rang out in every direction:

'Peaceful demonstrations against police violence aren't enough. What will hurt them is the money they will have to spend to repair all this. That's what will get their attention: losing money.'

'Don't waste this moment! The whole world is watching, we have the power; now everything depends on what we do with it.'

'You won't rob us of our values. We'll never apologize for bringing civilization to the world.'

'Anger is what you get when you oppress people for so long and nothing is done. If everything is so explosive right now, it's because it is hardly the first time this is happening. The police persist in its violence against Blacks. We have all seen the video, we were all forced to watch the execution. If we say nothing, injustice will continue. And we've had enough.'

'Look, there are a lot of young White folks who understand the situation and are demonstrating. They are the ones who will make a real change happen.'

'We are proud men, a credible alternative to the timid right. We will never accept people to trample on our values, to walk all over us.'

Those on the other side accused the Black, Jewish, and Muslim 'scum' of aspiring to the extinction of Aryans, of wanting the 'homogenization of peoples', warning them belligerently that they would always find them on their path to defend the values of the Christian West before sounding the charge. Others, undoubtedly anarchists and activists from Anti-Racist Action invited the demonstrators to destroy it all in order financially to hurt Capitalism. Still others, Ma Robinson, Authie and Stoke among them, called for remaining reasonable amid the outpouring of hate, to no avail, while the police caught between two opposing combustible factions were backing away as they awaited the reinforcements they had called for.

'The Milwaukee Events', as the press would refer to the frenzy that followed, reminiscent in some ways of the rebellion in Watts, lasted no less than three days and three nights. The rioting made the headlines for an entire week during which television vans camped out in Franklin Heights, on the lookout for just one word from the pastor who would never show up, at least not to be interviewed, as the ladies and gentlemen of the press had hoped. Yet, she carried on with her ministry, looking the journalists up and down who were harassing her before moving on either to the church or to Emmett's house where, forced to stay away from school, the girls were living barricaded under Auntie Authie and Uncle Stoke's protection. Both had been pretty beaten up during the clashes but were ready to do battle with the first unwelcome troublemaker who might approach the house.

That whole time Marie-Hélène was assisting the church from Chicago where she had taken refuge with her parents, split between their pride in seeing their daughter on television and their eternal worry, being immigrants, about keeping a low profile. She was working long distance together with Dan who had remained in Milwaukee to his mother's great joy, although she didn't fail to let him know how unhappy she was that he'd gotten mixed up in this whole business, so much so that he was forced to hide at home to get away from the journalists. He and Marie-Hélène were the pastor's spokespeople on social media, where she had chosen to express herself, delivering her messages of thanks in the name of Emmett's daughters as well as her own 'to all those who had taken part in the march, called on to stay in the annals of history', and her calls for calm to avoid seeing scorn spilled out over their heartfelt understanding that Sunday and their dream of a better humanity. Eventually, journalists packed up their equipment and left, and life went back to normal, Abigail and her sisters went back to school, Marie-Hélène returned to Milwaukee that, after an absence of three weeks, she desperately missed.

A long time later, when Ma Robinson was no longer of this world anymore, when Stoke and Authie, too, were gone and Emmett's name had been given to a street in this Midwestern city; when Dan, professor emeritus at the State University of Wisconsin-Milwaukee—true to his principles, he had steered clear of the private and Catholic Marquette—would speak of those days to his students both as witness and historian; when Marie-Hélène—now a best-selling author equal to her elders, Toni Morrison and Edwidge Danticat—had decided out of love not to return to Chicago; when the two of them would tell their grandchildren about it, who would be human beings first before being Americans, Jews, Haitians, Blacks, Whites—maybe together they would evoke The Milwaukee Events as part of an era that was truly gone.

SOME BIBLIOGRAPHICAL REFERENCES REGARDING, AMONG OTHERS, EVENTS MENTIONED IN THE NOVEL

BACHARAN, Nicole, *Histoire des Noirs américains au XXe siècle,* Éditions Complexe, « questions au XXe siècle », 1994.

BALDWIN, James, *La Prochaine Fois, le feu*, (*The Fire Next Time*), tr. Michel Sciama, Gallimard, collection « Du monde entier », 1963.

CAPOTE, Truman, *De sang froid* (*In Cold Blood*), tr. Raymond Girard, Gallimard, 1966.

COHEN, Jerry and MURPHY, William S., *Burn, Baby, Burn! The Los Angeles Race Riot of August 1965,* Victor Gollancz, 1966.

DANTICAT, Edwidge, *Adieu, mon frère* (*Brother, I'm Dying*), tr. Jacques Chabert, Grasset, 2008.

GUILLÉN, Nicolás, « Élégie à Emmett Till », in *Le Chant de Cuba, Poèmes 1930-1972* (trad. Claude Couffon), Éditions Belfond, 1984.

HUGHES, Langston, « Moi aussi », « La mère à son fils », (tr. François Dodat), in *Courage ! Dix variations sur le courage et un chant de résistance,* anthologie établie par Bruno Doucey et Thierry Renard, Éditions Bruno Doucey, 2020.

KING, Jr., Martin Luther, "I Have a Dream" (« Je fais un rêve », Bayard, 1998).

New World Translation of the Holy Scriptures, Watchtower Bible And Tract Society Of New York, Inc; January 1, 1974.

ROUMAIN, Jacques, « Sales Nègres » in *Bois-d'ébène*, Port-au-Prince, Imprimerie Deschamps, 1945.

ROUMAIN, Jacques, *Gouverneurs de la rosée*, Port-au-Prince, Imprimerie de l'État, 1944.

AFP, « États-Unis : À Milwaukee, les Noirs ont laissé tomber Clinton », https://www.lepoint.fr/monde/etats-unis-a-milwaukee-les-noirs-ont-laisse-tomber-clinton-22-11-2016-2084736_24.php

AUTRAN, Frédéric, « Obama et la question raciale : le désespoir noir », https://www.liberation.fr/planete/2017/01/19/obama-et-la-question-raciale-le-desespoir-noir_1541816

HANNE, Isabelle, « Après la mort de George Floyd, Minneapolis brûle sous la colère », https://www.msn.com/fr-fr/actualite/monde/apr%c3%a8s-la-mort-de-george-floyd-minneapolis-br%3%bble-sous-la-col%3%8re/ar-BB-14KSAw?li=AAaCKnE&ocid=mailsignout

LAJON, Karen, « Milwaukee trou noir de l'Amérique », https://www.lejdd.fr/International/USA/Mid-term-La-ville-de-Milwaukee-symbole-de-la-puavrete-aux-Etats-Unis-230338-3249041

CINEMATOGRAPHIC REFERENCES
IN ORDER OF APPEARANCE IN THE TEXT

Swashbuckler (The Pirates of the Caribbean), James Goldstone

Rasta Rockett, Jon Turteltaub

Guess who's Coming to Dinner, Stanley Kramer

Cry Freedom, Richard Attenborough

Twelve Years a Slave, Steve McQueen

The Hate U Give, George Tillman, Jr.

Roots, (based on the book by Alex Haley), Marvin J. Chomsky, John Erman, David Greene, and Gilbert Moses

I Am Not Your Negro, Raoul Peck

Author: Louis-Philippe Dalembert is a Haitian poet and novelist who writes in both French and Creole. His works have been translated into several languages and his novel, THE MEDITERRANEAN WALL was the French Voices Grand Prize Winner for best translation in 2021. He lives both in Port-Au-Prince, Haiti, and Paris, France.

Translator: Born in Indonesia (1936), raised in The Netherlands, and residing in the USA since the age of 22, Marjolijn de Jager earned a PhD. in Romance Languages and Literatures from UNC-Chapel Hill in 1975. She translates from both the Dutch and the French. Francophone African literature, the women's voices in particular, have a special place in her heart.

She was the Grand Prize winner in 2021 of the French Voices Award for Excellence in translation for THE MEDITERRANEAN WALL by Louis-Philippe Dalembert. For further information please see http://mdejager.com

TRANSLATOR'S ACKNOWLEDGEMENTS

My warmest words of thanks go to Timothy Schaffner for his ongoing support of my work that has found such a welcoming home at his press. I am deeply grateful for the way in which he tuned the various sounds in this symphony of voices, so strikingly composed by the author, Louis-Philippe Dalembert.

As always, my husband David Vita deserves infinite thanks for his time and enthusiasm as the first reader of this translation, to which his editorial comments and suggestions contribute so much.

—MdJ